SAFE LANDING

Safe Landing

ADVENA ABDUCTIONS
BOOK FOUR

HOLLIE HARTWRIGHT

PINDIKA PRESS

CANBERRA

Safe Landing (Advena Abductions Book Four)
Published by Pindika Press
Canberra, Australia

All characters in this novel are over the age of 18.

Paperback ISBN: 978-0-6456731-3-5

For the always-and-forever friends.

Author's Note

Safe Landing is the fourth and final book in the high-heat *Advena Abductions* science-fiction series, which began with the short novel *Count Down* and continued with *Into Orbit* and *Dark Space*. Though each book features a different human heroine and a resolved why-choose romance with a HEA, the *Advena Abductions* series has an interconnected series arc and is intended to be read in order. Please – I *beg* you – don't read this one first. *Safe Landing* is a series finale, and, as such, references characters and events from the preceding books.

Safe Landing is a super spicy, medium burn, insta-connection MMMF alien romance where the lucky human heroine will not be choosing at the end. It contains M/M, M/F, and group scenes, along with alien bits, chasing, light praise kink, very light breeding kink, knotting, tails, and swearing. It is suitable for adult audiences only.

Content warnings include accidental kidnap; a FMC with anxiety and insomnia who experiences anxiety attacks; near-death experiences; strained family relationships and toxic parents; violence, including battle scenes, personal violence, injury, and death, including death in battle; allusions to theft and criminality; medical scenes including pregnancy, birth, and reference to birth injury; reference to miscarriage (off page, in the past, no detail); references to incarceration. If you think I've missed anything from this list, please, *please* contact me and I will update it; I am committed to keeping my readers safe.

This series is written by an Australian author, using Australian English. Formal Australian English is largely based on the spelling and conventions of UK English, though sometimes US spellings will slip through for certain words, depending on which TV channels our parents let us watch when we were younger.

Terms & Definitions

Elya: a fundamental energy force existing throughout the known universe, seen and channelled only by a rare few.

Sidereal: a type of space craft commonly used by Darnagh families.

Divine Guard: a specially-trained soldier from Kjid, used as personal bodyguards for the Kjidja priestesses.

Mage: an Illisae with an above-average ability in wielding *elya*.

Circle of Mages/the Circle: the ruling body of the planet Ilis, made up of its most powerful Mages. The Circle is split into levels (First Circle, Second Circle, etc.) depending on ability and magical strength.

Empath: a Mage with the ability to both sense and manipulate the emotions of others.

The Spire: the only aboveground building in the Roth capital, Scytha City.

Ripples (in Scytha City): lines of rolling hills that spread out in a circular fashion from the Spire. These are caused by the Roth building underground.

CLAIRE

'WE'RE CLOSING,' JESSA SAID.

I coughed on a mouthful of water, setting my bottle back on the desk with a too-loud *thump*. 'What?'

The owner of Advena leaned back in her chair and crossed her long legs. 'We're closing,' she repeated. 'Advena, I mean. We've run at a loss since Maeve and Anna left. The new 80s club down the road is just the icing on top of the fucked-up luck cupcake.'

The 80s club had opened two weeks ago, and we'd barely seen a patron since. I didn't think it was the other club's fault, though. I considered voicing my suspicion that Advena's losses were due to Jessa's refusal to rehire replacements for Maeve and Anna, resulting in stretched staff, poor service, complaints, and at least one scathing online review that had gone viral. I didn't, though. Because Jessa was smart – this wasn't her only business, and it certainly wouldn't be her last – and because thinking about Anna made my chest constrict and my heart beat hard.

Acknowledge five things around you, my counsellor whispered in my memory.

I breathed in slowly. *The desk I sat at, heavy and expensive, with three shallow drawers on the left-hand side. The chair I sat on, leather and high-backed, with padded arm rests. The work laptop, a sleek silver thing I could never afford. The coat stand, draped with Belle's denim jacket, Ellis' mock tweed, and my black coat. The bookshelf, stuffed with folders and boxes of spare glass-ware for the bar.*

Maeve had gone north. After Tessa's disappearance, I got it. She needed space, needed time, needed a change of scenery.

But Anna?

I tried to understand that, too. Her grandmother's death would have changed her world.

But to not say anything? To just ... *go*, and have Maeve write a hurried email *two months later*, saying *I forgot to tell you, Anna is with me*, after we'd gone through the missing persons procedure with the police – for the *second* time? To leave her grandmoth-er's funeral arrangements to her lawyer and the state?

It was stupid, but I'd thought we were closer than that. When Anna had finally emailed me, I'd deleted it without reading. It was childish, probably, but my hurt was too raw.

Jessa uncrossed her legs, then crossed them again.

Pay attention, Claire, you're about to lose your job. 'I get it,' I said, clearing my throat, dragging my thoughts back to the present. 'Better to jump before you're pushed.'

'That's it, exactly.' Jessa smiled, her scarlet lips stretching. She was always impeccably made up, wearing the most ex-pensive cosmetics she could import, her hair always perfectly blow-dried, her couture outfits devastating on her hourglass figure.

I hadn't showered in two days, and I was fairly sure that the remnants of mascara darkening my lashes had been applied before that. I didn't want to think about the last time I'd washed my hair. I tried to tell myself that it didn't matter – *you're doing the best you can, Claire* – but I took another mouthful of ice-cold water while my free hand fidgeted nervously with the hem of my shirt. 'How long until we close?'

'A month.'

Fuck.

I wasn't afraid of finding work – I was a bookkeeper; I could always find it – but a month wasn't long, and my apartment lease would end around the same time. A quick mental check told me that I had the emotional reserves to handle a new job *or* a move, but probably not both.

I'd already given up vaping. *What more do you want from me, universe?*

Acknowledge four things you can touch.

I exhaled. *My shirt, the worn cotton soft beneath my fingertips. My water bottle, smooth and cold beneath my palm. The desk, slightly scored from years of use. My hair, tickling against the nape of my neck.*

'I want you to come with me, Claire.'

I frowned at Jessa, startled. 'What?'

She sat up straight, tucking her legs under the chair. 'Come with me. Well, figuratively speaking. We won't be going anywhere. We'll refit Advena with a different theme and a new name. I'm thinking either a speakeasy or a gin bar; we need to set ourselves apart again. Something chic, something elegant, something I can take to my other bars, too. I'm talking it through with a consultant tomorrow. Come with me right from the beginning. And as a sweetener, let me buy your *Pinup* series.'

'*What*?' I said again.

You're not a fucking parrot, Claire.

'Your *Pinup* series,' Jessa repeated patiently. 'Let me buy it. The whole thing. I want them on the back wall.' She waved her hand gracefully, as if gesturing to where the prints would hang. 'They'll fit perfectly. And we'll match the new bar's colour scheme to your work.'

I wrapped my fingers around my water bottle with exaggerated care, letting the coolness ground me as my body flushed with unwelcome heat. My *Pinups* were a series of digital paintings of models growing flowers from various parts of their bodies. It wasn't my favourite work, nor, I thought, my best, but it was a series that tended to stick in people's minds. Having it hung in a public place was my wildest dream and worst nightmare all at once: my work being seen, and my work being *seen*. Between near-constant anxiety and bouts of depression, I hadn't exhibited since art school. I'd lost my confidence, but I'd never stopped making new work.

'I'll take the job,' I said, after a long moment of silence. 'Let me think about the series.'

Jessa gave her curving smile again. 'Good. Can I trust you to keep this quiet until I tell the rest of the staff?'

'Of course.'

Jessa stood up, uncoiling like a cat. 'You won't regret it, Claire. You're the best bookkeeper I've ever worked with, and I'll do anything I can to keep you with me until you choose to leave.'

I flushed. I wasn't sure how many bookkeepers Jessa had worked with, as I worked across her other clubs, too, but asking didn't seem sensible, given the circumstances.

She left the room, her heels clicking on the polished wood floor, leaving the scent of her floral perfume behind.

I tucked my hair behind my ears and took another mouthful of water, willing my heart to slow its frantic beating.

Acknowledge three things you can hear.

The music from the club, some kind of indie electro pop. The gentle whirr of the reverse cycle heater, coming from the corner of the office. My own heart, thudding unevenly in my ears.

'Claire?' The stand-in head chef, Ellis, poked his head around the door. 'Kitchen's about to close. Do you want anything?'

I shook my head. 'I'll go home in a sec. Thanks, though.'

He lingered in the doorway. 'Jessa looked pretty serious. Everything okay?'

I forced a smile. It wasn't hard; I'd been forcing smiles since I was a teenager. *Yes, everything's fine, thank you. Look how many teeth I can show!* 'She's just worried about filling Maeve and Anna's positions. Nothing I can really help with, though. She'll work it out.'

He nodded. 'Want me to walk you to the bus?'

I repressed a sigh. Though he'd stopped asking me out, Ellis still hadn't ... stopped. It had been over a year now, and the attention was wearing. Ellis was nice, but I'd never been inclined to return his interest, and I didn't have the energy to manage other people's feelings, anyway. 'I'm fine, thanks Ellis. You should get everything cleaned up and try to get home early for once.'

'You sure?'

I gritted my teeth, then stood to rummage around in the top desk drawer, pulling out my bag before moving to take my coat from the hook and pushing my arms through the sleeves. 'Yep. Thanks.'

Mercifully for me, he nodded and disappeared. I waited for a few moments, pretending to be flicking through something on my phone, just in case he came back. When he didn't reemerge, I slung my bag over my shoulder.

Advena was dead.

There were a few small groups scattered around the tables, and a lonely-looking couple standing in a dark corner, but the dance floor was empty, and there wasn't anything resembling a line, either outside or at the bar. I waved to Belle, who was wiping down tables with an expression that suggested it wasn't the first time, said goodbye to the bouncers, and pushed my way out through the double red doors.

The neon-pink sign reading *hic sumus omnes advena* flickered, then went completely dark.

I shivered.

The night was chill; summer had ceded to autumn and there were stray leaves on the footpath. I didn't button my coat, though; it was my favourite kind of night, where the cold made me feel more alive.

There were still people everywhere as I got closer to the main road, another sign that Advena really *had* fallen from popular favour. Music poured from club doors and groups of tipsy women staggered on impressive heels from bar to club, club to taxi. A gaggle of men postured near a small cluster of women who looked barely legal, talking too loudly and pushing each other with exaggerated laughter in a sad attempt for attention.

I rolled my eyes and pushed my earbuds into my ears, though I didn't turn any music on. *Fucking dickheads*, Maeve would have said, loudly.

There were two young men and an older lady at the bus stop; the woman had a book open on her lap. I sat near her, ignoring the men, who held beer bottles in their hands. I put my bag next to me, taking out my tablet. I had two tablets: an expensive one I kept at home with more processing power, more storage, and better resolution, and the one I kept in my bag for ideas I had when I was out of the house.

Jessa had looked like a femme fatale from a film noir tonight, and I wanted to capture the memory while it was still fresh. I wouldn't draw Jessa, exactly, but rather take parts of her – the crossed legs, the tailored skirt-suit, the impeccable makeup, and blow-dried mane of hair – and give them to a new pinup. My stylus skated over the screen, sketching the outline. The curved figure, relaxed in the chair, the position both alluring and powerful. The tailored suit revealing long, shapely legs. The hair waving over shoulders and down to a tapered waist. Flowers growing from her eyes and parted lips, and more winding up her arms and legs. I added some colour, a deep splash of maroon for her suit, then softer pinks and apricots for the flowers.

'Hey there, goth girl.'

I continued drawing.

'He said *hey*, Avril.'

My nostrils flared as I took a deep breath. One of the men had stepped closer to where I sat, his hair shining blonde beneath the streetlights. His gaze burned the side of my face and sudden unease made my stomach churn. I glanced to the side; the older woman had left while I'd been drawing and I hadn't noticed.

Fuck.

Acknowledge two things you can smell.

Bitumen, from where the city council had re-sealed the bus slip lane, sharp and cloying. Beer, from where one of the men had spilled his drink, malt and yeast.

I clicked the stylus into place on the side of my tablet, then stuffed the whole thing in my bag, deciding to walk to a different bus stop. I stood, clutching the leather strap with fingers that had started to tremble.

'Where you off to, Paramore?' the other man – a brunette – slurred.

For fuck's sake. If you're going to taunt me, at least do it with references that aren't twenty years old.

I didn't respond, side-stepping the mean-looking blonde to walk as quickly as I could back towards the clubs, dropping my ear buds in my bag then pulling out my keys and clutching them in my fist.

Just in case.

'*I said hey, goth girl.* What, you too good to speak to me?'

There were footsteps behind me. My heart began to thump in my ears. *Don't freeze*, I begged myself. I quickened my pace, trying to put some distance between me and the men.

'I just want to talk to you. Why are you ignoring me? Rude fucking bitch.'

I heard footsteps rushing; instinct kicked in and I bolted. I could hear someone big coming from my right, so I dashed left.

Light flared, blinding. A heartbeat later, a horn sounded. I glanced up and took in the bus bearing down on me, its brakes screeching. My bag slipped from my shoulders, the strap falling from my boneless fingers.

Acknowledge one thing you can taste.

Blood, sweet and metallic, spreading over my tongue.

I didn't scream. I just closed my eyes and waited.

CLAIRE

THE LIGHT BRIGHTENED UNTIL I could see nothing but white.

Fuck. I'm dead, I thought.

I started to scream then, because I thought I might as well.

The light dimmed. I faltered as my eyes adjusted.

I swallowed a mouthful of blood, and I kept screaming.

I was standing on a platform in a large, dark room, and there wasn't a bus in sight. What I *could* see were three people who looked decidedly not *people-like*, and my scream continued.

The tallest was at least six-foot-six, which would be enough to make me stare – were they not also silver-haired, broad-shouldered, ripped as heck, and *mottled blue*. As an artist, I appreciated the depth and variety of tones in the hue; as a *human*, my brain shorted, because I'd never seen someone that colour, especially not someone who looked as if they should be playing prop for the national rugby team.

At least, I *thought* my brain shorted – until I looked at the next not-person.

They were shorter, with wide shoulders that made my body say *mmm, yes please.* They looked more human than the first, with a stocky frame, bronzed skin, deep brown eyes, and curved lips made for smiling. For half a moment, I relaxed – and then my eyes caught movement behind them, and I realised that the thing twitching behind their legs was an honest-to-God *tail.* A tail like a lion's, but with two tufts instead of one. A tail that – for all intents and purposes – seemed to be fixed firmly to their body and moving of its own accord.

The next not-person didn't have a tail, instead boasting ears pointed at the tips and hands ending in black claws. Those claws were digging into muscled thighs and their body was coiled tight, every slender muscle tensed beneath golden skin. The first two were regarding me almost expressionlessly, but the third was clearly distressed, their brow creased in shock – or possibly concern. As our eyes locked – theirs were wide and a beautiful green with slitted pupils, *like a cat* – their lips parted, and they *hissed.*

I kept screaming, because if this was death, then it was pretty fucking confusing. This wasn't anything like what I'd been taught in church as a child. My grandmother believed in angels, but her angels looked more human and less fuckable. Unless we were talking about proper, biblical angels, in which case these three were still lacking wings and the requisite number of eyes.

They might have been demons, and I suddenly got why artists in the past had made Lucifer so damn *hot.* Despite my shock at the claws, tail, and blue skin, it was all too easy to imagine following these three down to some fiery pit, my weak resolve dissolved by lust, and – let's face it – intense curiosity.

I mean, *a tail*.

This is not the time to fantasise about tails, Claire.

There was some kind of computer screen next to the platform and they converged around it. They were clearly communicating, gesturing and making eye contact with each other, but I didn't hear any words, just a jumble of *sounds*. The one with the claws kept hissing, the one with the tail was rumbling, and the blue one made noises that could have been words but were unlike any language I'd ever heard. He stepped forward, and I scrambled away until my back hit something cold and smooth.

His eyes grew wide and he gestured desperately. Stupidly, I noticed that his irises were a deep, swirling violet, his pupils white.

I turned around to see what I'd backed into.

My scream caught in my throat as I shifted from *flight* to *freeze*; a whimper escaped instead. 'That can't be ... That isn't ... No,' I said blankly.

My head swam and I stumbled, leaning against what seemed like a wall of thick glass for support. My skin tingled painfully at the touch of the icy surface.

The colours before me blurred as I blinked. Everything was shades of nighttime blue and pinpoints of white and yellow light, but the shapes looked suspiciously like shapes I knew, only I usually saw them from the ground. My city spread beneath us, lights flickering to life against the growing dark.

There were footsteps behind me and I whirled around, my hands coming up in some futile attempt to ward off danger.

It was the blue one. He met my gaze and said something, his tone soft and calm, clearly meant to soothe me. He held his hands out, palms up to make himself less threatening, but I had to crane my neck to look up at him, and the towering combined with his silver hair – shaved at the sides and braided back like a warrior in a fantasy novel – didn't exactly slow my heartbeat. He said something else and I cowered back, shaking my head.

He sighed, and his expression became resigned; he lowered his hands. His white pupils began to shine, and beneath his blue skin, his veins began to *glow*.

That didn't help my panic, but a moment later, a feeling of wellbeing spilled over me like a wave. Warmth swept up my limbs, even as I was overcome by an unshakable notion that everything was all right – that he would *make it* all right. I was safe now, safe with *him*. I could trust him, trust that he would make everything better. My body went loose and my head went light, like I was floating in a bath that was the perfect heat, and every single worry I'd ever had was washed away by the caress of the water.

He took a step forward.

A soft sigh escaped me, and I pushed my hair back from my face. It was all okay, really; what I'd seen through the glass behind me didn't matter. It didn't matter if I was dead, or something else; it didn't matter if I was somewhere strange, or on my way to some kind of hell, or if the people I was with weren't really people at all. My limbs were heavy and languid; I had to fight to keep my head up.

He held out his arms.

It was an offer, rather than a command, but he made me feel so *safe* and I wanted to be in them, so I stepped forward and let peace wrap around me even as his arms pressed against my back, cradling me, supporting me. I nestled my face into his chest and breathed him in, and with every inhale, it felt better: more calm, more warm, more *right*.

This was exactly where I was supposed to be.

His arms tightened, and he murmured something in my ear, the sound deep and soothing.

I tilted my face up. He stared down at me, his lovely violet eyes like glowing whirlpools. He gave a slight nod, his lips curving into a reassuring smile.

Fingers grabbed my chin, and red-hot pain shot through my skull.

'It's all right. You're all right. You're safe. Everything will be fine.'

I thrashed against the blue one's hold. He let me kick, let me scream, let me beat my arms against him, but he held firm.

'It will pass in a moment. Peace. All will be well.'

'*Well*?' I shrieked. '*Well*? What the *fuck*? Where the fuck *am* I? Who the fuck are *you*? What *the fuck* just happened to my ear? I thought I was *dead*, but *that fucking hurt, asshole!* How *dare* you tell me *I'm safe*?'

He winced and dropped his arms, stepping back. I touched my hand to the side of my head, where the searing pain had lessened to a dull throb. 'I am truly sorry. The pain will pass in a moment. We had to implant a translator so we could ask where to drop you; those human males are still in the same vicinity, and we didn't want to put you back down into danger.'

'*Back down?*'

'We picked you up before the transport craft could cause damage.' The voice came from my left, rough and rasping.

'You're on a Darnagh ship, a B-Class Sidereal. Can you tell us where you wish to be?'

I turned and stared at the one with the pointed ears. He stared back, his claws pressing deeper into his thighs. They all wore variations of the same silvery jumpsuit, cut slightly differently: his was short-sleeved, revealing defined biceps like those I'd seen on male dancers.

Which was to say that I had the sudden urge to sink my teeth into them.

This is why we don't go to the ballet, Claire. Stop being such a perv.

'We brought up a map from one of your Earth satellites.' The third not-person was standing by the screen. He gestured with hands that could easily span my waist – and I wasn't a waif. 'If you can let us know where to put you down, we'll start the sequence immediately.'

'Um,' I squeaked. 'I don't mean to be offensive, but are you wearing a tail? I think I'm seeing things.'

'One does not *wear* a tail, human,' he said arrogantly, the appendage in question thrashing from side-to-side behind him, its shining tufts matching his shock of honey-coloured hair. 'One is either blessed with a tail, or one is not.'

I rubbed my eyes. 'I just ... *What is happening*?'

'We're not human, little one,' the big blue definitely-not-human said gently.

'Ah,' I said, and stepped back. My tongue was heavy in my mouth, stinging from where I'd bitten it, and fear was narrowing my throat. 'Ah.' I rubbed my eyes again. 'I'm dead. I got killed because of some jerks drinking cheap beer at a bus stop. Fucking hell, how typical. I'm not the best person in the world, but I certainly deserved a better end than *that*.'

'You're not dead,' the blue one said. His voice was very deep and very calm, like he spent his life narrating meditation videos or romance audiobooks. 'All we want to do is put you back down. Can you show us on the map where you'd like to go?'

He gestured to the screen. The one with the tail stepped back to give me room, and I spent one gloriously insane moment comparing that movement to the men at the bus stop who had demanded my attention and cared so little about my personal space. It was a stupid thing to do – these not-humans had still picked me up without asking, not to mention the whole *translator* thing, which I would not be forgetting in a hurry. But they *had* possibly – probably? – saved my life.

When I closed my eyes, I could still see the bus bearing down on me, still taste the blood on my tongue. There was no way on Earth I could have moved out of the way in time.

I stepped forward shakily, swaying on my feet. The one with the pointed ears darted forward, ready to catch me, but he didn't touch me. 'Do you require assistance?'

'That depends. Do you have any benzodiazepines?' I muttered.

He frowned, then touched his ear. 'That isn't translating.'

I didn't answer, concentrating on stepping down from the platform without falling on my face or my ass. Cat-ears kept close, while Blue watched carefully. The tailed one gestured at the screen, where a map stretched over the glass.

I looked it over, swallowing. It was more blueprint than satellite map, and I wondered where they'd found it. I took a deep, steady breath, then touched the screen softly; it zoomed in on the place of contact, and from there I could move it around. My fingers trembled as I found the main street, and from there, Advena.

'Could you put me down near here?' I said, gesturing to the square on the map. Advena's kitchen would be closed, but the bouncers would still be there, and Belle, along with whatever patrons had held out for the night. 'Wait,' I added, as something occurred to me. 'Will you have to wipe my memory or something?'

The blue one frowned. 'Tampering with minds is banned in every Sector of the universe.'

'Good to know.' I paused. 'How is that different to whatever ... *calming* ... thing you did to me before?'

He flushed a lovely pastel blue; I tracked the movement of the colour, my fingers itching for my tablet and stylus. 'I'm an empath. Emotions aren't covered in the ban.'

I looked up at his face, narrowing my eyes. 'But emotions come from the mind. Human minds, anyway.'

'Yes, it's an interesting ethical conundrum,' the one with the tail said impatiently. 'Let's do this, so we can –' He broke off. 'So we can all go about our own business.'

'No arguments here,' I muttered. I wanted to go home, get into bed, pull the covers over my head, and pretend I'd been asleep all along; it was the only way I was going to deal with the fact I was now having full-blown hallucinations of places that looked suspiciously like *spaceships* and beings that seemed suspiciously like *aliens*. The sooner I was in bed, the sooner I could convince myself that this wasn't happening.

Blue moved to the screen – his muscled legs ate up the ground, and it only took him two steps – and his violet eyes peered at where I'd pointed. 'I'll start the sequence. You need to get back on the podium, little one.'

I ignored the pleasant shiver stealing over me at his words. *Little one.*

When I was back in place, his fingers danced over the screen. Cat-ears watched me, his expression closed. The tailed one watched Blue's swift fingers, his eyes narrowed.

The podium began to glow beneath my feet. At first it was soft, but it grew brighter and brighter, as if controlled by a dimmer switch.

'Farewell,' Blue rumbled, sounding oddly sad.

I closed my eyes against the light. 'Bye,' I mumbled.

From somewhere on a ship, a single, high-pitched note sounded.

LANIR

THE HUMAN FEMALE'S EYES flew open. She had long, thick lashes that cast shadows on her cheeks; I bemoaned the loss of her calm as her lips twisted once more and her fear licked over my skin. For a moment, she'd managed to push the feelings aside, but they came back, crashing like a wave.

She felt strongly, so strongly I almost couldn't block it out. She was a stranger; I should have held her emotions back with ease. As it was, my hearts began to race in sympathy with hers as the phantom of her adrenalin crashed through my veins.

A warning flashed across the screen in the Darnagh's complex symbol-based language. 'Ky?' I grated out, not able to tell whether the unease making my stomach churn belonged to me or the female.

Kyin jabbed his fingers at the screen, impatiently pressing any icon he could as his tail flicked behind him. 'What the fuck?' he breathed. 'It's frozen. *What the fuck?*'

'What's happening?' Gydion demanded, his claws retracting then extending.

'The systems are unresponsive,' I answered flatly, slowly translating the warning. 'Navigation, communication, the escape pods – and the transporter.' I glanced at the female, who was watching us, chewing on her bottom lip.

'The systems are *down*?'

'Not down,' Kyin grated out, still jabbing at the screen. '*Down* isn't possible. Things don't go *down*, not my systems, not on my ship. The controls have been overridden. *Frozen*. Blocked.'

'*Kyin*.' The voice came through the ship's communication system. 'Our timeframes have changed. You have what you came for. I have taken control of this ship. You have new coordinates. I will see you in Sector Nine.'

Kyin went completely still. Kyin was *never* still, not even while he slept; dread washed over me, dread drenched with a powerful mix of love, shame, and resentment.

The feeling wasn't mine.

'Ah,' I said, as evenly as I could manage in the face of Kyin's emotions. 'Your father.'

'You have new coordinates? What the fuck does that mean?' the female demanded.

The ship shuddered as its engines flared.

'*Fuck*,' Gydion hissed. Thinking more quickly than any of us, he leapt onto the podium and swept the human female into his arms – a bare moment before the ship swung around in a wild movement that had my hearts trying to climb up my throat and my hip slamming into the control screen podium as I scrabbled to stay upright. Kyin's tail whipped out, anchoring him like a third leg as he fought to remain standing; Gydion braced his back against the glass, holding the human tight as the thrusters rumbled to life and her planet began to recede.

'*What the fuck*?' she shrieked, gripping Gydion as the artificial gravity adjusted to the ship's sudden movement. 'What's happening?'

'Destination: Sector Nine. Planet: Scytha,' the ship announced. 'Enjoy your flight.'

'Kyin,' Gydion growled. '*Do something.*'

Kyin's fingers danced over the screens, his cheeks flushed a deep red. His emotions were a mess of anger and humiliation, and his frustration made my skin crawl as he tried to wrest back control of his own ship. 'That bastard,' he snarled. 'That fucking *bastard*. He's overridden all the access codes, all of the commands. He's even controlling the temperature and the gravity settings.' His tail whipped back and forth as he finally managed to pull up a diagnostic and flicked through the readings. 'I did everything that fucker asked of me, and he *still* pulls a move like this.' He looked across at me, hurt flickering across his expression. 'He could have just fucking *asked*.'

The female's fear pushed at me, running over my skin in cloying waves. I couldn't feel Gydion – his kind and mine had been at war for centuries, and Kjidja warriors all had mental barriers that denied the Illisae access to their emotions – but between the human and Kyin, my head was beginning to ache.

'Lan?' Gydion said softly.

I forced a smile. 'It's all right.'

He gave me a look that said he knew I was lying.

A low moan spilled from the human as she watched her city become nothing more than a blur of light.

'*No,*' she whispered. '*No.*' She thumped her fist against Gydion's forearm. 'I dropped my bag. I don't have my phone. I don't have my tablet.' She closed her eyes and whimpered. 'I thought the afterlife would be better than this.'

'Tablet?' I repeated.

Kyin frowned at Gydion. 'Are you sure you inserted the translator properly?'

Gydion hissed at him.

'I need some space,' the female said, squirming her way out of Gydion's arms. He let her go, his face unreadable. 'Is there somewhere I can sit down for a few minutes *without* seeing my home from afar while you fix this?'

I exchanged a glance with Kyin; a fresh wave of his shame washed over me, and I realised that *fixing this* might take some time. 'I can find you a cabin,' I said after a long, tense moment. 'Do you understand what's happening?'

'I'm not stupid,' she snapped. 'Someone else is controlling your ... ship. They've put you on a path you weren't expecting to travel, and you can't access any of the systems to change it back.' She took a deep breath. 'Look. I need ... I *need* some space and quiet, or I'm going to lose it. *Please*,' she begged, her deep brown eyes fixing on mine. I was struck by how alien she was, and how lovely. Her skin was a beautiful light gold, her hair a dark brown tipped with artificial pink, her features strong, her lips full. Her form was humanoid, like we all were, but curved, and wrapped in a variety of black garments, including chunky black boots that laced almost to her knee.

'We'll take you back,' I said, stepping towards her. 'I swear it. Once we have control of the situation, we'll take you back.'

She studied me warily. Cosmetic on her long lashes had smudged shadows beneath her eyes. 'Are you doing the emotion thing right now?'

'No,' I answered gently.

Her gaze dropped and she stared at her fingers. 'I believe you,' she said at last. 'I shouldn't, but I do. But *please* – please let me go somewhere quiet until you work this out.'

Gydion extended a hand. She looked at his claws for a moment; he retracted them without comment, and she placed her small fingers in his palm.

'Come, little one,' he said.

There were eight cabins on the ship: small, single-cot rooms with tiny private washrooms attached. We'd claimed three of them for ourselves; the others were empty.

'The beds aren't made up in the other rooms,' Gydion muttered. 'She looks as if she needs warmth.'

I considered her. The ship wasn't cool by our standards, but she was shivering, and the skin I could see was covered in tiny bumps like the ones Kyin got when he was cold. Her emotions were brimming like a wave about to break, simmering at a peak that she was holding in place with a thread of determination. There was a self-awareness about it that suggested she'd done the same thing before; the determination wavered as she looked around, her expression a mix of curiosity and bewilderment.

'Choose whichever cabin suits you best,' I said softly. 'Then you can take whatever you need from ours. Blankets, pillows – whatever you want.'

We showed her the empty cabins, and how to operate the door sensors. She chose a cabin at the end of the corridor, as far from ours as she could manage, which was, I thought, entirely understandable. I tried without success to adjust the heating as she rifled through the room's single cupboard, gazing at the jumpsuits stored there, her eyes going wide at the helmet used for spacewalks. She stared at the light shower and waste system through the open washroom door, and I sensed her control slipping.

'Is there water?' she said, her voice small.

I glanced at Kyin. 'Not in the cabins, no.'

She took a shuddering breath. 'It's fine, Claire, this is fine,' she said under her breath. 'You can live without hot water.'

There were some sheets in a pressure packet beneath the bed; Gydion pulled them out and made short work of covering the mattress. They were engineered for optimal temperature control, but the little human stared at them, her brow crumpling.

Comfort. She needs comfort. 'Why don't you come and choose some proper blankets – and anything else you'd like – from our rooms, and then you can rest,' I coaxed. I pushed out a tiny thrum of calm – with nothing like the force I'd used before – and she wrested back control, the wave of emotion holding at its peak.

Good girl, I wanted to tell her. *Look how strong you are.*

Some beings thought that *strength* meant never feeling at all. An empath knew what nonsense that was. Strength meant feeling *everything* and coming out the other side.

I wondered if that was something the little human was familiar with.

We'd been on Kyin's ship for months, so our cabins were all well lived-in, our personal tastes and glimmers of our home planets on display. Gydion had coaxed Kjidja ivy to grow over his walls and ceiling, and the bed was heaped with thick, soft blankets made of *feldi* pelt. Kyin's cabin was messy and sumptuous, the cot covered with neatly-tucked sheets of Ketruscan silk, the single shelf lined with a mix of defunct tech in varying states of working order. In a characteristically absurd contrast, a well-worn *erex* toy with woolly fur and beaded eyes sat upon his pillows.

My cot was covered in blankets made of heavy wool. I'd dismantled the main light; lamps of geode were fixed to the walls instead, with one bright lamp of rose quartz sitting on the shelf, bracketed by tiny ornamental fountains that made the water sounds I couldn't sleep without.

The female looked through our cabins. 'I … I just take whatever?'

'I think it's the least we can do,' I answered.

She stepped into Gydion's room, then stopped. 'Hang on. Wait. Why?'

I blinked at her. 'Because Kyin's father has accidentally abducted you and we put a translator in your ear without asking. We'd like to make you as comfortable as possible.'

'No, I mean why were you *here*? Why were you flying over Earth, when you're obviously –' she waved a hand at the three of us '– from somewhere else?'

None of us answered.

Her eyes narrowed. 'What were you doing? Were you …' She trailed off and took a step away from us. 'Were you abducting people?'

Kyin frowned. 'Why would we do that?'

Her cheeks flushed. 'I don't know, organ harvesting? As a food source? For sex?'

'That would break at least fifteen intergalactic laws,' Gydion said.

She cocked her head. 'But what you were doing was legal? Why won't you tell me, then?'

Kyin ran a hand through his honey-coloured hair. 'It was legal. For us, at least.' He paused. 'But maybe not legal for Earth.'

She took another step away from us. 'So I'm back to organ harvesting.'

'No,' Kyin said, exasperated. 'Do you even know if we have the same organs? My father just … My father just borrowed some of your bauxite ore, that's all.'

'Borrowed some of our bauxite ore,' she repeated.

Kyin waved his hand. 'You have a lot of it, relatively speaking. My home planet is all mined out. We borrowed some. Not a lot,' he added hastily, when her face darkened.

'Bauxite ore makes aluminium, doesn't it?'

'It has many names, but yes,' Kyin answered. 'Amongst other things.'

'And what does your father want with it?'

'His company makes things with it.'

The little human's lips pursed as she studied Kyin. Her lips were luscious, plump and curved, and I tried not to stare at them. After a moment, she shook her head. 'I don't think I can care about this right now,' she said.

She turned her back on him and took up one of Gydion's *feldi* pelt blankets, then took it to her cabin and spread the pelt out on the bed, tucking it neatly around the mattress. I felt her satisfaction as she ran her hand over the soft fur, soaked up the small pleasure she took in how it felt against her skin.

I thought she was done, but she headed back into the corridor. My hearts thumped when she entered my cabin; she grabbed one of my heavy woollen blankets and slung it over her shoulder, then carefully took up the quartz lamp.

She went back to the cabin she'd chosen, placing the lamp on her shelf before spreading the blanket over the pelt. The lamp cast a warm pink light over her room; she made a happy *humming* sound at it. 'Is there any more of that plant?' she said, gesturing at Gydion's cabin.

Gydion stared at her. 'I can make a cutting,' he answered eventually.

She nodded. 'I'd like that.' She stared around her room, her brow creased. 'Not quite right,' she muttered, and tapped her fingers against her chin.

We watched silently.

She headed into Kyin's room and gathered up some of his pillows. After a moment's pause, she took up the *erex* toy, too, cuddling it close to her chest. We followed her back to her cabin like flowers turning towards a sun; she arranged the pillows and the toy on the bed.

'Better,' she said. She looked up at us. 'Thank you.'

I inclined my head. I didn't think we needed thanks – we'd inadvertently abducted her, after all – but I wasn't sure how to verbalise that.

She reached towards the door sensor; her hand paused mid-air. She cleared her throat. 'Claire.'

I blinked.

'Claire?' Gydion echoed.

'Claire,' she confirmed. 'My name is Claire.'

Gydion's claws tapped on his thighs.

'Welcome to your accidental abduction, Claire,' Kyin said sourly. 'We'll be your hosts: Gydion, Lanir, and Kyin. We hope you enjoy your flight; we'll try our best to give you one hell of a time.'

'*Claire*,' I said, trying out the sound, and ignoring Kyin. I liked it; my tongue rolled on the *airh* sound.

She stared at me. A deep pink flush spread across her cheeks. 'Um. Okay then. Gydion, Lanir, and Kyin. Bye,' she squeaked, and waved her hand over the sensor.

The door closed.

There was a moment of calm, and then the wave broke.

Panic and confusion and fear spilled over me. It was so strong I staggered, bracing myself against the wall. The wave was buoyed on a base of something else that the female – *Claire* – carried bone-deep: an underlying sense of restlessness, of nervousness, a seemingly endless well of critical feeling turned inwards, eating at everything else that existed there.

I tried to sort through it all, to find who she was alongside that well. It was part of her, I saw; it always would be, but it wasn't *everything* she was. I felt Gydion slip beneath my arm, holding me upright as I cautiously reached out to her with *elya*, and searched.

I found curiosity, like a bright ray of sun. Shyness, a sweet pink blush. A deep blue determination. The scarlet of desire and a burnished orange of wonder.

She was a tangle of light and darkness.

I wanted to unwind her.

'Lan?' Gydion said, bringing me back to myself. 'What do you think?'

I straightened, finding my feet once more as the glow of *elya* beneath my skin settled. 'I'm not entirely sure,' I said at last. 'But this is going to be interesting.'

GYDION

'ANYTHING TO REPORT?'

Kyin turned to glare at me, his tail twitching behind him. 'My father is the king of all assholes,' he snarled. 'Isn't that enough?'

I rolled my eyes. Kyin enjoyed heightened emotions and all the drama that came with it; my patience for his theatrics only stretched so far. 'We're heading to Scytha. Why?'

Kyin looked back down at the control screen, examining the path his father had set us on as his tail twitched behind him. 'Rellyn must have sent my father another update from the peace summit. Perhaps the Council made a decision about the Roth.'

'Yes, but *which* decision?' Lanir gazed out into the black of space. 'Last we heard, there were two that seemed likely. Firstly, they refused the Roth King's request, and attacked Scytha outright while the planet was distracted by civil war. Second –'

'They granted his request and will send forces to fight with him, joining the war with all the weight of the Allied Planets behind them,' Kyin finished.

'Either way, we're heading for conflict,' I said quietly. I examined my hands, retracting and extending my claws. 'Why, Ky? Why did your father need that ore? Why take it to *Scytha*? And why *now*? What's the rush?'

There was a moment of silence as Kyin thought it through.

'He's selling weapons again,' he answered, his voice dead. 'Or rather, he's selling the ore to make the machines that manufacture the weapons. I know he's done it before – one of his *side projects* – and there's no reason he wouldn't do it again.' He slumped down, resting his forehead against the screen. 'I'm so fucking *stupid*. I didn't want to go to Earth – I wanted us to go to Natare for the summit – but he told me the ore would be used for medical equipment, and that it was *important*. And I fucking *believed* him.' His tail lashed back and forth, silently shouting his agitation. 'When will I fucking *learn*?'

'He's your father,' Lanir said softly. 'Of course you wanted to believe him.'

'Ky,' I said, when I could hold my tongue no longer. '*Which side will he sell to*?'

Kyin sat up and stared at me, then crumpled once more. 'Both,' he answered, burying his face in his arms. 'If I know him, he'll sell to both.'

Lanir and I exchanged an uneasy glance.

The notion that Kyin's father would drop his son into the middle of the Roth civil war – for *profit* – was one I wished I could be surprised by. Xanthin Crace was a ruthless genius, head of Darn's largest tech company, his name renown throughout the universe. Kyin had his father's intelligence, but not his heartlessness, which was where Lanir and I came in; we kept Kyin as safe as we could in the face of his father's cut-throat business decisions and any competitors who decided to threaten the son in place of the father.

It was a full-time job, and one we'd taken upon ourselves when times were different. We'd been willing – how could we not be, when we loved Kyin as much as we did each other? Keeping him safe was as much for *us* as it was for him; the notion of a universe without Kyin in it was unthinkable.

But three Kjidja months ago – three months, two days, and twelve hours, if I wanted to be precise – Kyin had ended things between us. *I can't do this*, he'd said. *It's not working.*

Lanir and I had stayed with him anyway, because without Kyin, we were like a ship without a navigation system, and we didn't trust anyone else to keep him safe. But things had been … *strained*. Not just with Kyin, but between Lanir and I, too, as if we needed Kyin to make us laugh, to make us *lighter*.

Kyin sat upright again. 'Oh, gods, Lan, the conflict,' he said, staring at the Illisae Mage. 'We can't take you into a war.'

Lanir lifted his chin. 'Where you go, I go,' he said calmly, but I saw his fingers clench into fists.

As an empath, battle would be unbearable for Lanir. All the pain, all the suffering, all the rage and regret and sorrow flowing over him, flowing *through* him, all without pause. The Illisae had mental shields to protect themselves, but they couldn't hold them forever – the shields required energy and *elya*, just like everything else the Mages did – and the sheer scope of the civil conflict on Scytha would break them down swiftly.

War would ruin him.

I shook my head. 'We'll work it out, Ky. We'll get Lan out before we arrive. Somehow.' I paused. 'And we have another complication.'

'The human,' Lanir said.

'The human.' I looked out the glass. We were in dark space now; the black was a void that always pulled at me. I loved it as much as I feared it. 'What happens to her when we arrive?'

'I might override my father's hack by then,' Kyin protested. 'We might be able to take her back.'

'And how much luck are you having so far?'

He glowered, which was a sufficient answer. 'My father builds safeguards on his safeguards, and he fights *dirty* when he hacks. He's set traps through every fucking system. If I override the controls on the climate, he'll fuck up the water supply. If I break through the hangar locks to get to the ore, that psychopath will redivert the oxygen.' He took a deep breath. 'I don't even want to think about what he's set up if I take control of the pilot console. I'll keep trying, but he ...' He trailed off. 'He's in full control. As always.'

'He's in control of the ship, Ky, not *you*,' Lanir said.

'Very helpful, Lan, thanks,' Kyin snapped.

'Regardless of whether Ky manages to break through, we need to plan for the eventuality that we end up in Roth airspace with a human female – with *Claire* – on board, during a civil war,' I said. 'What do we do with her?'

They were silent; Kyin's tail whipped through the air.

'Kyin's father might not enable the ship's shields when we fly into Roth airspace,' Lanir said reluctantly. 'If he doesn't, we'll be a sitting target, whether we're on terra or in orbit. This ship has only basic weapons. We'll be entirely vulnerable.'

'And carrying a tonne of ore needed by both sides,' Kyin muttered.

'The alternative?' I prompted, wanting it to come from them. I'd already thought this through and settled on what seemed the best plan, but I wasn't in charge.

We made decisions together.

'The safest place will be behind allied lines,' Kyin supplied. 'Regardless of where my father lands us, we *can't* have the human near the Roth. Whatever hold the allies have gained on the ground, that's the place she should be. *Far behind* the line,' he added.

I nodded. 'I agree.'

'So we get her there,' Lanir said slowly. 'Let Kyin's father land wherever he wants. If he wants the ore off the ship, then he'll need to let us off, too. We take her to the allied forces as soon as the ship is on the ground.'

'What if he lands behind Roth lines?' Kyin interjected. 'We just walk her through a fucking *warzone*? On *Scytha*? The place famous for kidnapping females and keeping them in chains? She doesn't look like a warrior. She's all ...' Kyin trailed off as he thought about it. 'Soft. *Curvy*. Like she should be draped in silk, not covered in armour.'

Lanir blinked at him, and I wondered which particular emotion of Kyin's had surprised him.

I tapped a claw on my thigh. 'How long until we reach Scytha?'

Kyin checked the screen. 'He's flying the ship at speed, but not as fast as we can go. Four weeks, four days, according to this.'

I smiled. 'That's plenty of time.'

'Plenty of time for what?' Lanir said warily.

My smile widened. 'For lessons.'

Claire stayed inside her room for two full days.

When she finally emerged, it was apparent that she'd barely slept – and that she was ravenously hungry. We'd left some water – along with some protein bars safe for most humanoid species – outside her cabin door, but we didn't know anything about humans, and we hadn't wanted to risk making her food that could be poisonous. Her rumbling stomach echoed softly around the corridor as I took her in: she had dark shadows under her eyes, and her hair was pulled into a messy plait that hung over one shoulder. She was still in the same clothes, despite there being several jumpsuits in the room's cupboard; her scent was fresh and clean, though, suggesting that she'd worked out how to use the light shower.

'What?' she said warily, when I'd been staring for slightly too long.

'I thought you might be hungry,' I answered, trying to close off my senses. The light shower hadn't erased her natural sweet scent; it was concerningly alluring. I fought the urge to bury my face in her neck and breathe it in properly.

She rubbed her stomach, considering. 'How long have I been in here?'

'Forty-eight of your Earth hours.'

Her lips twisted. 'No wonder I feel like crap.' She rubbed her eyes. 'Should I be scared?'

'Of us?'

'Well, I'm definitely not okay with the nonconsensual trans-lator insertion or the whole *flying through space away from Earth* thing. And I'm still processing how I feel about the em-pathic powers and the fact that I can trust my own emotions even less than usual. So yeah. I'd like to know if I should be scared of you.'

'This didn't start well,' I said. 'I understand that. I'm sorry about the translator, and for what it's worth, Lanir won't use his powers again without your permission. We have no reason to harm you, Claire, and nor do we want to. You're a guest in our home.'

She blinked, startled. 'God, I wonder if my actual housemates have even noticed I'm gone.'

'Do you have family?' I asked softly. 'Will they be worrying?'

She shook her head. 'My family doesn't ... We don't keep in touch.'

'Why not?'

She raised an eyebrow at me. 'Well, Gydion, since you asked, they were *disappointed* when I changed my degree from eco-nomics to visual art, *disappointed* when I dated a girl, *disap-pointed* when I got help for my mental health.' Her tone was acidic. 'They think my anxiety doesn't exist; they think I'm making it up. That I don't try hard enough. That I should just get over it. That I should be more like *them* and less like myself. It took me a while, but I realised they didn't want the best for *me*. They wanted a version of me that was better for *them*. A daughter who made good money and then got married and spawned kids like a good woman does. A daughter who accept-ed her lot and never had her head in the clouds. A daughter who wore dresses and went to church and didn't kiss girls as well as boys. A daughter they could brag about; a daughter who made them feel good. Feel *proud*. A daughter who made them feel like she was a reflection of everything they'd given her; like her success was somehow *theirs*.' She gave a thin smile. 'They have other kids, and my siblings are more inclined to be the way our parents want them to be, so my family leaves me alone, and mostly, I prefer it that way. Is that enough of an answer for you?'

'That's ... a lot,' I replied, trying to grasp everything she'd said.

She passed a hand over her eyes, her lips twisting. 'Sorry. That was an overshare.'

'You're welcome to share anything you want with me.'

She seemed mollified by my response. 'Do you have parents?'

'I suppose I must,' I said. 'My kind give up their kits once they're weaned. Younglings are raised communally until fourteen spans of age, then we are allocated to institutions: the government, the temple, the military. Most go to the government; it dictates the way Kjid is run, from food and environment to science and technology. But I went to the military. A specific branch of it, anyway.'

She studied me. 'Makes sense,' she said after a moment. 'You stand like a soldier. Straight spine, shoulders back, chin up, arms at your sides. But most soldiers stay with their units, don't they?'

My lips curled. 'Most do,' I agreed. I examined my hands. 'I took a period of unplanned leave many cycles ago.'

She gave an answering smile. 'You mean you're AWOL?'

I frowned at her in question.

She shook her head. 'Never mind.' The tip of her tongue grazed her full lips. I watched its movements, unable to look away. 'You mentioned food?'

'Food,' I agreed, giving myself a mental shake. 'Come.'

Kyin's ship was a model common on Darn, usually used by families for cross-Sector travel. He'd modified the Sidereal extensively, replacing its systems and its engines until he had a craft that could be used for elevated unit travel and was comfortable to live in for long periods of time. Since Lanir and I had been with him for so long, Kyin had also changed parts of the ship's design to make us feel more at home. Lan's species, the Illisae, lived on a planet with a toxic atmosphere. Though they were more immune to its poisons than other species, they spent most of their time in a series of complex cave networks complete with underground rivers. So that Lanir didn't miss the sound, Kyin had installed special screens throughout the ship over which water ran continually in a gentle cascade. My own planet was covered in dense forest, so Kyin built gardens to line the corridors, interspersed with small rockeries, and Kjidja ivy grew over every available surface. Kyin stamped himself on the ship, too; every gadget was the best his father's money could buy, and the ship had every convenience able to fit on board.

Which didn't matter now that his father had locked us out of most of them.

Claire looked around silently as we walked, soaking everything up. I knew that humans had mastered short-distance space flight and had a number of craft that stayed in the Earth's orbit, but I wasn't sure how familiar she was with space travel. She took it all in without comment, though I saw her fingers twitch against her thighs in an odd echo of my own habit when I was uneasy.

'Are you all right?'

Her eyes flickered to me. 'I'm still standing,' she answered, 'so I think I must be.'

I'd considered taking a variety of foods to her room – along with a healing wand in case something went wrong – but she couldn't stay in there. At the very least, she needed to exercise to ensure her bone and muscle density remained constant, but I also suspected that humans would be just as susceptible to the myriad dangers of space travel and long-term confinement as other species; she was mostly made of water, just like my kind was, and water needed to move to stay drinkable.

Not that I was planning to drink the human.

We weren't entirely sure what humans needed for sustenance, but as her body was closest to Kyin's, we figured we'd start there. The Darnagh ate a varied diet of meat products and vegetation, and while the ship didn't carry any *actual* meat, we could generate something that was a fair approximation of it.

'Looks just like a uni cafeteria,' Claire said as we stepped inside the small cooking and dining hall.

I didn't know what that meant, so I made a noise of acknowledgement and headed straight for the generator. Kyin was already there, wearing a frown as he studied the three dishes he'd made.

'This is going to be trial and error,' he said to Claire in greeting. 'We don't *think* any of it will be poisonous for you, but perhaps just take small bites, yes?'

She frowned at him. 'That doesn't inspire confidence.'

'No, but it's better than starving,' he said cheerfully, his lips pulling up into their usual irreverent grin. 'Probably.' He pointed to the first plate. 'This one is standard Darnagh fare – root vegetables and fake *erex* meat. The second is a little fancier: seasonal squash cooked with a bean-based protein and a dairy sauce. This one,' he went on, gesturing to the third, 'is my favourite. It's mock sea-creature with wheat-based strips, sprinkled with dairy flakes. Or something trying to be dairy flakes, anyway.'

Claire sniffed. 'Smells like seafood marinara. I'm in.'

Kyin placed the dish on a table, handing her the three-pronged utensil favoured by the Darnagh. Humans must have used something similar, for Claire didn't so much as blink, taking it from him and plunging it immediately into the food as she folded into a chair. I sat down opposite; she delivered a small amount past her lips and chewed.

'Well?' Kyin said, when she'd swallowed.

'A bit weird for breakfast,' Claire answered, 'but not bad.'

'Wait a while so we know it's not going to harm you,' I cautioned.

Claire put down the fork. 'Okay, but it does taste pretty similar to what I'm used to. Is there anything to drink?'

'Water, powered *umi* or *jynt* fruit juice, flavoured protein powders,' I said.

'Coffee?'

'*Coff-ee*?' Kyin echoed.

Claire groaned. '*Guys*. This abduction started as a zero-star endeavour. I graciously added one star just now for the fact I might not die of starvation, but I'm going to have to take it back if you don't have caffeine.'

'What is *caffeine*?'

'A stimulant. It's found in Earth foods like chocolate, and in drinks like tea and coffee. Tea is –'

'We have tea,' I interjected.

'Oh.' She closed her eyes. 'You are officially my favourite, Gydion.'

I suspected she was joking, but something pleasant twisted in my stomach anyway.

'Don't start picking favourites just yet,' Kyin said, his voice smug. He turned to rifle through the cupboard above the food preparation area, taking out a large packet made of blue foil. He opened it and sniffed appreciatively, then held it out to Claire.

She inhaled sharply. 'Oh, *Kyin*.'

The way she said his name made my skin break out in shivers. I rubbed my arms to hide it, but I needn't have bothered; neither of them were looking at me. Claire was looking at the blue foil like she'd just seen the Goddess, and Kyin was looking at Claire with – well, the same expression.

I shifted in surprise.

'It may not taste the same as your *coff-ee*, but this is a stimulant, too. Would you like me to make you some?'

'Please,' Claire begged. 'I'm desperate enough to start eating it by the spoonful.'

As Kyin prepared the drink, I studied Claire. 'I thought I could show you more of the ship today,' I said at last. 'You should know the place you're staying for the next few weeks.'

She nodded. 'I'll give you advanced warning that I'm feeling pretty fragile right now. If I freak out … just take me back to the cabin, okay?'

'If you *freak out*?'

'You know. Get anxious. Overwhelmed.' Her lips twisted. 'The Claire Special.'

Kyin frowned at her. 'The Claire Special?'

She shook her head. 'It doesn't matter. Just take me back to the cabin. I feel … I feel safe there.'

Wrapped in our blankets, with her head resting on our pillows.

Kyin glanced at me as my claws dug into the table, then put the finishing touch – *ici*, a Darnagh spice – atop the steaming drink. 'Here,' he said proudly. '*Limere.*'

Claire raised the glass to her lips and took a tentative sip. She wheezed.

I stood. 'Claire?' I said anxiously.

She began to cough, gasping for air as her eyes streamed.

'Kyin, water!' I hissed.

Kyin grabbed her a glass of water and clunked it down before her, his eyes wide, his tail thrashing.

'Fuck,' Claire croaked. '*Fuck*, Kyin. Is that topping made of *chilli*?'

'No, it's mostly made of *xydeth* leaves,' Kyin answered, confused.

'Tastes like dried chilli,' Claire muttered. She looked up in time to see Kyin's face fall. 'No, Kyin, thank you for trying. I really *like* chilli – I just don't usually eat it by the mouthful. Now that I know, I'm ready for it.' She picked up the glass again.

'Claire, you don't have to –' I started.

She held up a finger and took another sip.

This time, she didn't wheeze, or cough. She *did*, however, take a large mouthful of water straight afterwards. 'See?' she said faintly. 'Better. But maybe I could have it again without the topping?' She paused. 'And I do feel much more awake now, and hopefully it will fix the withdrawal headache. Thank you, Kyin.'

Kyin cleared his throat, turning back to the food preparation bench, but not before I saw that his cheeks had flushed with pleasure.

I watched Claire take another mouthful of her food, watched her tongue flick out over her lip, watched her long fingers wrap around the utensil. I glanced at Kyin, who had turned back enough that he could watch her do the same thing, his dark eyes alight in a way I hadn't seen in months.

In a way that made my chest tight; in a way that I'd *missed*.

I pressed my claws into my thighs and stood abruptly. 'We need to get into the screen library, Ky.'

He flicked a frown at me. 'More than we need control of the oxygen?'

I ground my teeth, not wanting to scare Claire. 'No. But it is important.' I let my eyes rest on Claire pointedly, as she took another sip of *limere*. 'We need more information.'

Kyin's frown deepened, but he nodded. 'There's no way in the hells I'll be able to access the maps,' he warned. 'But I'll try the others.'

'Good.' I aimed a smile at Claire, who was watching us curiously. 'When you've finished, would you like a tour of your first Darnagh ship?'

I trailed after Gydion and Claire, harbouring a strong suspicion that I looked like a sulky youngling.

Gydion had claimed the role of ship's tour guide before I'd had the chance, and he was making the most of it. Gydion had an answer to any question Claire asked, explaining everything from solar storms to space ice to freeze-dried protein powders to the medical bay. His voice was deep and rasping, his fingers occasionally grazing Claire's arm as he directed her around the ship.

Around *my* ship.

Other than picking her up to save her from the threat of imminent death, I hadn't paid much attention to the little human when she'd first come on board, too caught up in getting my father the ore he'd requested, before the asshole commandeered my beloved Sidereal. But when she'd picked up the *erex* toy from my cabin – the one my mother had given me, the one that came with me no matter where I went – the image of the fuzzy creature in her arms had begun to occupy my thoughts. When Lanir had suggested that I try to work out what to feed her, I'd started thinking about her more often, as a new puzzle to be solved, wrapped up in a luscious, curvy form.

And when she'd finished the *limere* I'd made her, licking the last drops from her lips, she began to occupy even more of my mind, interest sparking deep in my stomach in a way it hadn't done since I'd met Lanir and Gydion.

So I may have been a little bit resentful that it was *Gydion's* fingers lingering on the small of her back as he guided her around a corner, that it was *Gydion* who explained how the parts of the ship spun to create gravity, that it was *Gydion* she fixed her big dark eyes upon and blinked her long, thick lashes at as he ushered her through a sliding silver door. I could do *all* of those things, and I wanted her big dark eyes focused on *me*.

A growl rumbled up my throat; I swallowed it just in time.

'This is the simulation room,' Gydion was saying, gesturing around the empty space as the door hissed closed behind us.

Claire's eyebrows rose. 'Like, VR?'

Gydion frowned at her.

'Virtual reality,' she explained. 'On Earth, we have these helmets, and it's like being immersed in whatever world the program runs. The coding is beyond me, but I tried one at uni. It was an underwater world, and all these creatures were swimming past … A friend knocked himself unconscious trying to jump over a fish that wasn't there. He tripped and hit his head on a desk.'

'No helmets necessary,' Gydion said, his fingers sliding over the control screen. 'This is one of the smaller systems, so it can only manage a maximum of six participants at a time, but it uses a mix of holographic and sensory triggers alongside a partial biomesh to create an entirely immersive simulation.' He pressed a button. 'If it gets too much, say *finish*.'

'I ...' Claire started as the system *hummed*, initiating the program, then squeaked as the first tendrils of mist touched her skin. 'What –'

I took a deep breath as the air cooled, then from one blink to the next, we were immersed in green.

Claire made a strangled noise, quickly smothered by the palm of her hand.

Every landmass on Gydion's home planet, Kjid, was covered in thick rainforest. It wasn't the same as the woods on my own planet, Darn, or the tangled, stretching Forests on Tir; this was layer upon layer of plant growth fighting for life, creating a brilliantly verdant environment, impossible to tame. The Kjidja hadn't bothered trying, changing themselves to live in the rainforest rather than the other way around. Their claws helped them climb trees taller than Darn's high glass buildings, and they hunted the myriad creatures that lived alongside them in the thick green wilderness. They built houses high up in branches and collected water from where it pooled on the leaves of what they called *sky trees*.

'Oh my God,' Claire said. She reached up to touch a leaf bigger than her body, then shrank back when her fingers found something solid beneath their tips. 'Gydion. *What the fuck.*'

'This is Kjid,' Gydion said calmly, 'my home planet.'

'But I can *feel* it!' Claire's hair was curling in the mist; she reached up to smooth her hands over the waving strands. 'It's *wet!* What the *fuck!*'

'Like Gyd said, a mix of sensory triggers with a biomesh to make the simulation as real as possible,' I said softly.

Gydion's fingers moved over the control panel, and a moment later, the scene changed. We stood on a grassy hillside, overlooking a city of glass and shining metal.

My tail whipped from side to side. 'My home city,' I said, my voice suddenly strained. 'Arlight. I was born here.'

A sweet, warm breeze ruffled through my hair and dried the mist from Claire's. She inhaled, closing her eyes for a moment, then opened them to study the city, a slight crease appearing between her brows.

'This is … This is not that different to Earth,' she said, before yelping when a small transport carrier whirred over our heads, stirring her hair again. 'Okay. Maybe it's a *bit* different. Can we go into the city?'

I tried to smother my sense of dread as Gydion nodded and we 'walked' towards the outskirts. I knew that we were in a simulation, walking on the spot as the image adjusted, making it seem like we were gaining ground towards a city that wasn't real, but it didn't lessen my sense of trepidation. Arlight held everything I hated about my home: my father's wide-reaching, all-seeing corporation; a low, close sky that gave me claustrophobia; crowded public places where every step would see a screen shoved close to my face and, within minutes, my scowl plastered across public casts and chat networks, accompanied by a fresh onslaught of sordid gossip. All that alongside my mother's absence, which seemed to permeate the very pathways of the city itself.

But Claire wanted to look more closely, so instead of sprinting in the opposite direction, I walked beside her, as calmly as I could.

Gydion let her explore the outskirts for some time, following her down alleyways and through open-air markets and past screen halls, restaurants, shops, and simupodiums. The simulation didn't include any of my fellow Darnagh, which might have been eerie if I wasn't so relieved. I ignored my surroundings, watching Claire soak it all in, her expression one of rapt wonder.

Gydion watched us both carefully. When Claire turned to walk further into the city – towards where my father's headquarters lay – and every muscle in my body tensed, he turned swiftly to the screen and pulled us, without warning, into a different simulation instead – one of a place I'd never been.

The Illisae were an intensely private and self-protective species, so the only simulation we had of their home planet, Ilis, was one sanctioned by their Mages' Assembly. It showed one of their public cave networks, the one where they welcomed diplomats and other representatives from the Intergalactic Council. Those visits were always strictly orchestrated and monitored, and none of the visitors were allowed outside designated boundaries.

Lanir never bothered with the simulation of his home world; he said it was nothing like the planet he knew.

Claire spun around, a shuddering gasp escaping her lips as she took in the cave walls disappearing into darkness, the glow of the far-away light worms, the geode formations that made the cavernous space a rainbow of colour and playful light.

'This is Lanir's home?' she breathed.

'It's his planet,' Gydion agreed.

Claire swallowed. 'Wow. The colours are ... Wow.'

'The atmosphere on Ilis is poisonous,' I explained. 'Fatal, actually, for most species. But the noxious gases are light, and the cave networks go, well, *down*, and so the air within them is breathable. For the Illisae, anyway; I wouldn't recommend it for us. But the chemicals on the planet's surface leach into its minerals, which means they change the colour of the formation of rock over time …' I lost my train of thought as Claire reached up to touch one of the formations, her hand caressing the blue stone in a way that made my heart race and my body tense.

I want her hand on me, I realised. I wanted her long fingers skimming over my chest, over my stomach, over –

Gydion cleared his throat. '*Finish.*'

The simulation faded, leaving Claire standing with her arm in the air. She lowered it, staring at her fingers. 'Fuck me.'

My tongue darted out to touch my bottom lip.

Gydion peered at her eyes. 'How do you feel? Any disorientation? Dizziness? Nausea?'

'No more than usual,' Claire answered, flushing under his close scrutiny.

'Well then.' Gydion stepped back. 'I have a proposition for you.'

I suppressed a groan, my mind immediately leaping to a place it probably shouldn't have gone.

'What kind of proposition?' Claire said warily.

'Training.'

'Training?'

'You know that Kyin's father is currently in control of this ship, and that he's sending us to Scytha.' Gydion flicked on the simulation again, and a few moments later, we were standing in a red waste, heat beating down on our skin. In the distance, I could see a lake, thick with black algae and wholly undrinkable. Rocky outcrops broke the rolling, cracked clay; I could just make out doorways in the stone, leading down into one of the Roth's subterra settlements.

Gydion's fingers flicked again, and a Roth warrior appeared next to Claire. She yelped, jumping back into me; I caught her, looping my arm around her waist.

Her heartbeat thundered in my ears.

'Scytha is ruled by the Roth,' Gydion continued, walking around the warrior, who growled. Claire pressed back into me as she took in the muscled torso, the black eyes, the pearlescent scales, and the horns, which added an extra foot to his already-considerable height. 'The Roth are warriors. They always have been. But in the last few centuries, something has gone ... wrong. They are bent on expansion, desperate to save themselves, and they're employing violence to do so.'

'And Kyin's father is just ... sending us there. To where they live,' Claire said. Her back pressed against my chest, and I let my chin rest on the top of her head, studying Gydion, whose claws extended as he met my eyes.

'There is a new Roth King. He killed his father and is flying back to Scytha to try to claim his throne. Because Kyin's father has frozen our access to newscasts, we don't know which side the Intergalactic Council is on – the new King's, or the old regime – but either way, our ship will be flying to a planet in the middle of a civil conflict.' The Roth warrior gave a savage snarl; Gydion flicked off the simulation.

Claire pulled away from me. I let her go, trying to keep my tail still and only partially succeeding.

'So: training,' Gydion continued. 'Lan and I have fought since we could walk. Kyin is passable with a stunner and not half bad at close combat. We'll use the journey to Scytha to teach you everything we can.'

'So that if we land in the middle of conflict, I might not die immediately?' Claire said.

Gydion smiled, showing his elongated canines. 'Exactly.'

'I'm not –' Claire started, then took a shuddering breath. 'I'm not athletic, Gydion. I'm not *brave*. I've never done anything like this before.'

'Then it's the perfect time to start,' I said.

Claire turned and studied me. 'Fine,' she said crossly, after a short silence. 'It's not like I have anything better to do.'

It's not jealousy, I told myself, as I watched Gydion flip Claire onto the mat.

I don't care, I thought, as Claire threw a wild punch at his face and he caught it, smiling.

I'm fine with this, I silently insisted, as I watched her body arch under his as he pinned her down.

I couldn't tell whether I cared about Gydion touching Claire, or Claire touching Gydion.

She pushed at him, panting; Gydion leapt immediately to his feet, pulling her upright. 'See? You've improved.'

'I have – not,' Claire gasped. 'It's – been – two – hours, Gydion. I'm getting – worse.'

'You need a break,' he agreed. 'But it was a good start.'

She glared at him. 'I'm sore all over, covered in sweat, and I'm fairly sure you almost *bit* me. How is that a *good start*?'

Gydion moved, fluid as water, and feigned a strike at Claire's face. Her hands flew up to block it.

'See?' he said smugly. 'You couldn't do *that* two hours ago.'

He was right. Claire wasn't a natural fighter, but he'd coached her through the basic Kjidja blocking stances, and after some practise, she'd begun to move as if her body remembered them.

Claire lowered her hands, staring at her fists. 'No, I couldn't,' she muttered. She looked up, swallowing, her cheeks pinched with some sudden emotion. 'Can I go back now, please?'

Gydion turned off the simulation system immediately; I opened the door for Claire to stumble through. She leaned against the corridor wall, gasping.

'Little one?' I said anxiously.

She closed her eyes and took a deep, shuddering breath. 'Sorry,' she muttered. 'Sorry. I started thinking about home. I just ... I need to go back to my room. Please.'

Something wrenched in my chest. I offered her my hand. 'I'll take you.' I flicked a look at Gydion. *Get Lan*, I mouthed.

He nodded and slipped down the corridor.

Claire took my hand; I encased it with my own. Her fingers were long and thin, her knuckles pronounced; there were calluses on some. I was curious, but didn't want to ask her about her life when the mere thought of home had made her panic.

'The city of Arlight was built over hot springs,' I said instead. 'They're right at the centre, whole spans of them, circled by a covered walkway we call The Ring. In the beginning, the springs were sacred, a place of worship, and then they became a place of healing when my people realised they could lessen or cure some ailments. We don't need them for that purpose any longer, but they're still special, still a place that everyone loves to visit.'

She was silent as we walked. 'What colour are they?' she asked at last.

'Colour?' I said, surprised. 'Purple, like all the other hot springs.'

She peered up at me. 'Huh,' she said. 'The ones on Earth are blue or green.'

'Blue?' I repeated, wrinkling my nose. 'What kind of planet has *blue* hot springs?'

She snorted when she realised I was joking. 'God, I wish you had a bath on this ship.'

'I'll find you one as soon as we land,' I said, though I imagined that *baths* wouldn't be the first thing on our minds when we landed in the middle of a war zone.

Lanir was waiting outside her door, leaning casually against the wall, though his shoulders were tense. 'Claire?'

She stared at him. 'Gydion fetched you so you'd do your magic thing, didn't he,' she grumbled.

Lanir tilted his head slightly. 'Only if you want me to.'

Claire appeared to consider his offer for a few moments, taking her hand from mine to twist the hem of her shirt between her fingers. 'I do,' she said at last. 'I shouldn't, but I think I do.'

Lanir nodded. 'Whenever you're ready.'

Claire touched her fingers to the control panel for her room; the door slid silently open. 'Thank you for the food and *limere*, Kyin,' she said.

'You're welcome,' I said gruffly, and watched her walk inside her room.

Lanir followed her, and a moment later, the door slid closed in my face.

I looked down the corridor to see Gydion watching me, idly scraping a claw back and forth across his hard jawline.

'Enjoy the training, did you?' I sniped, pushing past him to return to the control room screen for another futile attempt to get past my father's overrides. 'Was it nice, having her pinned beneath you, squirming?'

Gydion caught my arm and pulled me close, until our breath was mingling and my hip was pressed to his. Gods, he always smelled so good, Gydion: like a thunderstorm, like springtime rain on a blossoming tree, with a hint of electricity in the air. He smelled like *mine*. My tail whipped from side to side as he stared at me, his green eyes slitted, his pupils dilated into diamonds. We were almost the same height, so I glared back, refusing to look away.

'Jealous, Kyin?' he hissed.

'Just surprised,' I snapped. 'What happened to the *forever* you used to talk about?'

'You were the one who ended it,' he reminded me, his eyes searching mine; for a moment, I wondered what he saw. He pressed closer, his free hand slipping down to grip my hardening cock through my jumpsuit.

'The one who ruined it, you mean,' I shot back, humiliated at how easily my body responded to him. It always had, but I'd convinced myself that it would stop with time.

Apparently, I was wrong.

'Your words, not mine, Ky.' His fingers traced my jaw with a feather-light touch even as his other hand squeezed my shaft, just below my head, hard enough that I hissed in pleasure-pain. He leaned in, so close that his breath brushed my lips when he spoke again, controlling the moment as he always did. 'So don't you *dare* get jealous when we move on.'

He pushed me away; I staggered back into the wall as he stalked down the hall to his room.

'*We*?' I called after him.

He looked back at me, hard and unyielding and devastatingly beautiful. 'Yes, Kyin. *We*.' He stepped into his cabin; the door slid shut behind him, and I was left in the cold corridor of the ship that belonged to me, but I could not control.

Alone.

CLAIRE

This is fine, I told myself. *Breathe, Claire. This is fine.*

My next thought was: *will I ever see a meme again?*

Lanir eyed me warily when I made a strangled half-sob, half-laugh sound and collapsed onto my cot. It was surprisingly comfortable, even though it looked like the kind of bed you'd find in a boarding school or a prison. The blankets I'd taken were soft and warm. All up, it could have been worse.

My anxiety, however, did not care.

I wanted to cry, but the tears wouldn't come. I had the notion that if I could just have one good crying session – a full-on, proper weep, with sobs and wails and snot and hiccups – I'd feel better, cleansed, almost. I couldn't do it, though. It felt like a betrayal; my body – well, my brain – threw so much at me, the least it could do was let me have a good, old-fashioned bawl. But it wasn't to be; my eyes remained stubbornly dry.

'You're trembling,' Lanir said gently, keeping himself by the door, giving me as much space as he could in a room so small I could feel the coolness of his body across it. 'And your heart is racing.'

'It's what I do.' I tried to take a deep breath. If I couldn't cry it out, I could at least try to calm myself down. *Acknowledge five things you can see.* I looked down at my hands. *The soft fur blanket I'd taken from Gydion's room, stretched tight over my mattress.* I looked to the side. *The heavy wool blanket I'd taken from Lanir, folded down at the end of my cot. The cute stuffed toy I cuddled at night, borrowed from Kyin, sitting atop a pillow. The dyed tips of my hair, falling over my shoulder in a loose braid.* I looked up again, and managed to inhale, deeply. *Lanir himself, his violet eyes whirling, his pupils glowing white as he studied me.* 'I'm always anxious. I've been like that since I was sixteen. But sometimes, it's worse. It's been ... bad ... lately. Before you abducted me, I mean. Usually, I try to self-manage, but I was having trouble. My doctor prescribed me meds. I bought the tablets, and kept them by my bed, but I never opened the packet.' I swallowed. 'Every morning, or when I got overwhelmed, I'd just ... remind myself that they were there. Waiting, in case I needed them.' I fidgeted. 'I wish I had them now. Even if it was just to look at the packet.'

'*Meds,*' Lanir repeated. 'Medication?'

I nodded, concentrating on controlling my breathing. *You're okay, Claire. You're okay.*

'I think I'm getting the hang of human,' he muttered. 'What made it bad just now?'

I winced. 'Gydion was teaching me to fight.'

Lanir frowned, waiting.

'At the end of the lesson, I protected my face. And I realised that I couldn't do that before. I realised that if I ever get back to Earth, I'll go back changed. Which made me think of home, which made me think of the fact I'm in an alien spacecraft travelling God knows how far across galaxies –'

'Which made your anxiety become heightened,' Lanir interrupted gently, before I could get too invested. 'I understand.'

I wasn't sure that he *did*, not entirely. Unless he, too, had been abducted from his home planet and separated from everything he knew to spend every waking moment in an alien spacecraft with complete strangers, he couldn't *possibly* know.

'That sounds like a perfectly reasonable response to me,' Lanir went on. 'Your world has been upended, little one. I can't imagine anything more natural to feel than fear. What I can do is help you when you need it,' he said, almost in answer to my thought. 'I can give you calm. But I won't do it without your permission, Claire. Not again.' He paused. 'You're doing an excellent job all on your own. But I can help whenever you wish it.'

I nodded, swallowing. I appreciated him seeking my consent, but I couldn't quite put it into words. 'Can you do it now?'

There was something else I couldn't tell him: that it wasn't just the distance from home and the differences in my environment that were making me anxious. It was the realisation that something I hadn't felt for years was simmering in my core, something delicious and hot, something that had steadily built while I'd been training with Gydion – something that I was afraid might boil over.

You can't have a crush on an alien, Claire. And you especially can't have a crush on three *of them.*

It didn't help, though, that they were all breathtakingly beautiful in their own – albeit different – ways. Gydion was all sleek, hard muscle, and the light furring on his skin made it silk-soft to touch. He had a hard, uncompromising jawline that any human actor or model would kill for, and cropped hair that matched the thick black lashes shadowing his cheeks. Kyin was broader, more solid, and his brown eyes were playful beneath a shock of loose honeyed waves; he had curving lips made for kissing, the kind you can't take your eyes off, especially when they were pulled up into a flirtatious grin. Lanir was all bulk and height; when he wrapped his arms around you, you were entirely encompassed, entirely safe. His face was made of even planes and angles, and he had the kind of collarbones that my fingertips itched to trace. His blue skin was becoming less of a shock; I noticed the depth to it, the way it shifted from eggshell to cerulean to navy depending on the light, and, I thought, his mood.

I wanted to draw all of them. Desperately. In an obsessive, consuming, *needing* way, the same way I *had* to breathe air and drink water.

'Do it,' I repeated. 'Please, Lanir.'

He nodded and closed his violet eyes; a heartbeat later, I did the same.

I wish I could have sensed some change in the air to know it was coming. The truth was that one moment I was beginning to fold under the weight of what I was feeling, and the next I found the burden lessened. My shoulders rolled back, my racing heart slowed, and the moment after that, warmth swept over me, the warmth of safety and calm and contentedness.

I didn't feel transformed, just ... free. The anxiety was still there, but it was manageable once more, as if Lanir hadn't taken my burden, just shared enough of it that it became bearable. With all of that came a sense of shelter, of protection, of ... home.

'Fuck,' I sighed, my eyes flickering open once more. 'That's incredible.'

Exhaustion weighed me down as my body finally realised it'd spent two hours fighting a large male with pointed ears. I lay down on my bed, yawning.

'I'll stay until you sleep,' Lanir said gently.

It was barely a minute until my eyes were closing and I was drifting off. I heard the soft swish of the door opening, and Lanir's deep voice whisper something as he walked outside.

It sounded like *Goddess help me*, but that couldn't have been right.

'What about this one?'

I leaned back in my chair and put my hands over my stomach. '*Kyin*. If I eat another bite, I'll explode.'

He eyed me warily. I bit my bottom lip so I wouldn't laugh; it turned out that mixing human metaphors with aliens was *fun*.

'I'm just trying to find your favourites.' He took away the dishes on the table and stacked them back inside the generator. The machine did this incredibly neat trick where *everything* was recycled, so it didn't matter if I'd only taken a mouthful of some of the meals Kyin made for me; it was all taken back into the machine to be turned into something else next time.

The food hadn't seemed to have any ill-effects, though Gydion had insisted I be taken to the medical bay and scanned, just to make sure. I wasn't sure how much help it had been; the three of them were clearly *not* trained medical professionals, and I was fairly sure that Kyin had been looking at the resulting scan upside down. I couldn't read the report – the translator only worked aurally – but I felt fine and wasn't too worried about it. I was probably eating way better than I had on Earth, anyway.

Though I missed my coffee machine, I missed my tablet even more. My fingers twitched almost constantly for something I could form an image with – a stylus, a paintbrush, a stub of charcoal – *anything*. But I'd been through the entire ship now – the parts Kyin's fucked-up dad let us access, anyway – and I hadn't seen one sheet of anything resembling paper. Not one stylus, not one pen, and definitely no charcoal or paint. Every night when I fell asleep, I held the images I wanted to draw in my mind, tracing the shapes over and over again in my imagination so I wouldn't forget them once I finally had something at my fingertips.

Gydion, the lines of him long and lean and strong, moving with supernatural grace as he demonstrated one of the Kjidja fighting moves against a backdrop of overwhelming green, with ivy growing up his limbs and over his pointed ears, his black claws extended and patterned with flowers.

Kyin, his eyes twinkling, sprawled with a mischievous grin in a chair, his hair falling into his eyes, a plate full of blooms before him and branches growing like antlers from his hair, his tail curling around a posy of wildflowers.

Lanir, glowing every imaginable shade of blue as he worked his magic, his veins pulsing white beneath his skin, his body growing flowers shaped like geodes with leaves made of emeralds, strong and solid as his eyes swirled an ethereal violet.

A new series, a triptych, and every work looking like something you really, *really* wanted to touch.

Maybe that was just me.

I was tired, too, my thoughts churning like water. I slept in fits and starts, barely enough that I could function. My body was exhausted from the sessions with Gydion, but my mind wouldn't relax enough to let me get six hours of sleep.

Fuck, I would have settled for three.

'Claire?'

I looked up. 'Sorry, Kyin?'

'I was wondering if you could tell me a bit about Earth? We don't know very much about it.'

Kyin, for all his cockiness and occasional inclination to pout like a spoiled child, was a good listener. He didn't seem to mind that I talked about Earth in a winding, round-about way, plucking at the sleeve of my jumpsuit as I spoke. After five days in the same outfit – at least, I *thought* it was five days; it was difficult to tell – I'd finally succumbed to the silver garments folded in the wall cavity of my bedroom. The jumpsuits were made of a magical, stretchy material that fit me as well as it fit Lanir, and seemed to support me in all the right places. When I examined it inside-out, it had multiple panels that would make it stretch or shrink to fit beings of all different shapes and sizes, as long as they were vaguely humanoid. There were even parts that opened to attach coverings for additional arms and legs, along with a panel at the back that looked to accommodate a tail. The jumpsuit felt cool and smooth beneath my fingertips, and once I put it on, I was never too cold; it regulated my temperature perfectly, which was a relief, because the air in the ship was always slightly too cool for my human ice block taste.

It seemed I'd be wearing the jumpsuits for a while. Kyin hadn't yet worked out how to get around his father's hacks, which, he told me, meant that the cleaning systems were stuck on their usual settings. For the jumpsuits, made for space travel and designed to be worn under proper suits for space walks, this wasn't a problem, but Kyin thought the spore wash would probably disintegrate my clothes.

I wasn't willing to risk my favourite jeans.

Kyin's tail twined against the legs of my chair as I spoke, and without thinking, I reached down and flicked my finger at it playfully. He snorted and flicked me back, the furry double-tuft at the end sliding over my knuckles.

'And when I went to art school, there was this –'

'Art school?' he interrupted, staring at me. 'Is that what I think it is?'

Nerves churned in my stomach, sudden and familiar. I could never really be sure how others would react to the fact I was an artist. Some people thought it was amazing; some people thought it was an indulgent waste of time; and some people never knew what to think about it, and therefore what to say to me afterwards. 'If you think it's a place where you occasionally make art, then yes.'

'You're an *artist*?'

I bit my lip and nodded.

His tail wound around my fingers. 'What kind of artist?'

I relaxed at the question, falling into a rambling explanation about digital painting and how much I loved working with oils, before launching into an overly-detailed description of my failed foray into lithography and my first ever show. His tail stayed twined around my hand as I spoke, and the longer its tips tickled my knuckles, the less odd it seemed – both his tail itself, and the fact he'd wrapped it around my fingers.

'Claire?'

I started, looking up.

'You drifted off for a moment there,' Kyin said, studying my face.

I hooked my hair behind my ears. 'It's been hard to sleep,' I said honestly.

He cocked his head, waiting.

'The sounds are so different,' I went on. 'As in, there aren't many. There's no noise from outside – obviously – and whatever climate-control system you have is whisper-quiet. I can't hear anything from the corridors. I never hear any of you.'

Kyin laughed softly. 'Because we've been tiptoeing around like fools, trying not to disturb you.'

'You have?'

His tail circled my wrist. Like Gydion's skin, it was lightly furred. 'Mmm-hmm. We can make more noise, if that's what you need.'

'I, um ...' I trailed off, my eyes fixed to the spiral of tail around my hand and wrist. It wound further, its tufts stroking the sensitive skin of my forearm.

I pressed my thighs together tightly as sensation bloomed there.

'Is there something else you need, Claire?'

His voice was deliciously smooth, and I didn't think I was imagining the invitation in it. *Fuck, can aliens read minds?* I thought, panicked, before I realised that it was probably my *body* he was reading. I'd unconsciously swayed towards him, and my eyes had fallen to his lips without me noticing. His tail tightened on my wrist as I flushed – partly from embarrassment, and partly from the realisation that *yes*, there was something else I needed.

'I, um,' I said again, swallowing. 'I wouldn't hate if someone stayed with me.'

'If someone stayed with you?' he repeated, his voice a rumbling murmur that resonated in my chest. 'One of us in your cabin when you slept, do you mean?'

I nodded, sucking my bottom lip between my teeth. 'For ... the noise.'

Kyin's mouth stretched into an arrogant, satisfied smile. 'For the noise,' he echoed. I held my breath as he leaned in close and tucked a stray lock of hair behind my ear. 'Lan!' he shouted without warning, sitting back.

I blinked in surprise.

Lanir appeared in the doorway a moment later, frowning. 'Ky? What's wrong?'

'Claire would like one of us to stay with her tonight,' Kyin crooned, his eyes still fixed on my face. 'In her cabin. To help her sleep. It should be you.'

I tore my gaze from Kyin to see Lanir's face go blank. 'Claire? Is that what you want?'

Had I completely misread the moment? Was I so desperate that I was imagining things?

I mean ... Lanir wasn't exactly a consolation prize; I wasn't about to turn down a night with him staying close.

'Only if you want, Lanir,' I said softly.

His lips twisted, and I wondered if he was going to say *no*, but he gave an uncharacteristically curt nod, then flicked Kyin an unreadable glance. 'I'll stay with you. Let me know when you're ready.' He turned around and disappeared.

I exhaled. 'Um, Kyin, I ... I'm not sure Lanir wants to stay with me.'

Kyin's lips twitched. 'Trust me, he wants to.'

I decided to bite the bullet. 'I thought *you* would stay.'

His tail wound further up my arm and pulled me gently forward, so close that I could see the flecks of black through his golden irises. 'Don't think for a moment I don't want to,' he said, his voice rough. 'But there's a reason it should be Lan.'

'Why?' I said breathlessly.

Kyin's lips curled up. 'Because, little one, of the three of us, he is the only one with any self-control.'

It was even more awkward than I expected.

I stood under the light shower for no fewer than *three* cycles. I'd been conditioned to think that *clean* meant using *water*, so it was difficult to convince myself that the light was doing anything, even though my hair shone afterwards. I didn't have pyjamas, so I got into a fresh jumpsuit and then – absurdly – pulled my blanket up to my neck when I climbed into the narrow bed, as if I had something I needed to hide.

I'd slept with people before. I didn't know why I was so nervous.

You've never slept with an alien, Claire.

Kyin poked his head through the door, wearing a shit-eating grin. 'Ready?'

I nodded.

'*Words*, Claire. We need your words. We *always* need your words.'

'Yes,' I said faintly. 'Yes. I'm ready.'

Kyin stepped back to allow Lanir through; the Illisae carried the mattress from his bed with him. 'I thought I'd put this on the floor, if that's all right?'

I nodded, then remembered what Kyin had said and cleared my throat. 'Yes.'

Kyin's grin widened. 'Sleep well, you two,' he said, and the door slid shut, leaving me alone with Lanir.

Lanir set his mattress down and arranged his blankets and pillow. He was also wearing one of the regulation jumpsuits, but he did some magic with his zippers and stripped away the entire top half, leaving him bare to the waist.

I didn't mean to stare, but I couldn't look away.

He was so perfectly proportioned that someone might have made him from clay. The dim light cast all kinds of lovely shadows across his skin in rippling tones of navy and black, highlighting the definition of his delicious muscles. He was *glorious*, and my fingers burned to draw him.

They wanted to do other things, too. Like trace the divots of his eight pack and circle his nipples.

I wasn't sure whether I wanted to do it with my fingers or my tongue first.

'I get too warm otherwise,' he said apologetically, taking my stunned silence as censure. 'I'm used to colder temperatures.'

'It's no problem,' I blurted, because it was *definitely* not a problem. Not in the way he thought, anyway.

He slid beneath the blankets, leaving the dyed wool bunched around his waist. He put one hand behind his head and closed his eyes, and my brain just about melted at the way his bicep swelled and his chest expanded.

Which was all well and good, except that I had an entirely new problem to deal with.

What's the etiquette on being heinously turned on by the alien who's come to help you sleep?

Not to mention – *can he feel what I'm feeling right now?*

I rolled so I was staring at the ceiling, trying to focus on keeping my breathing even, and waved the light off.

Lanir gave a barely-perceptible sigh.

I closed my eyes.

Then opened them again.

Then closed them and wriggled around to find a better position.

Then cocooned myself in a blanket.

Then unwrapped myself.

'Claire,' Lanir said, his voice tinged with amusement. 'It doesn't sound as if this is helping.'

'Seems that way, yep,' I said tightly.

'What *would* help?'

'I just ...' I trailed off. 'I honestly have no idea.'

'Would you, ah –' Lanir cleared his throat. 'Would you like a hug?'

Would I like a hug?

The last hug I'd had was from Anna, before she'd left. I hadn't dated for a couple of years, so friend hugs were all I'd been getting. Which isn't to say that friend hugs weren't lovely – they were – but they didn't have the bury-your-face-and-never-resurface feeling I was craving.

And even when I'd been dating, none of my dates had boasted a chest – or biceps – like Lanir's.

Yes, I very, *very* much wanted a hug.

'From you?'

'From me,' Lanir confirmed.

'If you're comfortable with it, I would like that,' I whispered.

'Then let me show you something,' he said.

He stood up, and a moment later, he'd gathered me up and set me gently on my feet. He lifted the mattress from my bed with ease, then pushed the thin base up until it sat flush to the wall; there was a gentle *click* as something secured it in place. He settled my mattress next to his and pulled back the soft fur blanket I'd borrowed from Gydion; my mouth fell open as I watched the two mattresses fuse together in the dim light, creating one reasonably-sized bed on the floor.

Lanir spread the soft fur across the now-double mattress, then pulled the wool-like blankets up and arranged the pillows, creating a comfortable-looking ... well, *nest*.

'That's ... That looks ... *nice*.'

Lanir sank down on the bed. 'Come here, then,' he said quietly.

I settled down next to him; he held out his arms. I snuggled in, unable to stop my sigh when his arms wrapped around me. His skin was cooler than mine, but not unpleasantly so; he arranged the blanket and covered me to the neck.

'Better?'

'Better,' I whispered.

I wasn't lying. I could hear the quiet thunder of a double heartbeat beneath my ear; the comforting rush of the sound outweighed my surprise at the notion he had two hearts. His fingers trailed hesitantly up and down my back, as if testing the waters. When I didn't complain, he did it with more confidence, until my muscles began to unwind and tiny shivers of pleasure made the hairs on my neck stand on end.

So much better.

'Are you doing your magic calm thing?' I said sleepily.

'No, little one,' he murmured. 'I'm not doing my magic calm thing.'

When I dreamt, my dreams were blue.

LANIR

I HADN'T LAIN AWAKE so long for years.

Claire was likewise awake for much of the night; she slept in short, restless snatches, and when she was conscious, I could feel emotions rippling off her like waves. Comfort, arousal, confusion, embarrassment, worry, acceptance – only for it to circle back to the start again.

I was glad she couldn't feel what those emotions did to *me*.

She felt perfect in my arms, warm and soft and curved; my body fit around her in all the right places. *He is the only one of us with any self-control*, I'd overheard Kyin say about me, but feeling the gentle hunger of Claire's arousal was seriously testing it. If I were to dip my chin and brush my lips across hers, I was fairly certain she'd kiss me back. If I were to slide my hand down her back to cup her rounded ass, I was fairly certain she'd let me.

But I didn't, and I wouldn't, because she'd accepted a hug, and nothing more.

Which didn't stop me wondering how soft her skin would feel beneath my fingertips, or what sounds she'd make if I worked my tongue over her breasts, or what she'd taste like if she let me lick down her body to settle between her legs.

I moved my hips away from her as my cock twitched, hard and aching.

I wondered how it would feel to bury myself inside her, to roll my hips until she shattered. I wondered what her climax would feel like as it rolled over my body; wondered whether she'd like it if I pushed the sensations of my own pleasure over *her*.

I wondered if she'd cry my name.

Eventually, I slept, but it was restless, fitful. Even wearing only part of my jumpsuit, I was too hot, but it wasn't as if I could strip further. Claire always wore clothes, no matter what; Gydion suspected it was a human thing, and so we'd decided to do the same to make sure she was comfortable.

I woke up well before the ship's systems stirred in its artificial morning. Claire was still asleep, curled up on her side, her cheek resting on my bicep. Her hair streamed out like a dark flag; I wanted to touch it, to stroke it back from her face so I could see the curve of her jaw, the shell of her ear. The artificial pink tips had faded slightly, but I liked it. It was a reminder that the delicious human female was real, flawed – and even better that way.

Stop staring, I chided silently. I gently disentangled myself, settling her head back down on a pillow, then rolled from the makeshift bed as slowly as I could, trying not to disturb her. When I climbed out, I knocked my quartz lamp off the shelf; it fell to the floor with a loud clatter.

Claire didn't stir.

I didn't bother being quiet after that. I pulled on the top half of my jumpsuit and left, tired and frustrated, my cock hard and aching, then headed to the kitchen. Gydion sat at the sole table, his eyes raking my face.

Kyin shot me a filthy grin as he made a cup of *limere*, his tail thrashing behind him. 'Rough night?'

It was too early for either of them to be up; they must have been waiting for Claire and me to wake. 'Fuck off, Ky.'

His eyes dropped below my waist; he sniggered. 'Should I say *hard* night, instead?'

In an uncharacteristic fit of petulance, I pushed a wave of what I was feeling at him – all my frustration, all my exhaustion, all my confusion, all my yearning, all my *lust*. Kyin staggered backwards, his eyes widening, his cheeks flushing. Gydion's spine went soldier-straight as he caught the fringes of feeling, his fangs sinking into his bottom lip.

'By the fucking *stars*,' Kyin said throatily. 'That's ... That's a *lot*, Lan.'

'I'm a First-Circle empath,' I grated out. 'That is *nothing*.'

He looked down at his crotch. 'Well, fuck,' he said to it. 'As if it wasn't bad enough without your input.'

Gydion hissed.

I looked across the hall at him and we stared at one another. The space seemed to shrink between our bodies; the air went taut. I rolled my shoulders, holding his gaze.

We were mates. We always would be. I loved him with every inch of my body, with every beat of my hearts. But we hadn't fucked for months – not since Kyin had ended it – and I missed it. Missed *him*.

Gydion's lips curled until they parted in a heavy-eyed grin; his tongue ran across his bared teeth. 'Remember the last time you looked at me like that?'

My nostrils flared. 'I remember.'

His grin widened. 'Then what are you waiting for?' He stood, his jumpsuit bulging over his crotch. '*Run, Lanir.*'

I turned and sprinted back down the corridor.

I was fast for my kind, but the Kjidja were hunters, and Gydion didn't have my bulk. He caught me halfway down the hall, hooking his arms around my legs so that I tripped in a heavy, tangled heap, my shoulder and hip taking the brunt of the fall. He pressed me down onto the cold floor, pinning my forearms above my head with one hand, his body wedging between my thighs, pushing them apart.

I could have thrown him off in a moment. We both knew it – just as we both knew I didn't want to.

His claws sank into my jumpsuit and ripped it straight down the back before his lips touched my skin. He ground his cock into my thigh, his fangs dragging over my shoulder. He played at being rough, but his claws were retracted and his fingers were gentle as he dragged them down my spine, stripping the ruined halves of my jumpsuit away until I was wholly bared.

'You're a miracle from the Goddess, you know that?' he growled. 'The most beautiful thing I've ever seen.'

'More, Gyd,' I demanded, grinding back against him. 'Hurry.'

'You're not in control here.' To illustrate that, he bit me, sinking his teeth into the flesh of my shoulder.

He knew I loved that, the fucker.

I rolled, throwing him off, and pinned him beneath me. He glowered, his green eyes lit with lust; I crushed my lips against his until his fingers were digging into my skin and he was panting into my mouth.

I stripped his jumpsuit down to his thighs, releasing his cock. I palmed it, working it up and down, brushing over where his tie would swell in the way I knew drove him crazy. I wished I could feel him, sense his emotions as I touched him, but the heat of his arousal was enough, making my own so heightened it was almost painful; my cock leaked pre-cum over his thighs.

'Lan,' he hissed.

I rolled us again, then let him push my knees together and thrust between my thighs. I hadn't taken him for months, and we were in the corridor, too far from the *zyda* oil we usually used; there was no way Gydion would fuck me without it, no matter how much I might beg. His cock was shaped like mine when it was flaccid, but when he was close to climax, a teardrop-shaped expanse he called his *tie* swelled on the under-side of his shaft and the base flared out. It caused Kjidja males to lodge inside their partner, locking them together to ensure the male's release stayed inside their partner's body. I could take his tie, but only when he'd prepared me for it. I felt it swelling gradually now, pressing against me as he thrust. I relaxed slightly, allowing it to slip between my thighs, then pressed them togeth-er, giving him the tightness that I know he craved.

He laced his fingers with mine. 'Lan,' he panted.

It was often this way between us: a hunt, a clash, and then tenderness. Gydion needed the chase, the *catch*, the control. And he knew I wanted the softness, his praise, his care, needed his *love* – and he always gave it. His hand came up to cup my cheek, the pads of his fingers brushing my cheekbone as my thighs locked around his tie. 'You're perfect,' he grated out, beginning to rock. 'Perfect.'

My cock was trapped between my belly and the hard planes of his, rubbed by Gydion's rocking motion. His free hand kept a bruising grip on my hip, anchoring himself – anchoring *me* – as he moved. Usually, this friction wouldn't be enough to tip me over the edge, but my body had been craving this for *months*, and I was desperately trying to hold on, waiting for Gydion so that we could come together.

I wrapped one arm around his shoulders and the other around his waist, then seized his mouth again, drawing his bottom lip between my teeth.

'Too good,' he hissed desperately. I felt his tie throb, his cock thicken. 'Lan –'

I came as the first spurt of warmth splashed between my thighs, groaning his name as I made a mess on my stomach. He rolled his hips like a wave through his climax, panting against my mouth. I kissed him as he shuddered, slowly moving to slow, languid kisses as his body calmed. He held himself over me, continuing to rock against me slowly as his tie softened. I knew he'd want to stay where he was – and that it would take a while for his tie to shrink – so I gave myself over to the soft caress of his lips, all but floating as he whispered praise between each nuzzling kiss.

Kyin's face appeared above us, split into a wide grin. 'You know that I love it when you fuck in my corridors,' he began, 'but I don't know how Claire feels about it, and I feel like we should warn her first. I can hear her moving around, so unless you think she's ready for this glorious surprise, you might want to move.'

Gydion grimaced and pulled away; I winced at the sudden loss of heat, and he dropped his mouth back down, brushing the lightest of kisses over my lips. 'Perfect,' he murmured again. 'You're perfect. My love. My heart.'

He pulled me up and guided me into my cabin. It looked emptier than usual, with my mattress in Claire's room and the bed frame pushed up, but I didn't mind. Gydion led me into the light shower and flicked the cycle on, though he also took up a soft cloth and dipped it in the tiny water fountain I kept in my bathroom, gently cleaning his release from my thighs. He didn't need to – the light would remove everything – but he liked to do it anyway.

I closed my eyes. 'I keep expecting Kyin to crack. I keep reaching for him. But he's not there, Gyd. I don't know why I keep thinking about it.'

'I know,' Gydion murmured.

'I just ...' I trailed off as Gydion found another clean cloth and dipped it in the water before running it over my neck and chest. 'I never thought he'd stick to what he said.'

I can't do this. It's not working. Not anymore. This isn't for me. It can't be.

'Do you miss him?' I blurted.

Gydion took my chin in his free hand. 'You are not second choice, Lanir,' he said quietly. 'What lies between us is not diminished by Kyin's absence.'

'I know,' I said thickly, because I *did* know. The link between Gydion and I had always been strong – unbreakable, even – but that didn't mean that I didn't crave Kyin, that I didn't want us all back together. And it didn't mean that Gydion and I weren't still finding our way through what it meant to be *two* again when for years we had been *three*.

'Good,' he said, and released my chin, returning his attention to my stomach. 'But yes. I miss him.'

'I just can't help but think there's more to it,' I said, staring at the wall.

Kyin's emotions had been a mess when he'd told us. Desperation, fear, love, grief. All things he still felt, though he tried to hold them at arm's length.

This isn't for me. It can't be.

'There might well be,' Gydion murmured. 'But Kyin made his choice, either way, and we have to respect that.'

'He wants Claire,' I said musingly.

Gydion snorted and pressed a kiss to my lips. 'Then he'll have to get in fucking line.'

'*Oof.*'

Lanir stirred uneasily. 'He's too rough,' he murmured. 'She's going to get hurt.'

Claire rolled onto her side, then pushed herself back up, grimacing as her arms shook.

'He knows what he's doing,' I said, though my stomach churned every time Gydion threw her down. 'She's tough, Lan.'

'She might be tough, but she's not indestructible,' he grumbled. 'She's a beginner. Gydion is treating her as though she's been doing this for years.'

'Because we're flying into a warzone,' I pointed out. 'We don't know how bad it's going to be, so he's preparing for the worst.'

Lanir's jaw was clenched so hard I was surprised he wasn't breaking teeth. 'She could just –'

'Lan,' I interrupted, sliding my hand over his knee, then immediately regretting it as my pulse began to race and my heart ached. 'We talked about this. We have no idea what course my father will take to get us on the ground once we reach Scytha. It's likely he'll shield the ship, if only to protect his ore, but once we're on the ground, we're sitting *erex*. Even *if* my father lands us behind allied lines, they might mistake us for an enemy craft. And if he lands us behind *Roth* lines, then we need to get Claire to safety. Which might mean taking her across an active battlefield. She needs to learn everything she can. It's the only way.'

'The only way *you* can see,' he argued.

'If you have another suggestion, Lan, I'm listening.'

He fell silent, because he did not, in fact, have another suggestion. There was no good answer for what needed to happen when we got to Scytha; we'd discussed it more times than was sensible, and this was the best way forward. Claire would be in danger – there was no getting around that – but so would *we*, and Gydion's teaching was the best gift we could give her, considering the circumstances.

Gydion stalked around her, his eyes glittering. Claire watched him warily, lifting her fists. One hand held a practise sword; the other, a light Tirian shield.

'He should be teaching her to attack, not just defend,' Lanir muttered.

I rolled my eyes towards the ceiling. 'Stars above, Lan. If you want to take over, talk to Gydion about it.'

Their partnership was a wholly unlikely one. Their two species had been at war over a collection of religious teachings for thousands of years before an uneasy truce was forged by their grandparents' generation. As a First-Circle mage, Lanir was escalated to the upper tiers of Illisae society before he was fully-grown, and as a gifted empath, he was shunted straight into his kind's illustrious diplomatic corps. Gydion was no less impressive: hand-picked as a soldier in childhood, then trained as a specialist guard for the Kjidja's beloved priestesses. He'd met Lanir when the Kjidja head priestess had visited Ilis, and something between the two of them had just … clicked. They'd left their home planets for each other – and weren't welcome to return.

It didn't mean they were immune to squabbling like untried younglings when the mood took them, though. It had been me who'd gently mediated, me who'd coaxed them from curses to kisses.

I took my hand from Lanir's knee, my fingers and tail twitching with loss.

Gydion feinted forward; Claire reacted, swinging the practise sword in a not-half-bad slash at his unprotected side. The Kjidja was too fast, and he dodged her attack, spinning to land a light blow on her hip. She staggered, pushed off-balance, and Gydion swept her feet out from under her.

Again.

Claire closed her eyes for a moment, struggling to catch her breath and clearly frustrated. Her brow was crumpled in a fierce frown, then she gathered herself, took a few deep breaths, and got back on her feet.

'See?' I murmured to Lanir. 'She's tough.'

My father said that to be successful, you didn't need talent – you needed sheer bloody-minded determination. You didn't need some kind of gods-given aptitude, you needed to never give up, and to keep going when you failed. Given his multiple business empires, I supposed he knew what he was talking about.

He hadn't started with money, just a solid idea and an un-bridled ego that had seen him approach multiple investors before one of them decided to back him. It had snowballed from there, seemingly unstoppable, until he had more money than several inter-planetary economies, and more power than was sensible.

He called what he did – designing complex systems and machines to meet a range of different needs – a kind of art. He often worked on them for years, and some were never used. I imagined that, as an artist, it would be similar for Claire: she'd labour over time, honing her skills, and sometimes create things that didn't work, but she'd keep going regardless, just as she got back up every time Gydion knocked her down.

She grounded her feet and raised her sword again.

Gydion chuckled. 'Good, little one. But you're swaying on your paws. Time for food. We'll keep going when you've rested.'

Lanir exhaled.

Claire dropped the sword. 'Oh, thank fuck,' she muttered. She glared at Gydion. 'I have *never* been this sore.'

'If you need a massage, Claire, you only need to ask,' I called from our seat at the far end of the simulation room, grinning.

She glanced at me, startled, then flushed a deep pink. 'Have you been watching the whole time?'

'What else would we be doing?'

She dropped her shield and rubbed her face. 'Literally any-thing, Kyin.'

'*Literally anything* isn't as pretty as you,' I crooned.

She flushed a deeper pink. '*Urgh*. You're insufferable, do you know that?'

I huffed a laugh. 'I think you like suffering me.'

'You need water,' Gydion directed. 'Go and sit down, Claire. We'll make you some food.'

She stomped towards the dining hall, throwing Lanir and I another suspicious look. When she was out of earshot, Gydion turned to Lanir.

'She's exhausted,' he murmured. 'How long did she sleep?'

'Two hours at most,' Lanir said.

'She needs to sleep tonight.' Gydion shut off the training simulation. 'Should someone stay with her again?'

'She was definitely calmer with someone there,' Lanir answered. 'I think it would be good for someone to offer.'

I didn't trust myself. 'You should, Gyd. That way, Lan can get some sleep, and be fresh if she wants him back tomorrow.'

Lanir blinked at me. 'That's ... That's very thoughtful, Kyin.'

I shrugged. 'I want the best for her.'

'If she agrees, me tonight – and one of you tomorrow,' Gydion confirmed.

We all nodded.

'Right,' I said, and grinned, tweaking Gydion's cheek with the tips of my tail as he scowled. 'Let's go feed our human.'

Even though Gydion had worked Claire until she could barely lift her training sword, she didn't sleep that night. Gydion slipped out of her room after an equally disturbed rest and disappeared straight into his bedroom to deal with the problem making itself known between his thick thighs. I laughed outright as his door slid closed, then made them both some *limere*.

Lanir and I watched her train in the morning. In the afternoon, Lanir delivered an in-depth and frankly snooze-worthy lesson on Roth history, somehow managing to make thousands of years of conflict, deception, murder, and violence dry and boring.

Which was actually a real talent, if you thought about it.

'What happened last night?' I hissed at Gydion when he sank down to kneel beside me, his eyes on Claire as she asked Lanir a handful of considered questions.

'I sat in the corner of her room for hours on end,' he said crossly. 'She slept for an hour, perhaps two. She was restless, moving all night long. It drove me insane.'

'Could you ...' I tapped my fingers on the side of my chair. 'Could you smell her?'

He shot me a glare. 'I could scent her *underwater*, Kyin. Of course I could smell her.'

'*And*?'

He lifted one shoulder in a half-shrug. 'Aroused. Confused. Unnerved. Repeat.'

'Hmm.' My tail swished behind me.

'*Kyin*,' Gydion said warningly. 'Whatever you're thinking, stop it.'

'I'm not thinking anything,' I said innocently. 'You know better than that, Gydion. I never think at all.'

'That's what I'm worried about,' he muttered. He paused. 'Goddess, Lan really has murdered this lesson, hasn't he?'

'Perhaps this is his way of getting Claire to sleep. She doesn't look too concerned about it.'

'She's a kinder being than me.' Gydion paused. 'I know you want her, Ky. But think about the situation. If something goes badly, there is no space on this ship to escape it. And when we get to Scytha, we'll have to work together. Our lives could depend on it.'

'I know, Gyd.' I stretched. 'I promise not to do a single thing our little human hasn't asked for.'

Claire's hair was always impossibly shiny after a light shower. I liked the rich brown colour at the roots, and the now-fading pink at its tips; I held myself back from touching it as she let me into her cabin that night. Lanir's mattress had stayed on the floor, creating a nest-like bed big enough for three. It took up most of the room, but I noticed that there was still enough floor space for another mattress.

'I know Gyd sat in the corner last night,' I said. 'Was that his choice, or yours?'

Claire flushed. 'His,' she muttered. 'He didn't even talk to me about it.'

'And where would you like me?'

'Not in the corner,' she answered crossly.

She slid down under the thick woollen blanket, then gestured. I climbed in next to her, leaving enough space between us that I'd have to roll to touch her.

Lanir and Gydion were right; she was restless. It took her a full half-hour to settle down, rustling with the blankets and turning over and over again until she was comfortable. When she stopped moving, she gave a barely-perceptible sigh.

'What's wrong, little one?' I said quietly.

'I don't know how to sleep with people,' she said, after a moment. 'But it's too quiet when there's no one here. My mind won't stop. My thoughts are in a washing machine that never finishes its fucking cycle. I'm so tired, Kyin.'

'Then come here,' I said.

In the soft light cast by Lanir's rose quartz lamp, she eyed me warily.

'Come here,' I demanded impatiently. 'Come here so I can hold you.'

I could have rolled over and gone to her, but it had to be her choice. The wait was excruciating – *will she say no? Will she throw me out?* – but a moment later, she was shuffling across the bed.

When her fingertips brushed my shoulder, I took her waist and positioned her so that she draped over my chest. She made a squeaking sound of surprise but let me move her, pressing her ear against me so she could hear my heartbeat. She was warm and her skin was smooth as sea worm silk and her hair was tickling my nose; it was *perfect*. It became even better when her sweet scent filled my senses and I realised that she liked it as much as I did.

'Better?'

'Better,' she said.

'Can I touch you?'

'Yes,' she answered. 'Lan did.'

I bit back a grin. 'Where did Lan touch you, Claire?'

'My neck. My back.' She cleared her throat. 'You can touch my hair too, if you like.'

Even if I'd never heard a cue in my entire life, I would have picked up that one. I moved one hand to her head, lightly massaging her scalp, and the other to her neck, making circles on her skin with my fingers. My tail went to her back, the tufts tracing up and down her spine.

She moaned; the sound went straight to my cock. 'That's … God, Kyin. That's … nice.'

I grinned into the dark. 'Good.'

She sighed, melting into me as she relaxed. 'That tail is really something.'

I bit down on my lip. *This is nothing*, I wanted to say.

'Sleep, Claire,' I said instead, pressing a kiss to her hair.

She was still for a while, but I could tell she was awake. Eventually, her fingers started tracing patterns over my ribs. She began with tiny circles, testing the waters, and then her caresses grew longer, her fingers searching further, until she was venturing across my ribcage and down onto the planes of my stomach. I let her explore until she was brushing dangerously close to my hip.

'That isn't sleeping, Claire,' I growled, catching her hand. I brought it to my lips and kissed her knuckles, so she knew I didn't really mind. 'If this isn't working, I'll have to try something different.'

'Something different?' she said breathlessly.

'Something different,' I agreed, my hand tracing out the bumps of her spine, right down to the delicious curve of her ass. She tensed, her breath catching in a tiny pant, so I moved my hand lower, cupping her. 'You'll tell me to stop, won't you, little one?'

'To stop?'

I grinned. 'I don't know how humans get to sleep, Claire, but I can tell you what *always* works for us Darnagh.' I flipped her over without warning, listening to her breathy gasp as I settled her on her back.

'What always works?' she managed.

'Orgasms,' I crooned. 'So many orgasms you can't think straight. Do you think that might help?'

'I – ah,' she breathed, as I brushed my lips lightly over hers, then traced a line from her throat to her collarbone. 'What if my body is different to yours?'

'I hope it's *very* different to mine,' I said, grinning. My tail traced up her leg, brushing over the apex of her thighs. 'But you look pretty similar to a Darnagh female with clothes on, so I'm betting you can't be *that* different beneath them.' I dropped my body down, letting her feel that I was already hard for her. 'We can find out.'

I could hear her heart beat faster, scent her arousal, sweet and heavy on the air.

I found the top of her zipper and let my hand still there. 'Claire? Orgasms or no orgasms?'

She swallowed. 'Orgasms,' she breathed. 'Please.'

Good answer. I surged back up and took her mouth, letting my mind go blank as I kissed her. There were usually hundreds of thoughts churning around my brain at any given moment, but Claire's sweet, complex scent made them quiet. She kissed me back, her lips nuzzling at mine until she became more confident and let her teeth sink into me. I rumbled in pleasure, sucking her bottom lip in return, then tracing its bow with my tongue. She sighed, opening for me, letting me ravish her mouth as her hands traced the shape of my shoulders.

'So, we've worked out the kissing,' I said, when I eventually broke away, trailing my lips down her neck. 'What next?'

'Touching?' she said breathlessly.

I let my teeth score her skin. 'How do you like to be touched, Claire?'

It took her a moment to answer. 'Gently at first. Softly. Teasing.'

'I can be soft. Well,' I went on, taking her hip in my hand and gently grinding against her, 'not all of me. What else do you like?'

She looked up at me, her eyes huge in the dim light. Her teeth worried at her lip. 'I like ... I like ...' She trailed off.

I dipped down and ran my nose up her neck, breathing her in before I nuzzled at her ear. 'Would you like to be worshipped, Claire?'

She inhaled, the sweet scent of her arousal intensifying. 'Yes,' she whispered.

'Then that's what I'll do.' I nipped gently at her earlobe. 'Is anywhere off limits?'

'No,' she breathed.

'Anything you don't like?'

'Proper pain. A little is fine, but I don't like a lot. And I don't like being shamed or demeaned. I have no issue with other people liking it,' she added hastily, as if she was worried that *I* might and she was trying to reassure me, 'but it's just not for me.'

I pulled back, feeling my eyes hood as I stared down at her. 'No pain. No shame. Just worship until you can't think straight. Yes?'

She swallowed. 'Yes.'

I bent back down to kiss a line along her jaw. 'Tell me if you want me to stop.'

I trailed my lips over her collarbone, letting my tail stroke up her thighs, never high enough to brush where I suspected she wanted it. I pulled her zipper down slowly, placing a kiss on every new bared inch of skin, until it rested just beneath the small scar of flesh on her stomach.

I didn't pull her jumpsuit away, instead trailing my fingertips up and down the strip of bared skin until she let out a frustrated huff.

I would worship her. But first, I was going to make her beg.

I pushed the halves of her jumpsuit aside, just enough that I could see the lovely swell of her breasts; Claire was all softness and beautiful curves. It was more than that, though; something inside her called to something inside me. I wanted my hands and my mouth all over her, wanted to make her quiver and shake and shudder until she couldn't take any more.

I wanted to stake a claim on her.

I traced the sides of her breasts, letting my fingers learn the landscape of her body, mapping out the ribs beneath. She squirmed and giggled when I drew patterns on her stomach, and I filed that information away for later.

I could see her nipples peaking through her jumpsuit, so I dipped my head and took one in my mouth through the material, bringing my hand up to cup her other breast. She keened as I sucked her hard, arching her back to press herself into my mouth, into my hand. I pinched as I sucked, pulling and kneading until her hips pressed up, seeking friction; her hands bunched in my hair, then slid over my shoulders and further down, one hand finding my ass and the other the base of my tail.

If she kept touching me *there*, I was going to lose what small measure of control I had.

'No touching, Claire,' I said mildly, pulling away, trying not to shudder as her fingers slid over my tail.

She blinked at me, confused, her cheeks marked by a deep blush of pink.

'This is about you,' I said. 'If you want worship, then you'll be still and let me give you what you asked for.'

It wasn't just about my negligible self-control. If Claire's churning thoughts were anything like my own, then I suspected that losing herself in pleasure would give her a small measure of peace and make the universe slow down, even if it never stilled completely. From what Lanir had said, she spent many of her waking hours fighting for control of her emotions, and the least I could do was push her to a place where she could surrender that fight, if only for a handful of moments.

I gave her a nuzzling, lingering kiss. 'Will you be still for me, Claire?'

Her breath caught; her tongue came out to wet her lips. With evident difficulty, she relaxed beneath me.

'Good,' I crooned. 'I'm going to strip you now. I want to look at you. And you're going to let me, aren't you?'

Her throat worked as she swallowed. 'Yes.'

She let me work her jumpsuit over her shoulders; I peeled the sleeves from her graceful arms and tugged until the suit bunched around her hips. Sitting back, I took her in; her lips were a dark rose in the dim light, her hair a swirl of shadows across the pillow beneath her.

Lust flared through me.

'Lovely,' I murmured. I trailed a finger from her collarbone to the twist on her stomach. Darnagh had a similar scar, made just after birth; I wondered idly if humans were the same. I let the tips of my tail circle one nipple, then the other; her skin broke out in tiny bumps as she shivered. That shiver ate at my control, and I leaned down to suck the sensitive peak into my mouth, sucking hard once more. Claire cried out, panting; her hips bucked and her hands fisted in my hair.

'Be *still*, little one,' I growled. I waited until she relaxed, then swirled my tongue around her, flicking the tip as a reward when she made a strangled sound but stayed still beneath me. I lavished the same care on the other breast as my tail quested down, toying with the skin above the cover of her bunched jumpsuit, then dipping below, over her soft stomach and lower.

She had hair there – tight, coarse curls. She caught her breath as my tail moved further down, finding a hot, swollen bud. Claire cried out as my tail trailed over it, her legs falling open to give me access.

'Darnagh females don't have this,' I said, biting gently at her nipple. 'Tell me what to do.'

'It's my clit,' she said breathlessly. 'Well, technically, it's only a small part of it. If you rub it –' she cried out as I spread the tufts of my tail to border it, moving gently on either side '– *ohmygodlikethat* – if you rub it, I'll –'

'Climax?' I supplied.

She made a strangled noise I took as assent.

'And do you have –' My tail quested further, finding delicious heat and slippery moisture; I stifled a groan – and a sigh of relief – as the lips of her sex gave way to an opening. 'You *do* have. Darnagh females get pleasure from a spot inside.'

'We have spots inside, too,' she panted as I teased her swollen flesh. 'But I need – pressure – on my clit to come.'

I nodded, bringing the tips of my tail together and letting them rest outside her entrance. She whimpered but didn't squirm, staying still like I'd told her. 'Good,' I whispered. 'Lift your hips. I want you naked.'

She did as I asked; I stripped the jumpsuit from her body and threw it across the room, not bothering to check where it fell.

She was the most beautiful thing I'd ever seen, lying still and spread out on the soft *feldi* pelt. I let my tail dip inside her, just slightly; her head tipped back and her eyes fluttered closed, but her body stayed still. 'So good,' I crooned. 'You're so lovely, Claire. Lift your knees for me, *cora*.'

She bent her knees and let them fall apart, opening herself to my gaze.

I wanted to sink my cock into her pink softness and rut until she couldn't walk straight.

Another time, I told myself. This wasn't about me. She wanted to be worshipped, and I'd give her just that. And probably spend the next day in my cabin with my hands on my cock at the memory of her perfection.

I mean, it wouldn't be the worst way to spend a day.

I sank my tail into her instead, biting back a satisfied smile at her wail. I found the rough patch that was one of the pleasure seats for Darnagh females and rubbed my tail against it, pressing gently.

'*OhmygodKyin – yes,*' she moaned, her hands bunching in the fur beneath her. Her neck corded with the effort of staying still.

'So good, little one,' I praised, and settled between her thighs, breathing in the intoxicating scent of her arousal. I dipped my head and huffed a breath over her, pleased when she cried out but did not move. 'Tell me how you're feeling, Claire.'

'Like I'm going to strangle you if you don't touch me,' she panted.

I laughed and withdrew my tail from her body. 'Try again, little one.'

'*Kyin*,' she whined. 'I'm feeling ... I'm feeling *worshipped*. But *please. Please.*'

'The worshipping hasn't even started yet, *cora*,' I told her, then dipped my head and licked straight up the centre of her.

I might not have seen a *clit* before, but I was yet to fuck a being who didn't lose their mind over a mouth caressing their most sensitive places.

She sobbed as my tongue found her bud and flattened over it, working up and down. 'Is this what you need, Claire?' I said against her slick flesh.

'Yes, *please*, Kyin –'

My name on her tongue sent a fresh wave of heat through me; I ground myself against the mattress mindlessly, seeking some kind of temporary relief as I dipped my tongue inside her. She was sweet and salty and fucking *delicious*, and I turned my attention back to her clit, my tongue flattening against it as my tail snuck back up to toy with her entrance. She was staying still, just as I'd told her, but it was evidently an effort; she was whimpering with every breath, her stomach tightening as she quivered.

I knew what *that* meant, even if she wasn't Darnagh.

I worked her faster, keeping up a rhythm, and let my tail slide down to brush her tight back entrance. She cried out, her hands fisting in my hair once more, and I pushed two fingers inside her slick channel just in time to feel it clench around me in the waves of her climax. She shrieked my name as I found the rough patch inside her, gently pressing there until she stopped shuddering and lay still beneath me.

I swallowed, pushing aside every instinct – every *desire* – to move up and thrust myself inside her. '*Cora*?'

'Mm-mn,' Claire answered thickly, her hands still in my hair.

'You have two minutes.'

She dragged my head up by her handfuls of hair and eyed me warily, her lids heavy. 'Two minutes until what?'

I grinned at her. 'Until I do that again.'

After her third orgasm, she fell asleep in moments. I curled myself around her, pressing her back to my chest, her round ass nestled against my aching cock, and I went to sleep smiling.

GYDION

I PACED UP AND down the hall.

Eight hours.

After Lanir gave me the dirtiest look he could muster, I paced in circles around the simulation room, instead.

Nine hours.

When Lanir stuck his head inside the door and snapped that I was giving him a headache, I went to the kitchen and began making Claire some food from scratch, choosing the most complex meal I could find.

Ten hours.

By eleven hours, I was going out of my mind. 'I'm just going to –'

'You're not *just going* to do *anything*,' Lanir said tightly. 'You're going to leave them to sleep.'

'All well and good for you to say,' I returned petulantly. 'You can't *smell* them.'

'No, but I can *feel* them,' Lanir shot back. 'You think it was fun for me last night?' He closed his eyes for a moment. 'I could feel every flush of heat, every strike of Kyin's excitement, every time she broke in climax, Gydion. You don't have the monopoly on suffering.'

'I thought your shield was better than that.'

'I have *limits*, and apparently Kyin found them,' he snarled. 'As if I should be surprised.'

I raked my hands through my hair. 'This is a problem, Lan.'

'Yes, I worked that one out myself, thanks Gyd.'

'He wants her, you want her, I –' my breath caught '– I want her. We can't get away from each other. What if she wanted one of us, but not both? What if she chooses him, and only him? This could be *every morning* for the next three weeks.'

'We'll deal with it,' he said, his voice calmer. 'We'll deal with it, because we have to.'

I started to pace again. 'I don't know if I can.' I stopped and took a deep breath, groaning as a trace of her scent filled my senses. 'Goddess above. This is driving me insane.'

'Get a hold of yourself, Gydion,' he said. 'I can *sense* you losing control. You can't do that, my love. Not with Claire on board.'

I dropped into a chair and cradled my head in my hands, digging my claws into my cheeks as he pushed a wave of calm over me. It wasn't quite as strong as usual, nor as steady; he must have been close to snapping himself. He was right, though; I couldn't afford to lose control.

The Divine Guard weren't supposed to take partners; while we could fuck whomever we liked – bar the priestesses – we weren't allowed to bond, and long-term relationships were strongly discouraged. Kjidja folklore was full of doomed love stories between priestesses and guards, lauding a love limited to lingering looks and the guards' devoted protection. I had honestly believed my life would follow that path; that I would be one of those stories. I'd believed that I would hold a fireless passion, a chaste, devoted love for one of the females I protected.

Instead, I'd met Lanir, and fallen so completely in love that I'd not only left the Divine Guard, I'd left my planet, too, and wasn't welcome back, a fact that had taken me some time to accept. My world was turned upside down again when we met Kyin, and both of us fell as one. It was worth it, though, because what I felt for them – what I was starting to feel for *Claire* – wasn't fireless. It wasn't chaste. It was overwhelming, consuming, *burning*. I wanted them like I wanted air in my lungs – to simply keep *existing*.

I *needed* them.

Alongside all that need sat my grief for Kyin's choice to leave us, and the memories of the three of us together. It preoccupied Lanir, but I couldn't let myself think about it too often. I usually pushed it away, because that was the only choice. Otherwise, the pain was simply too great, too overwhelming. Now, I tortured myself with the reminder of what we had been, dipping in to the memories to reminisce on how wonderful the universe was – and how much it could hurt.

I got up and started to pace again.

After twelve hours, I could hear stirrings of life from Claire's room. I caught the sound of her yawn, then Kyin's chuckle, and then a series of shiftings and shufflings accompanied by a low, desperate moan.

Despite myself, my cock perked up in interest.

'By the Light,' Lanir muttered.

I groaned and covered my ears, but it didn't help. I could still hear their gasps, hear Kyin give a muffled, wordless growl, hear the cry Claire gave when she shattered.

'They're getting up,' I said a few clicks later.

'Goddess help me,' Lanir said. He dropped into a seat and gestured for me to do the same; we sat, barely breathing as we waited.

Their steps echoed down the corridor. They walked into the kitchen, Kyin so close to Claire he might as well have been her shadow. He was grinning – as usual – but the expression faltered when he saw us waiting.

I hissed.

Kyin took in my expression and stepped in front of Claire, pushing her back. 'Claire,' he said calmly, 'go to your cabin. Lock the door.'

'What?'

'Go back, little one,' Lanir said, his voice level and soft. 'Walk. Don't run. We'll bring you food in a moment.'

'I don't underst –'

I stood, a growl rumbling from my chest.

'*Go*, Claire,' Kyin said sharply. He blocked the doorway with his body. 'Go *now*.'

Claire turned, but she made a mistake.

After two unsteady steps, she ran.

I was sprinting after her before my brain could kick in to tell me what a bad idea it was. Lanir shot to his feet and grabbed at me with more speed than I would have credited him, but I was faster. I dodged and made straight for Kyin, who planted his feet and bared his teeth.

Kyin was more solid than me, and the Darnagh had once been hunters, just like the Kjidja. Unfortunately for Kyin, he wasn't a Divine Guard. I took him down with one sweep of my foot and darted past him, my senses full of Claire, my heart beating in my ears, my claws extending, ready for the catch, every instinct shouting at me to take the female, bite the female, *breed* the female.

She skidded on the floor and hurled herself into her cabin, spinning to wave her hand over the sensor.

The door slid closed with a soft sigh, but I was already inside.

She backed away, as far as she could manage, though her glance around the small room told me that she knew she was making it easier for me to trap her. Her chest heaved as she struggled to catch her breath; her sweet scent had turned cloying with fear. She raised her chin and stared at me defiantly, though her fingers were trembling as she balled them into fists.

'What now, Gydion?' she said harshly.

I stepped towards her. She swallowed, but kept her chin high.

Brave little human.

When I was within arm's length, I dropped to my knees, dipping my chin so that I was staring at her feet. They were bare; her small nails were painted a glittery shade of purple. The sight of her skin made her seem even more vulnerable; I fought against the urge to move forward and touch her.

She was still for a moment and I closed my eyes, waiting for her to scream at me to leave.

'Uh – Gydion?'

I inhaled, letting myself unwind as her scent filled my lungs, returning to normal as she realised I wasn't going to hurt her. It relaxed every tight muscle, soothed every instinct, because it wasn't *just* Claire that I could scent. It was Kyin, too – he was all over her. He'd had his hands on her skin, his mouth on hers, his fingers between her legs – but the mouth-watering scent of his release wasn't present.

'Kyin didn't fuck you,' I said.

'Not in the way I suspect you mean,' Claire said warily. 'Would it be a problem if he had?'

I exhaled. 'No. It would just be harder for me not to touch you.'

Claire stepped forward and took my chin, forcing me to look up; her small finger dug into my jaw. Her expression was serious. 'What just happened?'

I closed my eyes. 'Kjidja males like to chase their mates.'

Her fingers tightened. 'Fucking *what*, Gydion?'

I swallowed. 'We like hunting. We like chasing. We like *catching*. It's an instinctual thing. We need ... We need to feel in control, and that's one of the ways we take it.'

A tiny sound escaped her; I opened my eyes to see her staring down at me. 'You need ... control?' she squeaked.

'Only as much as our mates allow,' I clarified hurriedly. '*Consensually*. Some Kjidja don't like it.'

'Okay,' she said, her free hand coming up to cover her heart. 'But I'm not Kjidja. Or your mate.'

'That doesn't seem to matter,' I growled. 'I want you anyway.'

Her lips parted. 'You want me?'

'Who wouldn't?' I studied her face. 'Did I scare you?' I asked, already knowing the answer but wanting to know what she was thinking.

Her flush deepened. 'At first.'

My fingers twitched with the need to touch her, but I didn't move. 'Just at first?'

She cleared her throat. 'I need warning next time.'

'Next time?'

She swallowed. 'Yes. Next time, tell me first.'

CLAIRE

'READY, CLAIRE?'

I raised the practise sword obediently, watching Gydion's face.

He'd taught me to do that – *watch their intentions, not their weapon*, he'd said – but it wasn't doing me much good, because my eyes kept straying to his lips.

'Block, little one.'

Gydion struck – slowly – and I half-heartedly parried, my arms absorbing the shock as my practise sword met his staff.

'Good. Again.'

I shivered, barely raising my sword before he was striking again. I staggered backwards, my eyes straying back to his lips.

I couldn't seem to think about much else; my mind was caught on what might have happened the previous day, had Gydion possessed even a thread less self-control.

He'd left my room with more grace than I'd been able to muster, pushing past Kyin and Lanir, who had rushed to make sure I was alright. I'd assured them I was, then asked them for space, and spent the rest of the day hiding. Someone – Kyin, I suspected – had left some food and a small screen outside my cabin, and I'd spent the long hours playing the only thing I could access on it – some kind of card game. The cards were marked with symbols I couldn't read and the game had rules I couldn't decipher; no matter how I played, it ended with a small, scaled alien popping up on the screen and eating my cards.

Someone had knocked on my door when the ship's lights started to dim, but I'd pretended to be asleep.

Mostly because I didn't trust *my* self-control. My imagination was running riot, offering a thousand different and delicious scenarios that all ended with me in bed with the three of them. I'd seen Gydion and Lanir exchange a heated kiss in the dining hall one morning, and Kyin seemed game for just about anything, so I didn't think my orgy fantasies were *too* outlandish.

I squirmed; Gydion raised an eyebrow.

My eyes flickered downwards before I could stop them. They traced over the dips and swells of Gydion's abs beneath his jumpsuit before I wrenched my gaze back up to his face.

I'd read alien and monster romances. The authors always made the non-human bits so they'd still fit in the humans – most of the time, anyway – but I didn't have the same guarantee. What if I was driving myself to distraction over parts that wouldn't fit with mine? What if they were so different that it simply wouldn't *work*? What if Lanir and Gydion's species didn't have sex at all?

I made a humming sound, remembering the feeling of Kyin's tongue between my legs, his fingers inside me, his hardness pressed against my hip.

'*Claire*,' Gydion growled, but the sound was amused. 'You're dead, little one. Many times over.'

I shook myself to find his hand at my throat. He pricked his claws gently into my skin before retracting them.

And even if our bits *did* fit, could I get past the differences? Gydion's need to chase, Lanir's ability to know my every emotion, Kyin's tail?

I hummed again. They weren't exactly negatives.

And I could *definitely* deal with Kyin's tail.

Then I remembered that I'd be going back to Earth when this was all over, and the realisation flooded across my skin like cold water.

There'd be no chasing on Earth. No skin in every shade of blue, with veins glowing underneath. No *tails*.

'Claire?' Lanir said sharply from the side of the room. Kyin sat beside him, white teeth flashing in his usual grin.

I took a deep breath, willing the churning in my stomach to subside. *Stupid*, I told myself. First, I was afraid because I'd been taken from Earth, and now I was panicking at the notion of going back? *Make up your mind, Claire.*

'I think that's enough, Gyd.'

Gydion eyed Lanir. 'If you're going to worry like an ancient, Lanir, I'm going to throw you out while we train.'

'I don't mind him worrying,' I said, and tossed Lanir a smile without thinking. He inhaled, then sucked his bottom lip between his teeth, his irises swirling.

Oh, fuck.

Gydion took my arm and gently unhooked my fingers from around the practise sword's hilt. 'I've changed my mind. I think Lan is right. Enough for today.'

Maybe he could chase me again instead.

A wave of warmth spread through my body.

'Claire,' Gydion growled, this time in warning; I shivered at the sound. 'I'm one wrong move away from ripping your jumpsuit to pieces and fucking you on the floor.'

I swallowed, staring at him.

I mean, yes, please?

'Um,' I squeaked instead.

'Why don't you have another shower, little one?' Kyin interjected. 'We're all a bit … tense. Some distance might help.'

Who knew Kyin had it in him to be the voice of reason? I nodded; Gydion let my wrist slip from his fingers, though his chest rumbled a discontented noise.

But … the floor, my ovaries complained.

I fled before I could listen, feeling three sets of eyes on my back, seeking the comfort of my cabin.

Again.

When I emerged from the shower, I'd worked myself into a panic. The worry simply wouldn't *stop*, constricting my chest, churning my stomach, closing my throat. Lanir was sitting alone on my nest-bed, his legs crossed, a screen in hand; he tossed it aside when I opened the door.

'I hope you don't mind the intrusion, but I could feel you from the dining hall,' he said gently. 'Would you like some help?'

I nodded, then dropped to my knees and crawled across the bed to him, not missing the way his jaw tightened and his white pupils blew out. It looked so different – so *alien* – but apparently my body didn't mind, my nipples tightening and rubbing against my jumpsuit as I moved.

When I was close enough, he swept me into a tight hug, cradling me on his lap. I inhaled deeply as wave of calm washed over me.

'*Oh*,' I sighed. I pulled away slightly. 'I don't want you to think I only come to you for the emotions, Lan.'

He snorted. 'I don't care if you do.'

'I shouldn't rely on you to make me feel better.'

His arms tightened. 'Claire, you've been accidentally abducted and are currently light years away from your home in the company of three strangers who aren't the same species as you. I think you're allowed to ask for help to make yourself feel better.'

I wriggled, nestling my head under his chin. Being in his arms felt so *right*, as if I'd been held by him for years, as if my body knew every hard plane of muscle. I'd learned the signs of him using his power – the intense focus, the glowing veins beneath his skin – so I knew that the feeling of rightness was all mine.

I sighed into the column of his neck, feeling his pulse drum beneath his skin. 'Thank you.'

Being so close to him was a mistake. I pulled back and stared at his fluttering pulse as desire flooded through me, chased by the unhinged notion that if I didn't touch his bare skin *that moment*, I'd die in need for it.

'Little one,' Lanir said hoarsely. 'You're killing me.'

Embarrassment slithered down my spine. 'Sorry,' I mumbled. 'I need –' I cut myself off. 'Sorry.'

'Why?' He pressed a kiss to my hair. 'What a way to die.'

I huffed a laugh and pressed an answering kiss to his jaw; when he groaned, I pressed another to his pulse. After a third, further down his neck, his hand came up and he tugged the zipper of his jumpsuit down, baring his collarbone to me.

I kissed him there, too, listening to his breath catch. 'Is this all right?' I whispered against his skin.

His hand cupped my cheek. 'It's more than all right. Do whatever you want to me, Claire.'

A stab of heat came with that statement, but surely he didn't mean it. 'Are you sure?'

'I'm sure.'

I inhaled, then pulled at his zipper. The jumpsuit parted, revealing a large swathe of blue skin covering an impressive set of chiselled pecs.

Oh, yes.

I snuggled against him, rubbing my cheek against his chest like a cat. His cool skin was smooth and soft but the muscle beneath was hard as rock.

'Is this what you need?' he murmured into my hair.

I tugged his zipper down further, stopping where my belly button would be. His stomach didn't have one, just delicious indents defining his abs.

Something stirred under me. I gave a soft gasp of surprise.

'Claire –'

I pressed down against it, feeling it – *him* – get thicker, longer.

It *felt* very much like a human cock, but bigger than I was used to.

'Claire,' he said again, but this time the sound was deeper.

I pushed his jumpsuit over his shoulders; he stripped it off his arms, then sat still as stone as I ran my hands over his shoulders, my cheeks going hot.

Oh, yes.

He all but glowed in the dim light, casting blue flickers around the room. I wondered if his cock would glow, too, so I trailed my fingers down his stomach with every intention of finding out.

He grabbed my hand. 'This isn't what I came in here expecting,' he grated out. 'This isn't about me.'

'Yes, you and Kyin are very selfless,' I said breathlessly. 'But I'd very much like to keep touching you, Lan. Do you want me to stop?'

He shook his head, his jaw clenched tight.

'Tell me if there's something you don't want.' I dipped my hand below his jumpsuit, wrapping my fingers around what I found there. He was so thick they were nowhere near meeting, but he *felt* like a human, with a silken softness covering the cool steel beneath.

'Holy shit,' I breathed. I drew him out, my mouth going dry at the sight of him.

He *looked* like a human, too, with a long shaft and a swollen head – except that he was blue, and, to my satisfaction, the veins beneath his skin were glowing like a fucking nightlight. Everything about his cock was delicious, from the way it felt to the way it looked, and I shifted my hips towards him without thinking, my body having its own ideas about what to do with it.

'*Claire*,' he rumbled.

I gave his shaft a few experimental pumps. He moaned, his hips twitching.

'Is this how you like it?'

He ground his teeth. 'I think I'd like anything you might do, little one. But I've been dreaming about all the things I want to do with you, and this isn't it.'

He dipped his head until our lips met, his mouth teasing softly over mine. He had a delicious fresh taste, almost like spearmint, and my lips parted to let him in, to taste him deeper. His tongue danced with mine until he broke away, pressing a line of kisses down my neck as I continued to work his cock, heat blooming between my legs at how he felt in my hand, at the way his breath caught.

'Claire,' he said again, then took my jumpsuit in hand, tearing it in two instead of using the fastening. I squeaked in surprise, then moaned as his head dipped forward to take a nipple into his mouth.

'Have you been talking to Kyin?' I managed.

His tongue laved over my sensitive flesh. 'He might have mentioned something.' He pulled away with a soft *pop*, then turned to my other breast. I was happy to let him do it, brazenly arching my back to give him better access. 'And when I say *mentioned*, I very definitely mean he bragged insufferably.'

He pulled my jumpsuit down further, the fabric giving way with quiet *rips* until he was able to pull the parts away from my body and I was in his lap, naked.

Gentle Lanir had a dominant side, and I couldn't pretend that it wasn't hot as hell.

His hands spanned my waist then moved down, brushing over my skin.

'You'll tell me to stop,' he mouthed around my nipple.

It wasn't a question. 'Yes,' I answered breathlessly.

As if I'd want this to stop.

One hand slid forward, and the other back. He gripped my ass in a firm hold as his other hand moved between my legs, his fingers brushing over my clit and slipping between my folds.

'So wet,' he groaned. 'Kyin didn't tell me *that*.' He trailed his tongue up my neck. 'I can feel where you're burning, Claire.'

'Then make it better,' I begged.

He sank a finger inside me, holding me still with the hand on my ass. I gasped, wanting to move, but he waited, letting me adjust before he pulled out and added a second finger. The stretch was delicious and I moaned, my eyes rolling back in my head as he found the sweet spot inside me and gently pressed, simultaneously applying pressure to my clit with the heel of his hand.

Oh, yes.

'Show me what you like,' he murmured.

The hand on my ass relaxed, urging me to move. I rolled my hips experimentally, listening to Lanir's wordless groan.

'By the Light,' he ground out.

'Are Illisae females different?' I gasped.

He nipped my earlobe. 'I have no idea. All I want to know is how *you* feel, in every way.'

Well, that was nice.

I rode his hand gently, my eyes almost closed as I watched his glow grow brighter from beneath my lashes. I took his cock back in hand and pumped my fist up and down as I moved, smugly listening to the noises he made. His head dipped back down to my breast and he sucked a mouthful of flesh between his cool lips, sending my body into overdrive as his tongue teased my nipple.

I ground my clit against his hand, feeling the heat inside me grow. 'I'm going to come,' I gasped. His hips jerked beneath me, thrusting into my fist. He surged up to swallow my cry as I shattered, my body clenching around his fingers.

'Gods, you're so hot,' he grated out, but it didn't seem like a bad thing, and a moment later my hand was covered in glowing white, jets of cum painting his stomach. I worked him through his climax as he shuddered, squeezing his shaft until he swore.

My lips curled up in satisfaction.

He studied me through hooded eyes. 'Kyin mentioned something else.'

'Did he,' I said wryly, keeping hold of his cock.

'Mmm. Something about three times?'

I laughed and rolled my hips, clenching my internal muscles around his fingers as he swore and his cock jerked in my hand. 'Kyin has a big mouth.'

He grinned. 'I heard he did something else with his mouth.' He dipped his chin and kissed me, nipping at my bottom lip. 'I think I should try it, too.'

'You should,' I agreed huskily. 'It's only fair.'

LANIR

'Have you noticed where we are?'

I looked up from my screen, where I'd been pretending to read a Kjidja drama while actually thinking about Claire coming on my fingers. 'Hmm?'

Kyin rolled his eyes. 'Snap out of it, big blue. Look at where we are.'

I followed his finger to the navigation screen. 'Oh, *shit*,' I said, scrambling out of my seat. 'How is that possible?'

Kyin poked at the screen and brought up the logs, the one thing we were still able to access. 'He's been switching the ship to elevated unit travel in the nighttime hours.' His lips twisted. 'Which means he must be piloting the Sidereal as we sleep. *Fuck*. That fucking –'

'Yes, yes, your father's a giant asshole,' I snapped. 'And a creepy one, too, apparently.' I took a deep breath, willing myself to be calm. 'That means we're only a week from Scytha.'

'A week from *war*, Lanir,' Kyin growled, as if I could have forgotten.

I stared at the nav screen. 'She's nowhere near ready.'

'No,' Kyin agreed. 'And neither are we.' He studied the screen. 'I wonder if I'm thinking about this wrong.'

'Thinking about what wrong?'

He gestured to his own hand screen. 'I've been trying everything I can think of to break his hack, to throw off his hold on our systems. But I'm getting *nowhere*, Lan. That fucker is like a walking glowfish: all tentacles, and every one with a poison tip.' He tapped his chin. 'He's distracting me with the battle so that he can win the war. But what if I changed my tactic?'

I could feel his growing excitement; it shivered over my skin. 'To what?'

He turned to me, leaning in so close he was breathing in my ear. It didn't help me concentrate; I had to resist turning my face and seizing his lips with mine. Kyin had a way of smiling as he kissed, the curve of his lips all but divine; I wanted to feel it so badly my hearts hurt. 'What if I took the fight to him?'

I covered my mouth with my hand; Kyin's father was clearly monitoring our systems, and that probably included surveillance. 'How, Ky?'

'What if I could find proof?' he breathed. 'If he *is* planning to sell to both sides, what if I could find it? The Council would *have* to do something. He'd be breaking multiple laws.' He flicked a glance at his hand screen. 'What if we let him have this battle, and focus on winning the war?'

'He still has the power,' I murmured warningly. 'For the next week, he has *all* the power. And not just over us – over Claire, too.'

'I'll have to be careful.' He pulled back; his eyes flared as they dropped to my lips. 'I can smell her on you,' he said. He took a deep breath. 'It's driving me fucking insane.'

He got up and left without saying another word, leaving me with a mess of his lingering emotions: lust, frustration, grief, regret.

But beneath them all: love.

I sat alone for a very long time, considering.

Something beeped.

I put my glass down and looked at my handscreen, frowning. 'Ky,' I called a moment later, leaping to my feet. '*Kyin*!'

A comm popped up, blinking.

'*Kyin*!'

'Gods, Lan, I'm here,' Kyin said grumpily, skidding into the kitchen.

I gestured wordlessly at the screen.

He blinked at it, then his eyes widened. 'Fuck,' he breathed. 'That's an encrypted channel.' He looked at it more closely. 'A *Tirian* channel.' He tapped the screen.

A Tirian Captain appeared, green-flushed cheeks lined with thorns. 'Kyin Crace,' they said politely. 'Mage. I am Captain Peony. She.'

'Captain.' Both Kyin and I bowed our heads.

'You seem to be locked out of your own ship, Crace. It looked a bit odd when we scanned it, so we thought we'd make contact.

My engineers are scrambling your audio and video streams, so you can speak safely if you have any worries on that score.'

'Thank you,' Kyin said tightly. 'We are locked out, Captain. I've been trying to regain control but haven't managed it yet.'

'If there's one thing I know about you, Crace, it's that you've earned your reputation,' the Captain drawled. 'I can only imagine a handful of beings in the universe who could keep you out of your own ship.'

'Then you can probably guess who is responsible,' Kyin growled.

The Captain nodded. 'Somebody close to home, I suspect. Would you like us to break the lock?'

Kyin's eyes widened. 'Why, Captain Peony. That's against intergalactic protocol. And given what's been done to my ship, probably a very illegal skillset for your systems engineers to possess.'

She nodded. 'Yes, I am aware. I always hire the best, Crace. But you'll need control of your Sidereal if you're flying into Roth airspace. There's more junk up there than black. I'm sure your father will understand, given the circumstances.'

'Yes,' Gydion growled from behind us, startling me. 'Break it.'

Captain Peony nodded to him in greeting. 'Divine Guard.' She paused. 'Crace? What say you?'

Kyin inhaled. 'Captain ... Thank you for your offer. If you're willing to help us, there's something else I would ask instead.'

The Captain raised an eyebrow. 'I'm listening.'

'Five years ago, there was a case the Intergalactic Council oversaw. A Severn warlord was selling ammunitions to both sides in the Amirla civil war.'

A line appeared between the Captain's brows. 'I remember it.'

'This ship has a hold-full of bauxite ore and is headed straight to Scytha.'

Her frown deepened. 'I see.' She looked away; there were some murmurs in the background. 'Your trip to Earth wasn't sanctioned by the Intergalactic Council, Crace.'

'What?' Kyin's tail twitched in agitation. 'But I checked the approvals my father sent myself. Everything was stamped and signed.' He glanced at me. 'The timing did seem odd, but since we had the approvals, I didn't think too much about it.'

'I think this is worth looking into.' The Captain's eyes flickered to me, then Gydion. 'Are you sure you don't want me to break the hold? It might be safer for your family.'

'He took over once, Captain. He'll just do it again, and there will be repercussions if you break the lock, repercussions that could affect everyone on board. But if you could look into the approvals, and whether there are any trails about the upcoming sale of this ore ...'

'Already on it,' the Captain said. She looked aside. 'My engineer is sending you the latest news on Scytha, with updated battle lines and the locations of allied forces. On that point,' she continued, her eyes narrowing, 'we can see the other being on board, Crace.'

'That's right,' Kyin said calmly. 'Lanir and Gydion's mate.'

'*Human* mate,' the Captain said sharply.

'We had a notion to leave her with the new Roth Queen when we landed on Scytha,' Kyin returned. 'She's human, too, isn't she? I also heard that one of the Tirian peacekeeping ships has a human female on board. That was *your* ship, wasn't it, Captain?'

The Captain's lips pursed. 'Your friends' *mate* would be safer on Kjid, or Ilis, or Darn,' she said sharply. 'But if you can't manage that, then dropping her with the Roth Queen is not the worst plan you could formulate. The last we heard, the King was on the verge of taking back Scytha City, and the Queen was staying close behind his forces. I'd try there first.'

Kyin gave her a short bow. 'Many thanks, Captain Peony.'

The Tirian nodded. 'We'll scramble your audio and video for another hour,' she said, then blanked the screen.

I exhaled slowly as a Tirian news stream popped up on my screen. It was information that would only be available to the peacekeeping ships and the Intergalactic Council, not broadcast across the galaxy. 'The Intergalactic Council's allied forces have joined the Roth King, and there's heavy fighting across Scytha City,' I murmured. 'They've retaken the southern outskirts, but not without a heavy cost. A weapons cache exploded; someone close to the King was badly wounded.' I flicked an image onto the wall. It was blurry, but a Tirian medic was crouched over a Roth warrior, suturing his wounds with a bandage gun. 'The King is holding ground for the moment.'

'Which means he'll probably be ready to move further into the city by the time we get there, if not before,' Gydion said grimly. 'There'll be more fighting, more casualties.'

I flicked an updated map next to the image. 'We'll need to head behind their lines. From what I can see, the King is gaining ground slowly and at a large cost, but he hasn't *lost* any ground yet. If we head to the south, we can leave Claire where it's safest.' I frowned as a gossip stream popped up alongside the map. 'Fuck. Apparently the Nataran Prince *also* has a human consort. He's fighting alongside the Roth King – and his mates are staying with the Roth Queen. This says the Nataran Prince's mates refused to leave him, even the human one – who is *pregnant* to him.'

'Then it will be a fucking party,' Kyin said sourly. He tapped his fingers on his chin. 'We still have no idea where my father will land us. We can't even make a *plan*. And Claire –'

'What about Claire?' she said sharply, padding softly into the room. She blinked in surprise at the images on the wall. 'Fuck. Are they other alie – other *beings*?'

'A Tirian. You've seen a Roth before,' Gydion said softly.

Her eyes flickered between the two beings. 'The Roth are still scary motherfuckers.' She studied the Tirian. 'This one looks like an elf. But like, a hot fantasy elf. Not a Christmas elf.'

Kyin's eyes narrowed as a stab of his jealousy hit me in the stomach. We knew what she meant, and she wasn't talking about temperature. 'A *hot fantasy elf*?'

Claire waved her hand. 'Not as hot as you three, obviously.'

Kyin sniffed; a wary satisfaction rolled through the room.

Gydion pointed at the map. 'This is Scytha. This is where the King is now,' he said, gesturing to a small section, which was demarcated with an orange line. 'This is the territory he holds, according to the Tirian reports,' he continued, indicating a section bordered with green. 'And this is where the worst fighting is.' His finger made a wide circle around an area coloured red. 'It's worse than I expected, honestly. From this, it seems that the rebellion is widespread, both in numbers and in territory. The Roth King has the support of allied troops, but civil unrest is messy; you can't just sweep in and wipe the board clean. You must take power and *hold* it, then convince the ones you took it from that *you* deserve it – either by right, or through fear.' He considered the map thoughtfully. 'The King hasn't had long to do either. I imagine that he'll have his supporters spreading information about the legitimacy of his claim and his plans for the future, but that kind of change takes time, and from what I know, the Roth have been set in their ways for centuries. So, he'll probably be focusing on the military campaign – no easy task when you're trying to subdue a warrior species.'

'His troops will be thinning the more he pushes forward,' Claire said, realising. 'Because he'll have to leave soldiers in every place he takes in order to *keep* it.'

'That's exactly it,' Gydion said, pleased. 'I imagine that's what the bulk of the Allied Planet forces will be doing – following behind and helping to consolidate the territory the Roth King wins.'

'So where will we land?' Claire said, looking at the map. 'There?'

I exchanged a loaded glance with Kyin and Gydion.

'We don't know yet, *cora*,' Kyin said. I stiffened at the endearment; *my soul*, it meant, in the dialect Kyin's mother had taught him, one spoken by so few Darnagh that the translators didn't recognise it. I knew the meaning, though, because it was what Kyin used to call Gydion and me. *Cora*, my soul, female. *Core*, my soul, male. *Corae*, either gender neutral or my souls, plural – the word he used to cry out most often when Gydion pushed him to a shattering climax as I swallowed his cry with a kiss. 'We can't access our navigation path, and even if we *could* see where we were going, there's no guarantee that my father wouldn't change course along the way.'

'So we go in blind?' Claire said, incredulous.

Gydion shook his head. 'We plan for the worst and hope for something better.'

I let her emotions wash over me. Fear, anticipation, dread, and the ever-present anxiety, heightened now. I twisted my lips and strode across the navigation room, pulling her into my arms. She started in surprise but let me do it, relaxing as I stroked her back and nuzzled at her hair.

'We won't let you get hurt, Claire,' I said.

She pulled away. 'That isn't what I'm worried about,' she snapped. 'I don't like that *you* could be fighting. I don't like that *you'll* be in danger. *That's* what I don't like.'

'Aww, Claire,' Kyin said, grinning. 'You're *worried* about us. Is it because of the orgasms? It's because of the orgasms, isn't it?'

Claire scowled at him, but her cheeks went pink.

'It's Gydion's turn tonight, yes?' Kyin said, his grin growing wider.

'I'm not a merry-go-round, Kyin,' Claire snapped. 'But yes, it *is* Gydion's turn. If he wants it.' Her eyes flickered between us nervously. 'But ...' She trailed off.

A mix of nervousness, embarrassment, and anticipation washed over me, buoyed by a heated arousal so strong I caught my breath. Claire chewed on her bottom lip, her cheeks flushing, then looked away.

'But *what*, little one?' I prompted softly.

'It's nothing,' she said, too quickly.

Kyin quirked an eyebrow. 'It doesn't sound like nothing, Claire. Do you want to sleep alone tonight?'

'No, I just –' She blew out a breath.

'*Oh*,' I said, realising as her eyes flickered between us once more and her arousal warmed my skin. 'Do you want more than one of us to stay?'

Gydion went statue-still.

Her flush strayed down her neck. 'I –'

'One not enough for you?' Kyin said, but his grin had wavered.

I inhaled. 'I think –'

'– that whoever you want to stay, Claire, will stay,' Kyin interjected. 'Do you want Lan and Gyd? Or all of us?'

Claire swallowed audibly. 'All of you.'

Kyin stood. 'Then I'll go make our bed.'

'I know there's some tension between you,' Claire said, when he was gone. 'You don't have to do this.'

'It's not Lan and me that you need to worry about,' Gydion said, tapping his claws on his thigh. He glanced at me, searching my face. 'We want to.'

Claire studied us. 'Would it help if I asked him about it?'

Gydion shrugged. 'It can't *hurt*, little one. But I don't know if he'd tell you.' He turned to me, reaching up to touch my cheek. 'But if you find anything out, we'd like to hear it.'

GYDION

I was the last one to make it to Claire's room. The Tirian Captain had sent us a wealth of information, ranging from gossip streams to historic blueprints of Scytha City straight from the Roth archives, which Kyin had swiftly backed up to a screen he'd managed to disconnect from the Sidereal's internal network. I spent our precious, scrambled hour poring through it, trying to find something – *anything* – that might help us once we landed.

It was likely we'd be landing in the desert, so we'd need to wear temperature-regulating spacesuits. The air on Scytha had less oxygen than Earth and Darn, so both Claire and Kyin would need converters, which were worn over the mouth and nose and changed hydrogen molecules to oxygen via an electric pulse. Though it would be uncomfortable in the heat, we would need helmets and Kjidja body armour for protection from the atmosphere and any Roth we might encounter. We'd need to carry food and water, as there was no guarantee we would make it somewhere safe quickly. We'd need small blanket packs, as temperatures plummeted at nighttime. Our helmet comms would need a link to each other, in case we got separated.

And we'd need weapons. All of us.

I wasn't worried about myself. I'd trained since childhood to protect the priestesses. I'd fought in more bouts than I could count, had undergone endurance tests, and could use a range of weapons with deadly accuracy.

Kyin was strong at hand-to-hand combat, and had a decent mind for strategy, but he'd never had to live on wild terra. Lanir could protect himself, but he'd be distracted by the emotions of the beings around him – and he'd feel every single one of their deaths as their souls were plucked from the Light.

And Claire ...

I was proud of what she'd achieved on the ship, but I couldn't fool myself and say that it was *enough*. She'd be vulnerable, and because of that, we'd be vulnerable, too.

I stiffened as a scent filled my mouth. The control room was cool, but my body flushed with heat – with *want* – as the sweet, heady scent of Claire surrounded me.

I breathed in deeply as my cock hardened. I shifted from one foot to the other, trying to ignore it, trying to concentrate on reading the reports, but it became all but impossible as Kyin's spice coated my tongue.

My mind ran riot, imagining all the things he could be doing with her.

The delicious metallic tang of Lanir's arousal began to twine with the other two scents, and I wondered what Kyin and Claire were doing to elicit *that*.

I tried to read the reports – one of us had to plan for Scytha, after all, and planning usually fell to me – but my eyes strayed continually to the doorway, and my nose was twitching at the mix of thick aromas, my claws extending and retracting against my jumpsuit.

Moments later, I gave up, striding from the control room towards the scents that were driving me to distraction.

A sweet moan came from behind Claire's closed door. I paused, my heart racing, before I waved over the sensor.

Kyin was cradling Claire's face in his hands as they shared a kiss that was both tender and desperate. The tip of Kyin's tail was tracing over the swell of Claire's breasts, tweaking her nipples through the jumpsuit.

'Gods. Kissing you is my new favourite thing,' he said, breaking off as Claire arched her back, offering his tail better access. Kyin took full advantage, sliding his hands down to add his fingers to the mix, strumming his thumbs back and forth over the hard peaks. He glanced at the doorway. 'Took you long enough, Gyd.'

My claws pricked my thighs as the door slid closed behind me.

'How do you want this to go, *cora*?'

Claire glanced at Lanir, then at me, her cheeks flushed a deep pink. 'I don't … I haven't thought about it.'

I had the feeling that might not have been true.

Kyin snorted. 'You mean you haven't thought about all three of us worshipping you until you scream? Because I guarantee that *we* have.'

Claire's breath caught.

'But if you want that, you have to tell us,' Kyin continued, 'so there's no misunderstandings, and we're all on the same page of the make-Claire-come systems manual.'

'How ...' Claire began, her voice strangled. She cleared her throat. 'How do you feel about it?'

I caught Lanir's eye from where he stood in the bathroom door, leaning heavily against its frame. His cheeks were paled with a blush, his pupils blown out and spinning with desire.

'Lanir and I are here for whatever you want, Claire,' I said. 'If you want to go to sleep, then that's all we'll do. If you want something else, then you just have to ask.'

'I think you know how I feel about it,' Kyin said, his fingers playing over her breasts. 'I want to see you come on Lanir's hand.'

Claire shuddered.

I pressed my claws further into my thighs. 'Have you done something like this before, Claire?'

'No,' she answered, her voice unsteady. 'But I want it. I want *this*.'

'Then we're going to work you until you scream, *cora*,' Kyin said, grinning. 'Gydion? Where should we start?'

I twitched at the words, ones he'd said so many times before, but always with Lanir stripped and panting before us. *Where should we start?* with Lan spread out over the bed. *Where should we start?* with Lan face-down and trembling with want on the floor. *Where should we start?* with Lan bent over a chair in the dining hall.

Where should we start?

'You're so beautiful, Claire,' I purred, ruthlessly pushing aside the memories. Kyin was here for *Claire*, not us, and Claire needed my worship, not my pain. 'All flushed and ready for us to play with. But you're wearing too many clothes. Lan?'

Lanir stepped forward then fell to his knees next to her. 'Claire?'

Claire reached up and touched his cheek, then pulled her zipper down.

I exhaled, retracting my claws. I wasn't sure what I'd expected, but it wasn't *this*. I'd imagined she'd need longer to adjust to the idea of more than one of us touching her, but she sighed as Kyin palmed a breast while Lanir gently stripped the jumpsuit away from her skin. She was perfect, the curve of her hips and softness of her stomach contrasting with the sharpness of her collarbone and her long, strong fingers. Her flush reached down her neck, spreading across her chest as I studied her naked body.

'What next, Gyd?' Lanir said quietly.

'Would you like to be kissed again, Claire?'

She nodded, swallowing.

'Words,' I said. 'We need words. Always. If you say *yes*, then we will kiss you. If you say *no*, or *stop*, everything halts. Immediately. There are no special terms here, just *yes* and *no* and *more*. Do you understand?'

'Yes, Gydion,' she said, her eyes heavy.

'So would you like to be kissed, Claire?'

'Yes, Gydion,' she repeated, and held out her hand.

Kyin moved aside, leaving her before me. Lanir pressed his lips to her hair and stroked his fingers across her stomach. I took her hand and gave a soft kiss to every knuckle, then turned it over to press another line of kisses from her wrist to her elbow.

She watched, her throat working as she swallowed. My lungs were full of her scent, heady and addictive, sweetened by her arousal. The combination of her, Kyin, and Lanir was chipping away at my control; everything – every*one* – that I held dear was in one room, in various states of undress and arousal, and my instinct were shouting to *claim*, to fuck and tie and *breed*. It didn't matter that it wasn't possible with Kyin and Lanir, nor that I had no idea what Claire thought about children – I wanted it anyway, to prove that they were mine.

Fuck.

I pushed the thought – and my possessiveness – aside, taking up Claire's free hand and giving it the same soft attention as the first. I flicked a glance at Lanir, whose fingers spread up to cup her breasts and work her nipples, gently plucking and pinching and kneading until Claire whined. She spread her legs in a blatant invitation, already swollen and wet from Lanir and Kyin's teasing; my cock pulsed at the sight of her, flushed and begging and perfect.

'Please, Gydion,' she whispered. 'I want you inside me.'

Part of me wanted to give her what she was asking for, to sink myself into her and move until her body tensed around me and she whined with pleasure. But while Lanir and Kyin were used to my tie, Claire wasn't; I didn't know what human males looked like. I wanted her to squirm and sweat and sob and beg, but I didn't want to *hurt* her, no matter how much I wanted to be buried inside her.

'Hold her on your lap, Lan,' I said.

Lanir pulled her into his lap, one arm banded around her waist. His free hand pushed her knees apart then rested lightly on her thigh, an anchor if she needed it.

A wave of love and appreciation flowed through me. Lanir wouldn't feel it – Illisae Mages couldn't get past the Kjidja's natural mental shields – but I let him see it on my face, biting my lip before I dropped to my elbows and blew a soft breath over Claire's pink, swollen flesh.

She whimpered.

Lanir had told me about the bud at the top of her sex, so I concentrated my attention there, nuzzling the soft curls on her mound and pressing kisses all around, just missing the place she needed pressure until she was shuddering and squirming, pushing against Lanir. He held her firm, whispering praise to her as I teased, telling her how beautiful she was, how well she was doing, how good she felt under his hands. She was flushed from his praise and from frustration, the pink turning to red the longer I tormented her.

I traced my fingertips up the inside of her thighs, skirting the moisture there, until I was just shy of her lower lips.

'*Please*, Gydion,' she begged.

I could have teased her for hours – *days* – but I took pity on her and skimmed my thumbs over the outer petals of her sex. She panted, squirming; Lanir tightened his hold, whispering more praise.

I started at the base, close to her second tight entrance, and worked my thumbs in soft circles over her, moving slowly up. She keened, her thighs quivering; she was so wet her flesh was slick and slippery and divine, her arousal trickling down between the round globes of her ass. I worked my thumbs around her bud, avoiding it completely, then, without warning, brushed a finger around her entrance.

Her hips bucked; she whimpered. Beside her, Kyin's tail thrashed back and forth behind him. He groaned and pulled his cock from beneath his jumpsuit, working it up and down as he watched. Lanir was more collected, but his eyes were closed and

I could see the swell of his cock beneath Claire; he was almost unnaturally still as he tried to keep control.

Another time, I'd work to break that control, to make him groan and sweat and give himself up like a sacred offering, just like Claire was doing. I'd work until both of them were desperate, pleading messes, until they were so wound up that their climax would feel as if they were being broken open, made anew, and they were broken and healed *together*.

But tonight wasn't for that; it was for Claire, and making sure she felt safe – safe, and so wrung out and exhausted that she slept for hours.

'Gydion,' she choked out.

'I've got you, Claire,' I murmured. 'I've got you.' My eyes flickered to Kyin, then Lanir. 'We've got you, little one.'

I sank my thumb inside her.

She whined, her hips pushing down, trying to take me further. Lanir held her fast, letting me touch her in shallow, slow thrusts, always soft, never far enough, just teasing her entrance. Even so, her muscles clenched around me; I withdrew, waiting until her body calmed.

'What –' she sobbed.

'Not yet,' I said gently.

'You're edging me.'

'I don't know what that is,' I answered, my thumbs going back to their small circles over her lower lips. 'But if it means you won't come until I let you, then yes, I am.' I paused. 'Do you want me to continue?'

A frustrated sound tore from her throat. '*Yes*, dammit.'

I hissed my approval, flicking another look at Lanir. His hand came up to cup Claire's chin; he tilted her head to the side, then ran his nose up her neck.

'I wish you could see how beautiful you are,' he murmured. 'All flushed and swollen and pink. Look at what you've done to Kyin.' He tipped her head gently towards Kyin, who gave a savage, wordless snarl, squeezing his swollen head. Pre-cum was sliding down his shaft; he touched himself unselfconsciously, without restraint, as if he'd known Claire for years. As if she knew what pleased him and he, her; as if we'd done this together before.

Claire whimpered as I touched her, making my way slowly back up to the peak of her sex. This time, I let the pads of my thumbs stroke the sides of her swollen bud – stroke, pause, stroke, pause – never fast enough to let her build to a climax. Her thighs were a constant quiver and her body was wound tight; her eyes were fixed on me, fixed on where I was touching.

I slid my fingers back down, circling her entrance, then dipping further. She cried out wordlessly as I brushed over the tight pucker of her ass. 'Do you like being touched here, Claire?'

She nodded, panting.

'Words, Claire.'

'Yes,' she ground out. 'Yes, I like it there. Yes, you can touch me there. Yes, you can fuck me there.'

I laughed. 'You're not ready for fucking, little one.' I pushed my finger gently against the resistance; the tip slipped inside. She was so hot, so tight, that I couldn't stop a shudder of my own. Kyin wasn't the only one damp with pre-cum; I could feel it gathering against my stomach. I withdrew, then circled her rim gently, teasing and tickling until her hips bucked again.

'Would you like to take Kyin in your mouth, Claire?'

She gasped, her eyes darting to Kyin. 'Yes. Yes, please.'

I nodded at Kyin, who rose onto his knees. Lanir kept his hand cupped around Claire's jaw, guiding her to the side; she looked up at Kyin, her brown eyes wide, and took his swollen head in her mouth.

Kyin swore as her lips moved further down. He stayed still, letting her take what she could, groaning when she moved back up, then down once more.

'Good,' I praised. I pressed down lightly on her bud in reward, then slipped a finger inside her, pushing the one at her ass back in at the same time.

Claire moaned around Kyin's cock. I could tell that he was close; he glanced at me, almost for approval. I gave him a nod; he thrust once, twice, into Claire's mouth, then growled wordlessly as he came. Her throat worked convulsively, swallowing his release.

'Fuck,' Lanir whispered.

I found the rough patch inside her and began to press lightly, withdrawing and pushing my finger back inside her back entrance in tandem. Claire whimpered; Lanir turned her back toward him and swallowed her sounds with a kiss. Sweat was dampening the hair at her temples and droplets had gathered between her breasts; she looked wrecked and tormented and every kind of exquisite.

I dipped my head and sucked gently on her bud.

'Look at how gorgeous you are,' Lanir crooned softly. 'How well you took Kyin, how beautifully you're stretching around Gydion's fingers. Such a good girl for us.'

She came immediately, her body clamping around my fingers in strong, even waves. I felt her release pulse beneath my tongue and I ground myself on the mattress in answer, purring so she'd feel the vibration. She tasted like paradise, so I left my mouth where it was as she sobbed and her body eventually calmed, licking her thighs and petals clean when she was done, then dipping lower and licking her there, too.

'*Fuck*, Gydion,' she said, collapsing back against Lanir. '*Fuck*.'

Lanir pressed kisses up her neck. She turned in his lap, settling herself on the mattress, her legs still around his hips, so that she could fish beneath his jumpsuit for his cock. I moved forward and pressed myself against her back, taking her earlobe gently between my teeth as I watched her fist Lanir's hard length, his own hand reaching out to touch between her legs, his fingers disappearing inside her as her breath caught.

'Perfect,' I breathed, catching Lanir's chin to crush his lips to mine. Claire's hand began to work and he groaned, his hips angling up so he could fuck into her fist. It was desperate and clumsy and divine; she was so wet that I could hear every movement of his fingers as they pushed in and out of her.

I would have kept watching, except a hand slid over my ass, caressing, then gripped my cock from behind.

Kyin's teeth sank into my neck, not enough to hurt, but enough to keep me still as he unzipped my jumpsuit to fist me properly. I was so hard his movements almost ached, but the feeling had nothing on the confusion and pleasure and *hope* spilling through my chest. The fingers of his free hand swirled over my swollen head, gathering up my pre-cum, then slid between my legs.

'You're fucking amazing, do you know that?' he growled in my ear, no hint of his usual irreverence in his tone. 'So sleek and strong and perfect. Watching you is *everything*. Touching you is *better*.' He used my pre-cum to make my entrance slick, then pushed a finger inside. 'Remember how good it was? When we'd take turns fucking Lan senseless, then fuck each other? I remember how you feel around my cock. How your tie felt inside me. Perfect. Fucking *perfect*, Gydion.' He swiped his tongue up my neck as his hand worked; pleasure built at the base of my spine, ready to spill, ready to *explode*. 'Next time, you could take Claire as I fucked you. Or I could take Claire as you fuck *me*. Or we could fuck Claire and Lanir together, side by side, make them squirm, make them beg, make them shake.'

'Ky,' I grated out, barely holding on. 'Ky, I'm –'

'I know, *core*,' he rumbled. 'I know you're ready. I remember. I remember fucking *everything*.'

I broke at the sound of his endearment, spilling into his hand. He made a satisfied noise as Claire cried out again, rocking against Lanir's hand as he covered hers in thick, glowing ropes. I leaned back against Kyin, my eyes pricking as his arms wound tightly around my waist and he nuzzled my cheek. Lanir looked up, his expression a crease of confusion and relief; he schooled it quickly, easing Claire back into his arms and whispering praise as her eyes fluttered closed.

I didn't know what was happening, but I didn't want it to end. I let Kyin hold me as I closed my eyes, and I let myself pretend that Kyin had come back to us and Claire was ours, let myself pretend that this was every day, and every night, and everything was as it should be.

I woke up gasping for air.

I was the only one awake. Claire was snuggled into Lanir's arms, and Kyin was still curled around my body, but something was wrong. I raked in a breath, but my lungs were still screaming for more, and my heart was thundering.

'Ky,' I croaked, shaking him. '*Ky!*'

Claire's skin had an odd blue tint, and Lanir was going white. I couldn't think straight, couldn't *breathe*. I pushed myself to my feet.

'Kyin,' I managed, forcing my voice louder. '*Kyin*. Lan. *Lanir*. Wake *up*.'

It was Lanir who stirred first, groaning before inhaling desperately, his hand flying to his throat when he realised what was happening. 'Masks, Gyd,' he grated, his mind working faster than my own. 'The masks.'

I cursed myself for not thinking of it, then stumbled across the room, banging a fist on the wall to open the hold where the emergency equipment was kept. I pulled out several masks, dropping them on the floor. Claire gave a mumbling protest as I fit one over her face and activated it; she inhaled sharply, her eyes flying open, as the air started to flow.

Lanir got shakily to his feet, half falling on the door sensor. It slid open, and air gushed into the room from the corridor. I inhaled in relief, fitting a mask over Kyin's face regardless.

'Ky,' I said, shaking his shoulders. '*Kyin*.'

He woke a few moments later, pulling at the mask before he realised what it was. He sat, his arms trembling. 'What the fuck,' he croaked.

'Breathe slowly, Ky,' I said, laying a hand on his chest. 'Your heart is beating at twice the speed it should be.'

Lanir stuck his head into the corridor, taking several deep breaths. 'The airflow in the room must have failed,' he muttered. 'It's fine out here.'

Claire sat up, trembling, linking her arms around her legs. 'What's happening?'

'The airflow must have failed as we slept,' I said. 'It's all right now. It's –'

There was a hiss from the ceiling as the airflow turned back on, then a soft click as the ship's audio system engaged.

'You did this, Kyin,' a male voice said mildly. 'I let the first time with the female go, but I will not be ignored. Remember what we talked about.' The audio clicked off, and we were left in silence.

Kyin staggered to his feet, trembling, but I didn't think it was from fear. 'That *utter* bastard,' he snarled, his fists clenched. 'You *utter* bastard!' he roared at the security camera in the corner. 'You could have *killed* them! You selfish fucking *psychopath*!'

'That was your father?' Claire said, her voice small.

'That asshole has officially ceased to be *anything* but the being currently in control of this ship,' Kyin snarled. 'How *dare* he ...' He trailed off, his jaw clenching.

'He cut off the airflow?' Lanir said slowly. 'Why?'

Kyin didn't answer.

I stepped towards him. 'What did he mean by *remember what we talked about*, Kyin?'

Kyin ran a hand through his hair. His eyes were wide and wild; he turned his back on us and faced the wall, his chest heaving.

'Kyin,' I said sharply. 'Your father just tried to harm us. *Why?*'

For a moment, I thought he wouldn't answer, then he spun and collapsed to his knees, bowing his head. 'He handfasted me,' he said to the nest-like bed beneath him, his voice empty of emotion. 'Without my knowledge, without my consent. He handfasted me to the daughter of another tech company's director. It's supposed to be a merger via bonding. They supply products, my father supplies his name, and the daughter and I – I don't even know her given name – live together in mutual resentment ever after.'

Shock rippled through me, followed by pain so strong I thought I could crumple beneath it. I refused to, forcing my spine straight. 'What does that have to do with us?'

He glanced at me, his expression full of despair. 'A gossip stream on Darn posted an article about me. About *us*, Gyd. They didn't name you, but they had a still of me and Lanir from a security cast when we were in Sector Four.' Kyin swallowed. 'The other director saw it. Said he wouldn't see his daughter shamed and threatened to end the handfasting.

'My father apparently didn't want that.' Kyin stared at the wall. 'He contacted me. Told me I had to –' his breath caught '– told me I had to end this. End *us*. Or he'd take matters into his own hands to end it *permanently*.'

Lanir drew Claire close, his brow creasing in pain.

'I didn't want to walk away,' Kyin said, his voice desperate. 'I've *never* wanted to walk away. I want it even less now,' he went on, his eyes straying to Claire. 'But I had to, don't you see?'

'You should have told us,' Lanir said, a faint hint of reprimand in his voice. 'We could have thought it through together. We could have helped you, Ky.'

'There is no help for me,' Kyin said despondently. 'I'll never escape him.' He searched our faces one by one – me, Lanir, Claire. I wondered what he was looking for. 'I'll never have what I want. He'll take it from me. I can't be selfish, can't resist, because he won't hurt me – he'll hurt *you*.' He strode to the door, his tail thrashing behind him. 'This can never happen again.' He raised his face to the room's camera. 'You hear that, you fucking monster? *This will never happen again.* You can torture me all you like. But if you touch them –' his voice faltered; he took a moment to collect himself '– if you *fucking touch them*, I swear to the stars that I will *destroy* you.'

He left the room, and he didn't look back.

The ship was tense.

There was no other word for it, and no escape. It was as if Kyin's guilt and sorrow and anger were permeating every room, every corner, as if the ship itself was holding his emotions and amplifying them, pushing them through the silver corridors until they hit us square in the chest. It could have been Lanir, I supposed, letting his own emotions leak through what he called his *shield*; he certainly seemed stretched thin with regret, his eyes sad and his jaw tight.

After taking me to the medical bay to make sure there were no lingering effects from the oxygen deprivation, Gydion kept up with my training, but all the joy had gone. He was perfunctory and thorough, and I was quiet and obedient. I couldn't fool myself into thinking that I'd ever be good at it – I didn't have the instincts, nor the steel to deliberately hurt another being –

but if I was attacked when we reached the ground, I might have a slim chance of – well, not dying immediately.

I felt as if the hurt was curled into a ball in my chest, a ball that was gradually gaining weight until I'd be crushed beneath it. Being with all three of them had been every fantasy come to life, something that had always been an ember, never permitted to burst into flame before I met them. It had been perfect – being anchored and praised by Lanir, pushed to my limits by Gydion, and used and worshipped by Kyin. Everything had been bright with new hope, then that light was swept away by the machinations of Kyin's father and the complicated history between my three males.

I shook my head at myself. They weren't *mine*. But it was hard not to think of them that way, especially when I remembered how it had felt to be pinned between the three of them, encased and surrounded and entirely *safe*, indulged and cushioned by the combined force of their desire.

Such a good girl for us.

I wanted it to happen again. Badly. But given the mood of everyone on board, I swallowed my hope back down.

'Claire,' Gydion called one morning through my closed door. I'd gone back to sleeping alone, and I'd refused Lanir's help when my chest tightened and my heart raced; he had enough going on without me making things worse. 'Do you want to see?'

'Do I want to see what?'

There was a short silence. 'Scytha,' he answered at last. 'We're coming into orbit. You can see the planet from the navigation room.'

Do I want to see the planet where I might die?

'May as well,' I muttered.

I didn't know for sure, but Scytha seemed bigger than Earth. Its sun shone blindingly to our right as we approached, the rays dulled by the ship's special glass, like driving with the afternoon sun beaming straight into your side window.

We could see the planet's red continents, wide and stretching, encasing small, black seas, obscured by a dirty grey fog and the occasional drift of darker, thicker pollution. Scytha was how I imagined Earth might be in a few hundred years: its resources depleted, its water spoiled, most of its fauna living underground and all but its most hardy plant life burnt to a crisp. It wasn't like a desert, with its own ecosystems and its own abundance; this was desolation. It was shocking to see, and impossible not to imagine Earth's continents like that, baked red by the sun – stripped, bare, dying.

'Fuck,' I breathed.

'We'll be flying into orbit soon,' Kyin said tightly. He ran his hands through his hair. 'Usually, we'd bring up images of anything we might need to avoid. But we don't have access to do that.' He glanced to the side, meeting my eyes briefly before he looked away. 'We're flying blindfolded. Let's hope my father remembers to grant us a safe landing.'

'It's not your fault, Kyin,' Lanir said softly.

'*Of course* it is,' Kyin snapped. 'I agreed to get the ore, didn't I? I was the one who saw Claire running, saw the vehicle coming from the other direction, and beamed her up. I'm the one who can't break my father's hold on my own ship. I'm the one who was selfish enough to let you and Gyd keep travelling with me after I broke it off, even though I *knew* how much it hurt you, knew how much it *cost* you, because I wanted you close. *Needed* you close. Fuck,' he said, blinking. 'I'm just like him. Just like my father. A self-absorbed monster who –'

'*Ky*,' Lanir said sharply. 'You are *not* like him. He is responsible for too many scars to count. Your only mistake was trusting your own father. Those are *not* the same things.'

'It doesn't matter,' Kyin said. 'It doesn't matter if I'm different to him. I've still brought you here, into a danger we might not escape from.' He stood up. 'I'm sorry. I'm so sorry.' He strode across to me and seized my chin, stealing an angry kiss; my lips parted in surprise. His eyes blazed as he looked down at me. 'I think we would have been good together, *cora*, all four of us. Not just good. More than that. Incredible. Perfect, even.' He released me, looking across at Gydion and Lanir. 'I might not be allowed to have what I want, but I will *never* stop loving you, no matter what happens. And if I have to handfast –' he swallowed '– if I have to handfast another being, I swear to the gods that I will *never* touch them. There is nothing in this universe for me but you.'

'His penchant for drama is flourishing,' Gydion remarked, when Kyin had left the room. 'Anyone would think we were moments away from certain death.'

Lanir snorted, but his eyes were so sad it all but broke my heart.

I took a deep breath. 'Gydion. What should I be doing right now?'

'Firstly, breathe,' he said. 'I can *see* you tensing up, Claire. Second, we're going to go and pack what we need. Once that's done, we're going to change into our spacesuits and we're going to help you into the shell armour and helmet. Then,' he said, gazing outside the ship, 'we're going to wait. We have no idea how long it will be before we're on the ground, nor how we're going to get off this craft.' He flicked a glance at Lanir. 'We need to be ready for all eventualities.'

I didn't want to be ready for all eventualities. I wanted to be back in the bed on the floor six days ago, with my biggest problem being when Gydion was going to let me come. But we didn't always get what we wanted, and the chances of me getting *that* ever again were slim to none, so I followed Gydion and Lanir silently to my room and let them arrange the things I needed inside the small, light backpack I'd be wearing.

I had to admit that their gear was impressive. I'd have everything I would need – a week's supply of food and water, a kind of digital compass, a tiny lantern that radiated some sort of battery-powered heat for warmth and cooking, a water purifier, a blanket, a high-tech swag that inflated to the size of a normal bed and folded itself back up at the push of a button, distress flares, a spore spray that could be used both to wash and to clean food and utensils, weapons, *and* a spare suit – and everything fit in a vacuum-pack backpack only slightly larger than a laptop case. It was light, too; I didn't think carrying it would bother me in the slightest. Gydion's pack was bigger, containing multiple weapons and a tent for us to sleep in.

The jumpsuits we wore on board the ship turned out to be the first layer of the more complex spacesuits. They weren't as bulky as I'd expected, and the gloves and shoes were close-fitting, so it wasn't too hard to move around in. The spacesuit and body armour added weight, but it was evenly distributed and there was no way I was stepping foot on the ground without it. The most uncomfortable thing was the oxygen converter, which covered my nose and mouth, and the sleek helmet, which made my scalp itch. It wasn't the bubble helmet we were used to seeing on Earth astronauts, but rather a close-fitting collection of metal plates with a wide, glassed visor that looked like something from a superhero movie.

When Gydion was satisfied with our packs, our suits, and our weapons – there were two stun guns strapped to my thighs, along with some kind of hand-held shocker that released an electric pulse circling my wrists – we went to find Kyin. He was wearing his suit and armour, and he'd packed a bag, but his helmet was sitting on the table before him as he stared at a cup of *limere.*

'He might not open the doors,' he said, without preamble. 'He'll have to disable the shields to unload the ore, but it doesn't follow that he'll open anything but the hold.'

'We know,' Lanir said gently. 'That's why we're here. Just like you are.'

Kyin spun his cup. 'The waste disposal system.'

'The waste disposal system,' Gydion confirmed. 'It has its own shield controls and manual overrides that we can access. If he won't let us off, that's how we escape.'

Kyin nodded. 'I want you to have something, Claire.' He slid a thin band of what looked like rose gold from his thumb. Taking my hand, he stripped off my close-fitting glove, then pushed the band over my middle finger, pinching the metal until it moulded to my skin. 'This will read your heartbeat. If it's too high, it will activate a personal shield around your body. You can activate it manually – or deactivate the shield if your heart is racing for other reasons – by pressing here.' He turned my hand and brushed over a tiny stone set in the metal. 'Your suit has its own shields, so this is only if they fail. If they fail, you turn this on, and you *leave it on*, Claire, yes? You leave it on until you're safe.'

I stared at the band, snug on my finger. 'Kyin. This is yours.'

He shook his head. 'It belongs to you now.' He brushed a kiss across my knuckles, carefully refastened my glove, then let me go.

A low sound rumbled through the ship.

Lanir closed his eyes. 'We're descending.'

Fear made my stomach churn. 'So quickly?'

'My father does everything on his own time,' Kyin said, cracking his jaw. 'Which means *immediately*, if that's what he wishes.'

I forced myself to swallow as my ears popped.

Gydion tapped his fingers on his thighs as Kyin settled an oxygen converter over his face, then pushed his helmet on.

Lanir scooped me up out of my seat, then resettled me on his lap, his arms tight around my stomach and chest. 'Nothing will hurt you,' he said. 'We promise.'

The sentiment was comforting. *But you can't promise that*, I thought.

The ship shuddered. 'We're landing,' Gydion said tightly. 'Be ready.'

A low, grating groan echoed through the corridors; the hairs on the back of my neck rose.

For a moment, everything was silent and still.

Kyin broke the tableau, getting up to wave his hand over a sensor opposite the preparation area. A beep sounded, and a moment later the door slid open, revealing a small airlock.

'He's letting us out?' Lanir whispered, his surprise evident.

'Don't be too triumphant,' Kyin returned, his voice strained. 'This can't be the ore drop. This is a dare. He's betting we're not stupid enough to walk out into *that*.'

That turned out to be desert, red clay stretching forever in every direction, draped in clouds of brown and grey. We stood together in the airlock, gazing out at an environment where *nothing* survived. There were no trees, no scrub, no animals, no visible water sources. There weren't even any rocks for shelter.

'Fuck,' Gydion said, neatly summarising what I suspected we were all thinking.

Kyin inhaled. 'We have a choice,' he said quietly. 'Stay here and stay at my father's mercy, hope the ore drop takes place somewhere better, and that we can escape there. Or we risk this.' He waved his hand at the stretch of red outside. 'We risk this, we risk our lives.'

'Kyin, we're with you,' Lanir said immediately. 'We're always with you. Whatever happens, *wherever* happens, we're with you.'

'Agreed,' Gydion said quietly.

Kyin turned to me. 'Claire, what do you think? We can't guarantee your safety either way.'

I stared out at the desert. I'd never even been *camping* before, let alone dealt with something like this. But Kyin's father could choose to drop us in the middle of an active battle zone next, or somewhere worse, if that were even possible.

I studied each of them in turn. Lanir, with his comforting height and bulk and his beautiful blue skin and striking violet eyes. Gydion, all lean muscle and grace, his cropped dark hair starting to grow out, his lovely green irises split by their diamond pupils. Kyin, his usually-laughing eyes serious now, his curved lips thinned with worry, but still so gorgeous it was almost painful nonetheless, his tail moving slowly behind him as he waited for my decision.

I hadn't expected *any* of this, but I'd expected to care about them even less. I'd been the victim of an accidental abduction – which, thinking about it, was *exactly* the kind of thing that would happen to Kyin – but there was more to it than that. My body had trusted them, and they'd read it like a book; I had never felt so understood, so *worshipped* as I had the night I gave myself into their hands. I told myself that I wasn't falling in love, but I was certainly falling into *something*, and I knew – regardless of the decision I made about when to leave the ship – that all three of them would protect me with everything they had.

If we left now, Kyin would be free. He wouldn't be trapped by his father's control. The three males would have the time and space to mend the tear between them, to be together again if they wanted to. Surely that was worth risking the middle of a desert waste – especially knowing that the alternative might be just as bad.

'We're getting off here,' I said quietly.

Kyin pulled me into his arms and rested his helmet against mine. 'Well, at least your accidental abduction hasn't been boring,' he said over the suit's internal comm. 'I'm going to give you so many orgasms you won't see straight for days.'

'When we get somewhere safe,' Gydion growled.

Kyin waved an irreverent hand. 'Yes, yes.' He grinned at me through the glass in his helmet visor and mouthed *tonight*.

I bit my lip, trying not to laugh.

Lanir closed the airlock door behind us, then laced his fingers through mine. 'Last chance to back out.'

I shook my head.

'Words, Claire.'

'No,' I said evenly. 'I'm not backing out. Let's go.'

Kyin waved his hand over the sensor; the external door slid open, and a gust of air washed over us.

I couldn't feel the temperature through the suit, but I knew it had to be dangerously hot. Gydion had been right to insist on the spacesuits; they were designed to regulate temperature in the void and to protect from solar rays, so the blistering sun wasn't an issue, either.

'Over to you, Gyd,' Kyin said. 'Nature is *not* my thing.'

'First, we get away from the ship so we don't get caught by the engines,' Gydion answered dryly, dragging Kyin and I away from the ship as Lanir followed. The clay was baked rock-hard beneath our feet, and every step jarred my ankles.

We followed Gydion until we were some distance from the ship; I turned around as it took off, seeing it from the outside for the first time. It looked – as much as it could look like anything but a fucking *spaceship* – like a beetle, with a rounded, belly-like middle, and what must have been the navigation room protruding from the front. I'd expected noise, but I didn't hear *anything* as it took off, just felt a slight shudder through the air.

'Well, that's done,' Kyin said matter-of-factly. 'Hopefully forever, though that may be expecting too much. Farewell to the mechanical love of my life: my perfect, determined Sidereal. I'll always remember the night Gyd fucked me so hard on the control panel that that we accidentally flew to the wrong Sector. I'll never find another ship like you – the control panel was *exactly* the right angle to bend over.' He turned to us. 'What are the chances one of you has accounts we can access? My father will freeze mine and probably empty them as well. I have one account my mother set up for me, but I'll have to go to Darn to access it in person. She knew my father might try to take it, so she added bioscans to the access requirements.'

'I don't think credits are our most pressing concern,' Lanir said with a smile. 'But I have accounts.'

Kyin exhaled. 'Thank the gods. You know what I'm going to do with them, right?'

Lanir's smile turned wistful. 'You're going to buy us presents. I remember.'

'*So many* presents.'

'Are presents a Darnagh thing?' I asked.

'Presents are a *Kyin* thing,' Gydion said.

'I know *exactly* what to get you first, *cora*.' Kyin gave me a filthy grin. 'The biggest, *thickest*, fanciest –'

'Ky,' Gydion interrupted. 'The desert.' He took out his digital compass. 'South is that way,' he said, pointing. 'We really should rest during the day and walk at night, but we don't know how far we are from anything, so it's my feeling that we should walk as far as we can now, while we're fresh.'

'Do we know if we're on the right *continent*?' Lanir asked.

'No,' Gydion said. 'We don't know anything. If you have any better ideas, I'm listening.'

Lanir shook his head. 'We should head south on the chance we're on the right landmass and can find Scytha City. Surely we'll find *something*. Eventually.'

Kyin readjusted his pack. 'Let's go. The faster we're there, the faster I can spend your money, Lan.'

Gydion snorted. 'Forward, then. Let's go.'

We settled into a plodding rhythm – Gydion at the front, Lanir by my side with my hand in his, and Kyin behind us. I was – embarrassingly – far less fit than the other three, and under the weight of the spacesuit, body armour, and helmet I began to tire quickly. I didn't say anything, though, just sucked gratefully on the spacesuit's internal filtration system every time it processed enough sweat to turn into a mouthful of water.

I tried very hard not to think about the first time I had to pee.

After a while, I fell into an almost trance-like state, hearing nothing but my own breathing and the gentle thud of each footstep. The landscape became oddly beautiful, the soft, undulating red at once alien and familiar, the relentless blue sky a colour I didn't think I'd ever be able to capture on canvas, smeared by the odd cloud of pollution. There were signs of plant life, when I began to look more closely: a kind of black moss grew from cracks in the clay, and one small rise was covered in a vine-like plant that glowed a lovely cobalt. I didn't see any signs of animals, but the sun was directly overhead, and I supposed they'd be smart enough to stay underground in the oppressive heat of the day.

We didn't talk; when he began to chat, Gydion told Kyin – with a stern tone that sent shivers down my spine – to save his energy. Kyin mock-pouted, but he must have seen the sense in it; after a few hours, there was no way any of us could have kept up a conversation, anyway. Gydion and Lanir swapped packs every now and then, sharing the heavier bag containing the tent, and when the sun was starting to dip below the horizon and my stomach was a constant, empty rumble, Lanir took mine off me, wearing it on his front.

I made a half-hearted protest, but as Gydion showed no signs of slowing down, I didn't resist *too* hard.

Night had fallen completely when Gydion came to a stop. He'd chosen a place sheltered by gentle hills and offering some protection from the wind, which had picked up as the sun set.

'We're not sleeping,' he said. 'Have a mouthful of water from your flask and a quarter of a protein meal. Claire, is your filtration system working?'

I nodded, flushing. It was working just fine, but I'd be glad to drink something that wasn't filtered liquids from my own body. It was an impressive technological feat, but …

Eck.

'How far do you think you can go before you need a proper rest?'

'Maybe a few more hours,' I answered.

'Good girl,' Gydion said. My cheeks grew hotter. Apparently, the context praise was delivered in didn't matter; it made me squirm with pleasure regardless. I'd never known I had a praise kink; I added it to the growing list of things I'd learned since my abduction. *How to block a punch. How to hold a mother-fucking sword. How to not die of embarrassment while talking to an empath. How to drink straight chilli. How not to lose your mind when you're sandwiched between two hot aliens.* 'We'll sit down, eat, drink, and then keep going.'

We folded down directly onto the red clay, each grabbing our flasks and a protein bar from our packs; Kyin helped me with my helmet, then pressed a kiss to my forehead. I took the converter off my face; I could still breathe without it, though it was noticeably harder than I was used to, every breath seeming too shallow, my lungs aching faintly from the exertion. Even with the regular mouthfuls of filtered water during the walk, I could have easily emptied my flask. I didn't, taking two bites of the protein bar – flavoured vaguely like almond butter, which wasn't the worst – then swallowing three careful sips of water before replacing the cap.

'Look at those stars,' Lanir said softly, tipping his head back.

I looked up, my breath catching at the stretch of indigo sky, broken by a million points of twinkling light. There were *three* moons – one large, two smaller – all at varying stages of waxing or waning.

'This must be the only place on the planet we'd be able to see them.' Gydion took a final sip from his flask then stowed it back in his pack. 'I heard that there's so much pollution elsewhere that the Roth can't see the sky at all.'

'Lucky us,' Kyin said. 'So far from civilisation that we can still see beauty.' He grinned at me, pulling me against his side. 'Though there's something *much* lovelier right here.'

I pressed my face into his shoulder to hide my burning cheeks.

Gydion stood. 'Let's go before Kyin gets any ideas,' he said dryly.

'Too late,' Kyin said. 'I already have ideas. *So many* ideas. Enough ideas for *years*.'

Gydion's face fell, before he shoved his helmet back on his head. By the time his eyes were visible once more, he was wearing an easy smile. 'Come on,' he said, offering me a hand. I took it, and he pulled me up; I frowned at him, questioning.

He simply handed me my pack, then took up his own. I fitted the converter back over my face, a feeling I couldn't name settling heavily in the pit of my stomach.

When we were ready, we started walking once more; Gydion continually checked his compass to make sure we stayed in the right direction. For a while, Kyin hummed a surprisingly lovely tune over our connected comms, the sound rich and full, but he eventually fell silent as we continued to trek.

And *trek*.

I had *never* walked so far.

I suspected that without the suit regulating my temperature, I would have stopped hours ago. As it was, my feet and legs ached with every step, fire spreading up my calves and thighs. Even my core and back hurt, unused to the weight of the pack and the helmet.

At some stage, I felt tears start to slip down my cheeks. I could have asked Gydion to stop, I knew, but I didn't want to feel like I was holding them back.

Lanir took my hand. 'You're doing so well, little one,' he said; from the lack of reaction from Kyin or Gydion, I suspected he was using the comm to speak directly to me. 'You're so strong, Claire. Do you think you can make it until dawn?'

'Yes,' I whispered, refusing to think about it.

'Good,' he murmured; a wave of his approval washed over me. 'I know it seemed like an accident that we found you, but the more I'm with you, the more I suspect that the Goddess intended this all along.'

Lanir had told me a little about the goddess the Illisae and Kjidja believed in, the source of their universal magic, *elya*. She had many faces and many purposes, including bestowing bonds between fated lovers. She wasn't really like any Earth goddess I knew; a kind of merging of Aphrodite with Hecate and the Moirai, with the Illisae's apparent fixation with *balance* thrown in for good measure.

Despite my upbringing, I wasn't religious, but both Lanir and Gydion seemed to believe in their goddess in the same way they believed in gravity; for them, she existed on a fundamental and indisputable level, and every action within the universe – no matter how small – was proof of that.

I wasn't about to argue; I'd seen the veins beneath Lanir's skin glow and he could read my every emotion like an open book. Who was I to say that power *didn't* come from a goddess?

'The Goddess intended for us to be marooned on a war-torn planet in the middle of a desert?' I said, smiling.

Lanir gave a one-shouldered shrug. 'We could have taken a different flight path the night that we found you. We could have flown over your city but never noticed you or those males. You could have left earlier, or later, or chosen a different place to wait, and been safe, made it home and carried on with your life as it was. But we *did* take that path, and you *did* wait at that place, and we *did* see you, and we decided to intervene. And because of that, you have brought Kyin back to us, and given us something all your own.' He turned to give me an answering smile that melted my insides. 'A centre. A tether. A soul. Does it matter where we are, if you are with us?'

My breath caught.

The way Lanir talked about fate was ... seductive. Maybe it was luck – or maybe I *was* supposed to be at that bus stop, and they *were* supposed to pick me up.

Maybe I was where I needed to be.

'The Kjidja and my kind had been at war for centuries, did you know?' Lanir continued. 'We fought over differences in our holy texts. A peace treaty was signed when I was small, but our two species have always had something other than the Goddess in common.' He paused. 'We're not allowed to fall in love.'

'What?'

He gave a single, sharp nod. 'On Kjid, the elders from two clans will negotiate matches. They say they base their decisions on the personalities of the young ones involved, but Gydion thinks they don't bother, making matches that are political and practical more than suitable. One clan lacks a baker, so off goes the baker's son, matched where he's needed, that kind of thing.

Over time, those matches might grow into affection, but they don't start that way.

'It's different again on Ilis. We're not even allowed to partner. The Mages' Assembly simply has us mate.'

I stumbled. 'What?' I said again.

He glanced at me. 'The Assembly chooses two who have complimentary gifts and tells them to do their duty. They breed us like *erex*, always aiming for stronger Mages.'

'But that didn't happen to you.'

'No.' I could hear the smile in his voice. 'Gydion's Priestess came to Ilis for a diplomatic visit. I was a junior Mage in the diplomatic corps, assigned to help make her comfortable during her stay. We didn't like one another at first,' he went on, 'me and Gydion, I mean. I thought he was too stern, and he thought I was too gentle. But over a few weeks, we became friends, and when he kissed me one night, it was as if my entire universe realigned, and I just ... *knew*.

'We fled,' he continued. 'We had to. How could I do my *duty* once I'd met him? It's why we can't go back to Ilis or Kjid. We broke the rules – it was especially bad that we'd broken them with someone who was once the *enemy* – and we're not welcome.'

I squeezed his fingers, sorrow churning my stomach.

'No need to feel sorry for us, little one. We have no regrets.' He looked forward. 'We met Kyin at a space station in Sector Two. We were eating, and a being crashed into our table – running from a bounty hunter who wanted to ransom him back to his famous father.

'How could we leave him alone?' Lanir chuckled. 'Who could feel the warmth of Kyin's smile and walk away? We couldn't. But even in the best times, we were three beings who loved one another, functioning independently within a shared life. But now?' he went on, gesturing to Gydion and Kyin, walking side-by-side, ahead of us. 'We're functioning *together*. Moving together, working together. Because you give us a reason to. And it feels –' his breath hitched, his cheeks paling in a blush beneath his helmet visor '– it feels *right*.'

I couldn't answer; I didn't know how. My heart was racing and my stomach was fluttering; no one had *ever* said something like that about me, *felt* something like that about me. I knew that Lanir was taking a risk being so open and vulnerable, and there was no way I wanted to hurt him by blurting out something he might misinterpret.

'I know it's fast,' he continued. 'But I don't want you to misunderstand. If you want us, you have us.' He pressed my fingers. 'If you choose to fall, we'll catch you, Claire.'

I swallowed, my mouth as dry as the clay I was walking on. *I'm going back to Earth – aren't I?* 'Lan –'

'You don't need to say anything,' he said gently. 'I'm a patient being. And you're worth waiting for. No matter what.'

The butterflies in my stomach went into a frenzy. *Fucking hell.*

'I mean,' he said, after a pause, 'Kyin will annoy you constantly until you give in, but Gydion and I will wait.'

I laughed, and suddenly, my feet didn't hurt so much.

KYIN

WE STOPPED JUST AS the sun was rising for the desert dawn.

Gydion said that he was tired, but I could see how exhausted Claire was from the drag of her feet and the slow flutter of her eyes, and I knew he'd stopped for her. I would have taken one look at her and set up camp hours ago, but Gydion had a knack for knowing exactly how far he could push someone, stopping just before they broke, and he knew that Claire was strong. She hadn't so much as whispered a complaint; I'd been grumbling incessantly to Gydion over a direct comm since we'd last eaten.

I helped Claire pull her mattress and blanket from her pack as Gydion set up the tent. The tent was almost obscenely comfortable, large enough for the four of us, its structure made of some kind of alloy which was both flexible and strong. I always picked the best when I was outfitting my ships, even if it was something I didn't ever expect to use; I was glad for the habit, now. The wind had picked up as we walked; though we couldn't feel it inside, its constant howls were unsettling.

It only took a few minutes to set up our beds. Claire collapsed on hers, a look of relief evident from behind her oxygen converter. She and I would need to leave them on while we slept; I hoped we could take them off once we arrived in the biodome covering Scytha City.

For kissing, obviously. But they were also fucking annoying to wear.

'Drink before you sleep, little one,' Gydion said softly, reaching out to touch Claire's cheek. She shook herself with a start, clearly almost asleep already, and obediently took a sip of water from Lanir's offered flask.

'Should we eat someth –' I started to ask, but Claire was already sinking down on her mattress, her eyes fluttering closed.

'You go ahead,' Gydion said, amused. 'Our human is apparently ready to sleep.'

I chewed my way through a bite of a protein bar, then took a mouthful of water from my own flask. If we continued eating like this, we could stretch the food out to last weeks, but the water was another matter. And our bodies, of course. Neither Gydion nor Lanir had any fat stores to speak of, and my own would be gone relatively swiftly.

'When do we risk a distress flare?' I said softly, not wanting to disturb Claire. I pulled her blanket up to her shoulders.

'When we're dying,' Gydion answered bluntly. 'We have no idea who will answer it, Ky. Are you willing to take the chance before that?'

I shook my head. 'No. No, I'm not. But we should let Claire know, so she's prepared.'

'Agreed,' Lanir murmured.

'We've walked over eighty Kjid miles since we left the ship,' Gydion said. 'We won't be able to sustain that distance, not with depleted food, water, and adrenalin. But we should push forward as far as we can while our bodies are still able.'

I nodded. 'What did you two talk about?' I said to Lanir. Claire was expressive when she spoke, moving her hands and tilting her head. That they'd had a conversation was obvious, even if I hadn't been able to hear it.

He gave me a measured look. 'I told her what I was thinking,' he said softly. 'That we were ready to be together, all of us, whenever she was.' He glanced between me and Gydion. 'Was I right?'

'Yes,' I said immediately.

Gydion's jaw tensed. 'Don't you think she'll want to go back to Earth? She hasn't once voiced the possibility of staying with us. What is there to stay for? We don't have a ship. We don't have a home. We can't go to Kjid, can't go to Ilis, and now we probably can't go to Darn, either, not long-term, at least. What can we offer her?'

'Us, Gyd,' Lanir said. 'We can offer her *us*.'

'Is that enough?' Gydion gave me a level glance. 'Is there even an *us* to offer?'

My stomach twisted as a rare feeling of uncertainty stole over me. I'd assumed – because my feelings for them hadn't changed – that Gydion and Lanir would be happy to pick up where we left off. I'd expected the addition of some grovelling apologies – and present buying – on my part, neither of which would be a hardship, because I *was* sorry, and I *lived* for buying presents.

Perhaps I'd been wrong. 'I, ah –'

'Of course there's an *us*,' Lanir interjected calmly, clearly taking pity on me. 'There always will be. I know you're still angry, Gyd, but lashing out isn't the way to deal with it.'

Gydion inhaled. 'Fine.' He turned to me. 'Kyin, I understand why you did what you did. I understand that you did it for our safety, and I appreciate your bravery and self-sacrifice. But you could have told us, and it *hurt*. I'm not sure I'm past it yet.'

'I understand,' I said, swallowing.

Gydion sighed. 'But we missed you.' He held out his arms.

I crawled into them, letting myself rest on Gydion's strength, breathing in the summer rain scent of him. Lanir smiled, then lay down between our legs, resting his head on my thigh.

'See?' he said, sounding equal parts happy and exhausted. '*This* is what we can give her.'

I went to sleep with my fingers in his hair and a smile on my face.

'Ky. Kyin. *Kyin*, wake up.'

I started awake, made instantly alert by Gydion's urgency. 'Did he cut off the oxygen again?' I mumbled, before I realised that we weren't on the Sidereal and my father had left us in the middle of a desert waste.

'Can you hear that?' Gydion hissed.

I listened, picking up the telltale *whoosh* of engines in descent. 'Fuck, that isn't the wind.' I shook Lanir. 'Lan, *core*, wake up. Some kind of craft is nearby. It sounds small, but I can't tell what it is.'

Gydion checked the weapons strapped to his thighs, then pulled another gun from his pack. 'Come on, Ky. Lan, stay with Claire. Get everything packed.' His lips twisted. 'Be ready to run.'

'What –' I heard Claire say sleepily, as we pushed outside the tent, my helmet in my hand.

There was light over the horizon, and for a moment I couldn't tell whether it was dawn or dusk. A check to my suit's clock – adjusted to Scythan time – showed that we'd slept through the entire day *and* night, and the fiery halo in the distance was the rising sun. My stomach growled loudly even as I swallowed to ease my parched throat; I didn't know whether I needed water or food more. Gydion was a sleek shadow beside me, soundless as he padded away from the tent, his head cocked as he concentrated on the barely-audible whine of the craft.

'It's approaching,' he murmured. '*Fuck.*' He flicked me a glance. 'We have no way to tell whether they're allies, the Roth resistance, or something else entirely. They shoot, we shoot, yes? We can't let them get close to Lan and Claire.'

I gave a terse nod, pulling a stun gun from its holster. After a few moments, I could hear what Gydion's sharper senses had picked up: the whine was getting louder.

Gydion tensed.

My tail thrashed behind me.

'There.' Gydion pointed to a barely-visible speck on the horizon. 'I can't see …' He stepped forward. 'I don't think it's a Roth scuttler, but that doesn't mean anything.'

'How the fuck can you even see that, Gyd?' I muttered. I shielded my eyes, as if that would help in the dim light. 'It looks like a tiny fucking circle to me.'

'That's because it is,' Gydion said slowly. 'It looks like a Tirian craft.' He stepped in front of me, stalking back and forth. 'That doesn't mean anything. We still don't know who's flying it.'

'Hopefully a Tirian.'

Gydion glanced at me long enough to roll his eyes. 'Obviously.'

I grinned at him. 'Hey. Here I am, risking my life to be your backup when I would *much* rather be curled up in bed playing with Lan's cock. Where's the gratitude?'

Gydion's lips twitched. 'You're incorrigible, do you know that?'

'It's my defining characteristic, yes.'

'If they're Tirians, they'll be wearing armour.' Gydion returned to his usual seriousness, tapping his gloved fingers against his thigh. 'Aim for the –'

'Neck, groin, ankles. It's like I've never been in a life-threatening situation with you before, Gydion.'

'Put your helmet on, Kyin.'

I grinned again, and shoved my helmet on my head.

As the craft got closer, I could see that it was, indeed, one of the half-sphere Tirian craft. Gydion planted his feet in front of me; I had around half a minute to admire his protectiveness – and his ass – before the wind whipped up and the craft landed on the clay, barely a handful of metres away.

A door slid open. 'Hello,' said a deep, rough voice. 'Kyin Crace?'

'That's me,' I said warily; Gydion moved to block me from the being's line of sight.

A head emerged; Gydion visibly relaxed, letting his hands fall to his sides.

The Tirian jumped from the craft. They were tall and broad-shouldered, with silky brown hair and hazel eyes. Their cheekbones and ears were lined with thorns, and they were dressed in regulation Tirian bark armour. They took in Gydion's guns; their hands came up to show they were empty.

'Ashton McCarthy. He. Captain Peony thought you might need some assistance.'

'Oh, thank the fucking *gods*,' I said. 'Yes, that would be more than welcome. Can you take us literally anywhere that isn't here?'

The Tirian's lips twitched. 'We're based in Scytha City.'

I turned to Gydion. 'Well, this day just got better.'

A blonde head poked through the open door of the Tirian craft. Gydion tensed; Ashton stepped back in answer, raising his hands higher.

'Does anyone need medical attention?' the blonde Tirian said hopefully.

The first Tirian – Ashton – gave a barely-perceptible sigh. 'You've got to give me longer to ask, Will. You're going to surprise someone with a loaded gun one day, and *you'll* be the one that needs a doctor.'

The second Tirian jumped down from the craft. They were pale, paler than most Tirians, and their features were familiar enough that I suspected they had Illisae blood. They were pretty, holding a travel med kit in one strong hand.

'Well?' Ashton said. '*Does* anyone need medical atten-tion?'

'We're all hungry and dehydrated,' Gydion answered. 'But no one is injured or ill.'

The blonde Tirian's face fell.

'I'm sure they all need to be checked anyway,' Ashton said soothingly. He eyed me and Gydion. 'You need to be checked anyway, right?'

'Definitely,' I said at once, recognising the cue of a male desperate to please his mate. 'Probably thoroughly. I think I have a blister. It might even need ointment.'

'The Captain said there were four of you.'

Gydion tensed again. 'Our ... mates ... are still inside.'

'We know you have a human,' the blonde Tirian said gently. 'We're here to help, not to judge.'

Gydion gave a short nod. 'Then I would appreciate you checking her first, doctor. Her arrival with us was ... unexpected ... and we're not sure how to best care for her.'

The doctor nodded, glancing at Ashton. 'We can help with that.' He put a hand to his chest. I'm Willow, by the way. He.'

'This is Gydion,' I said, jerking my chin. 'Inside the tent are Lanir and Claire.'

'Lanir?' Willow eyes widened. 'You have an Illisae mate?'

'A First-Circle empath,' I said proudly.

'Green gods,' Willow said, surprised. 'I didn't think the First Circle left Ilis.'

'They don't,' Gydion said grimly.

'Ah.' Willow cleared his throat. 'Don't worry, I won't ask. My birth mother was a Fourth-Circle healer who left Ilis for Tir. I didn't get her gift, but I did get her passion.'

'Lanir will be happy to see you,' I said. 'He hasn't seen another Illisae in a very long time.'

Willow's expression turned stoically polite. 'Most Illisae don't acknowledge me,' he said, his voice carefully matter-of-fact. 'I'm Tirian to them.'

'Lan isn't like that,' Gydion said. He turned and headed back to the tent. 'Come.'

The Tirians waited outside with Gydion as I slipped inside. Claire and Lanir had packed all the beds and blankets away; Claire was pacing anxiously while Lanir watched her. When she saw me, she gave a soft cry.

'Are you all right?' she said breathlessly.

'Completely,' I said, drawing her close before pulling off my helmet and nuzzling her ear. 'The ship is Tirian. There's two of them; one is a doctor. With your permission, he'll check your vital signs, and then ours. If you don't want that, then we'll say no. What do you think?'

Her hands went to my hips as she thought about it. 'Okay,' she said slowly. 'You won't leave me, right?'

'No,' Lanir rumbled, at the same time I said '*Never.*'

Gydion held back the tent door, letting the Tirians inside. Ashton's eyes went straight to Claire; Willow fixed on Lanir, swallowing.

'Empath,' he said, bowing his head.

Lanir's violet eyes widened in surprise. 'Brother,' he answered, stepping forward to give the traditional Illisae greeting, placing his right hand on the Tirian's cheek. Willow returned the gesture tentatively, his expression flickering as he struggled with some strong emotion. 'Ah,' Lanir went on. 'Nira's son. I know of your mother.'

Willow stepped back, breaking the greeting. 'No doubt,' he said expressionlessly.

'You mistake me,' Lanir returned gently. 'Nira was brave, breaking free of the Circle to follow her heart. I've seen the casts of her addresses to the Mages. She was passionate and articulate, and an excellent healer. I was sorry to hear she had joined the

Light.' He tilted his head, studying Willow's face. 'I know you think you didn't get her gift, but I see its shadow in you. And it will come again in your daughter.'

Willow blinked. 'Daughter?' he said hoarsely.

'Most of your paths show two,' Lanir said, looking over Willow's shoulder at something only he could see. Lanir didn't get glimpses of the future very often – it had only happened three times since I'd met him – but I knew to shut up and listen when he did. 'One of your body, and one of your heart. Both will glow with *elya*, gifted by their birth mother. The daughter of your body will be Nira come again –' Lanir glanced at Ashton, who was watching silently, his hands bunched in fists '– but will follow her heart-father and heart-mother's path. There is a spear in her hand and fire in her soul.' Lanir smiled. 'The daughter of your heart will be far easier to raise, if it's any consolation.'

'Fuck,' Willow said, staring at Lanir in shock.

Lanir nodded. 'Best start preparing now,' he said kindly, patting Willow on the shoulder. 'Though I wouldn't mention it to your *karia* just yet.'

'She'll lose her fucking mind,' Ashton muttered, seemingly in agreement.

'I am looking forward to meeting her.' Lanir glanced back at Claire, his lips twitching in a small smile. 'This is Claire. She will also be happy to see your *karia*.'

'Claire,' Willow echoed, shooting her a kind smile. 'Your ... mates ... said I should ask to check your vital signs.'

Claire's hands tightened on my hips, then released; she turned so that her back was close to my chest. 'You can check them.'

Willow didn't waste time, checking her pupils, her tongue, and her ears before asking permission to check her pulse. When he placed his fingers on her wrist, I stiffened, but it wasn't because he was touching her – it was because I had no idea that was where Claire's pulse *was*. I knew which protein bars she liked the best, and how to make *limere* that made her sigh. I knew that she liked to cocoon herself in a blanket when she slept, and what she sounded like when she broke into pieces with pleasure – but I didn't know where her *pulse* was.

How could I keep her happy, keep her safe – *keep her* – if I didn't know *that*?

My tail whipped behind me in sudden agitation; Lanir shot me a frown, then sent a wave of calm. I let it wash over me as Willow stared at Lanir in surprise.

'I've ... I've heard of an empath's gifts, but never experienced them,' he said thickly. 'That's ... It's incredible.'

'How did you know?' I blurted. 'That her pulse was there?'

Willow's lips curled up; he fished in his medical bag and pulled out a hand scanner and a foil of dehydration tablets. 'Our *karia* is human. I almost died of worry when I first looked for her pulse and couldn't find it. Tirians have pulse points along their spines,' he explained to Claire, pressing a tablet into her hand, then distributing the remainder to Lanir, Gydion, and me. I popped the tablet straight in my mouth, my body reacting instantly as it dissolved on my tongue in a flood of sweet salts. 'And humans don't. I thought her hearts had stopped beating.' He flicked me a glance. 'Humans have one heart only. And the easiest pulse points are on their wrists –' he showed me where he gently pressed two fingertips to the inside of Claire's '– and their throats.' He demonstrated, tipping Claire's chin back slightly so I could see her heartbeat fluttering beneath her skin. He gave Claire a serious look. 'You'll need more sleep than your Kjidja, to eat more carbohydrates than your Illisae, and take in more vitamin D than your Darnagh. You'll need less protein and more vitamin C than all of them. I'm glad to see this –' he gestured to the oxygen converter '– because you'll need it here. The Spire is oxygen regulated for the Roth Queen, but the biodome over Scytha City isn't functioning right now, and you'll get dizzy if you don't take a converter with you. Be warned, the Spire temperature isn't regulated; the humans find it too hot in the day *and* too cold at night.'

Gydion frowned. 'The temperature isn't regulated? I thought the Spire was sacred. Aren't the Roth priests there?'

'There have been a number of attacks on Scytha City,' Ashton said. 'Some have caused no damage, but some have taken out systems used by the Spire. The climate system was damaged a week ago. The water filtration system was damaged three days ago, which means we have water to bathe, but not to drink. The comms system was damaged yesterday. We're trying to work out a way to bounce signals off an existing satellite system, but the main brain behind it is ... distracted.'

'His mate is pregnant,' Willow said with a smile. 'Heavily.'

'I can help with the systems,' I said slowly.

Willow's smile widened. 'Honestly, we'd hoped you'd say that.'

'But is it safe?' Gydion broke in, his gaze flickering between me, Claire, and Lanir. 'If there are attacks on the Spire, why is the King risking himself – and his Queen?'

'Because it's swaying those who were inclined to rebel,' Ashton answered. 'The longer he's there, the more Roth switch sides to stand with him. Like you said, the Spire is sacred to the Roth – and it's also a symbol of the King's legitimacy. I won't guarantee you that it's safe, because it isn't. But I will say that it's saf*er* than staying here to die of thirst.'

'Comforting,' Gydion muttered.

'When you see it, you'll understand.' Ashton glanced at his wrist screen. 'We need to move, Will.'

Willow moved his hand screen around Claire's face and chest. 'You're slightly dehydrated, but nothing too bad,' he confirmed. 'Your heart rate is elevated, but I suspect that's normal, given the circumstances.' He gave her a kind smile. 'Is there anything you're worried about?'

Claire shook her head. 'Not at this moment.' She went still, blinking as if surprised at herself. Lanir shot her a smile, at once understanding and proud.

Willow nodded. 'If your mates are happy, perhaps I can check them once we get to the Spire?'

We were only too happy to leave, and a few moments later, Ashton was helping Gydion dismantle the tent and pack it away as Lanir chatted quietly to Willow. I took the opportunity to hold Claire close, nuzzling her neck.

'How are you feeling?'

'I honestly have no idea,' she whispered. Her arms linked around my neck as she pressed herself against me. 'Relieved, I suppose. I'm not much good at camping. But I'm trying not to get *too* excited about the prospect of running water.'

'Running water?'

'A *bath*, Ky.' She closed her eyes, her lips parting. 'What I wouldn't give for a hot bath.'

'Do humans need baths?'

'Need?' She smiled. 'No. *Want*?' Her smile widened. 'Very, *very* much so.'

I hoisted her up over my shoulder. She shrieked in surprise, drawing the eyes of everyone else. I patted her thigh, resisting the urge to sink my teeth into her rounded ass. 'Claire needs a bath,' I announced. 'Apparently, baths are a human thing, and she needs one.'

Ashton's stern face split into a wry smile. 'We might be able to help you there.'

GYDION

When I saw the Spire in Scytha City, I understood what Ashton had meant.

Scytha City was different to anything I'd ever known. Kjid was covered in lush rainforest, so thick and so wild that cities – as most beings thought of them – were an impossibility. My kind built their houses in the trees instead, high off the ground to avoid some of the predators that roamed our planet. We had bottomless lakes amidst the forest, tangled with ancient tree roots, and trees with huge, curved leaves that collected rainwater.

I could see no water here.

Red clay stretched in every direction, disrupted only by odd, ridged ripples, evenly spaced and circling out from a centre point. Beneath them, the Roth lived and worked in their network of underground buildings, sheltered from the unrelenting heat of their sun. At the centre point from which the ripples spread sat the only aboveground building on the entire planet.

I'd seen a lot during my travels with Kyin and Lanir. The glassed cities of Darn, gleaming silver in the light, with small craft darting around skyscrapers like fireflies; the onyx towers of the Zeddik, so tall they reached into the clouds; the half-terra, half-aqua buildings of the Enterocti, where the sea lapped at your door. But I'd never seen a building like *this*, one that was so commanding, so magnificent, and yet looked as if it had grown out of the land around it.

Round red walls stretched for what seemed like miles. Black moss and blue ivy grew like a stretching web, shielding black-glassed windows from the harsh sun. The entire structure grew in height towards its centre, which was a tower marked by a climbing ridged spiral, overlooking the desert around it in every direction. One of the drifting clouds of pollution we'd seen from orbit was seemingly settled over the city, turning the sky grey and the air a murky brown.

It was odd and forbidding and beautiful all at once.

'Fuck me,' Kyin breathed. 'Do you have anything like this on Tir?'

Willow shook his head. 'Nothing,' he said softly. 'Even our tallest buildings wouldn't reach a quarter of this height.'

Kyin looked towards the rippling city outskirts, barely visible through the air pollution. His tail twitched, and his expression settled into one of focused intensity, one I knew to be Kyin having *ideas*. 'Direct air capture,' he muttered under his breath. 'It would minimise the pollution immediately, and clear the city air completely over time, if they stopped making more. I'd have to analyse the components –'

'I hate to state the obvious,' Claire said, gazing up at the Spire, 'but why haven't the rebels attacked it yet?'

'Because they need it for legitimacy if they win,' Ashton said grimly. 'The Roth believe that their Kings are their dread gods' chosen, and their priests reside in the Spire. Attacking it would be like attacking their gods. So, while the outskirts of the city aren't safe, the Spire remains entirely intact.'

The landing pad was some way from the Spire, which made my hackles rise, but I could see a group waiting for us – different species, all armoured. Lanir took charge of Claire when we landed, sweeping her into the safety of his arms; we were ushered off the Tirian craft and straight into a sub-terra tunnel.

'Fucking hell,' Claire breathed, taking in the red walls all around us, and blinking at the soft lighting lining the floor. 'It's like being in a cave.' She frowned at me over Lanir's shoulder. 'Will you be okay? I know Kjid isn't like this.'

An invisible hand gripped my heart and squeezed; for a moment, I was speechless. Knowing I cared for *her* was one thing; knowing she cared enough to ask *that* question was another. I swallowed the lump in my throat. 'I'll be fine. Thank you, little one.'

She nodded and went back to looking around, but I couldn't recover so easily.

It made me all the more determined to do what I was planning.

'This leads into the Spire,' Willow said, politely making conversation as we walked. The armoured guards around us were determinedly silent; I saw Claire eye them warily, her fingers curling in Lanir's hair. 'The King has allocated quarters for you in the guest wing. As we said before, there's no cooling or heating, you can't drink the water, and we're using the Great Hall for a dining room. Also – stay with your mate, yes?' He flicked me a glance. 'Because the new Roth Queen is human, there's been … interest … in the other human females. Our *karia* can take care of herself, and the other human female has a starling mate who doesn't leave her side, but just be … wary. Some of the Roth males are … hopeful. There's no danger,' he added quickly, seeing Claire's face. 'You might just find a few courting presents left at your door, is all.'

Ashton snorted. 'A few? We could barely get out of our room until Mae –'

Willow elbowed him. '*Ash*. Don't overwhelm them. This way.'

The tunnel branched into three; we followed him down the left-hand side. There was a noticeable incline and Claire protested until Lanir set her gently down. She took her place behind Kyin, grabbing hold of his tail and grinning when he gave a mock-growl over his shoulder. A moment later, he'd wrapped it around her waist like a rope, keeping her close.

My heart constricted again; I looked away.

'This is where it gets harder, I'm afraid,' Willow said. The tunnel opened into a huge, black-glassed atrium, one wall showing the sky and a stretch of the rippling underground city. Ivy grew over the glass in a blue, winding shadow. Willow gestured at a set of glassed elevators. 'We'd usually use these, but their power supply was damaged last week, so we need to take the stairs instead. It's six storeys.' He eyed us, his gaze lingering on Claire. 'Will that be all right?'

'I'm not *that* unfit,' Claire grumbled.

'I'm not concerned about your fitness. You're dehydrated and have barely eaten in the last few days,' Willow said gently. 'If you've got any water left, it would be a good idea to have some now.' He pulled a flask from his medical bag. 'I certainly will be.'

We all followed his lead and had a few mouthfuls of water before we started on the stairs. The stairs were made for the Roth – most of whom stood as tall as Lanir – and so the steps themselves were twice – maybe three times – the height suitable for Claire's shorter legs. She didn't complain, though she began to pant and her cheeks flushed pink as she half stepped, half jumped up each and every stair.

Kyin's tail swiped through the air. 'There's a lift here whenever you need it, little one,' he said, holding out his arms.

She raised her chin stubbornly. 'I can do it.'

'I know you can,' Kyin said. He leaned in closer. 'But the *bath*, Claire. You need to conserve your energy.'

She raised her eyebrow at him, brushing her hair back from her face. The pink tips had faded since she'd been with us, leaving them a washed-out cream colour. 'Baths aren't that tiring, Ky.'

He grinned at her, then ran his tongue suggestively over his teeth. 'Are you sure?'

Claire swallowed; I bit back a hiss as the sweet scent of her arousal perfumed the air. 'I can still do it,' she said, and turned her attention back to the stairs.

I took her pack from her without speaking, wearing it on my front. She shot me a look – half exasperation, half gratitude – and continued her struggle.

Willow kept up his easy chatter as we climbed, though his face flushed green and his breath came faster as he pointed out parts of the city through the small stairwell windows. Ashton loped just behind him, seemingly completely unaffected by the exertion. Eyeing the muscle shifting beneath his armour, I suspected this was nothing at all to him.

By the fifth floor, even *my* muscles were beginning to protest. Kyin's grin was looking forced, and Lanir's neck was covered in a slight sheen of sweat.

'Thank the green gods,' Willow panted, when we finally reached the sixth floor. He eyed Ashton, who was entirely unruffled. 'Do you know, sometimes you make me unfairly resentful.'

Ashton smiled. 'You can always join us for training, my love.'

'Not a chance in the shadows,' Willow returned. 'This way.'

The stairwell opened into a wide red corridor, marked by long, black glass windows. The corridor ended in what seemed like a small hall, its ceiling stretching two storeys high, its walls covered in huge frescoes showing what must have been Scytha before the planet began to die.

The painted landscapes were nothing like Kjid; they had far more bushy forest, and the lakes and seas were a deep blue, not their current lifeless black. Animals I'd never seen before gathered on their shores and lounged beneath the stretching boughs of trees; birds sang from the branches and flew over verdant grassland, the green peppered with purple and white wildflowers.

'Beautiful,' Claire breathed. 'Fuck, it almost looks like home.'

'These frescoes are hundreds of years old,' Willow said. 'Alcide said they were made in the time of the Sun King, one of the last great rulers of Scytha. He has plans to restore them, and for new frescoes to be painted in other parts of the Spire.'

When I looked more closely, I could see what Willow meant by *restore*; the paint was faded and chipped away completely in parts. They were breathtaking from a distance; you had to get closer to see the cracks.

'This is the entrance hall to the guest wing,' Ashton said. 'We all have quarters here, even the Roth King. Well, everyone except for the Enterocti Prince and his mates. They're sleeping on the outskirts of the city, close to an underground spring.'

The armoured guards fell away as Ashton and Willow led us through the hall and into another set of corridors. We followed them down the right-hand branch of the hallway until they finally stopped in front of a door.

'This room was put aside for you,' Willow said, waving his hand over the sensor.

The room was large – as might be expected, given the size of the Spire – but bare; the only furniture was a huge bed, low to the ground, and a water filtration unit. Claire clearly didn't care, sighing happily when she saw the sunken pool in the far corner of the room, full of water that was steaming into the air. She pulled her converter from her face and took a deep breath, then shot me a smile that made me weak at the knees.

I straightened my spine and turned to Ashton and Willow. 'You should know that Claire isn't here by choice,' I said.

Kyin made a surprised noise behind me.

'We accidentally abducted her,' I went on, ignoring Lanir's sharp inhale. 'She was in danger on Earth, and we beamed her up so she could escape it. When we were about to put her back down, Kyin's father took control of his ship and we were locked out of the Sidereal's systems. We promised to take her back to Earth as soon as we could.'

Ashton and Willow exchanged a glance. 'We'll talk to our Captain,' Ashton said after a moment, 'but you have to know that the conflict here is our first priority.'

'I understand,' I said. 'My point is that Claire may not wish to remain here. In this room. With us.'

There was complete silence.

'She had no choice along the way,' I continued. 'But she should have one now.'

Lanir made a small, pained sound.

'Claire?' Ashton shifted forward. 'We can find you other quarters if you need.'

I kept my eyes on the door – until Claire's face appeared before me, furious.

'Are you trying to get rid of me?'

I frowned at her. '*What*?'

'I said, *are you trying to get rid of me, Gydion*?'

'Claire,' I said, my stomach suddenly hollow at the notion of her gone. '*No*. Of course not. But you –'

'Don't you think I would have spoken up, if I wanted to be elsewhere?'

'I –'

'I am a *fully grown woman*. Yes, I'm an anxious one, and yes, I occasionally need help with that, but on Earth I had a job and a home and friends and an art practice and though I might not have been amazing at functioning, *I did it*.' She crossed her arms. 'Have I – even *once* – given you reason to suspect that I can't speak up if I truly need to? Do you remember what you said to me? *There is no special word, just yes, no, and more*?' She glared at me. 'It's *more*, Gydion. That's the word I want to use. *More*.' She flicked her hair over her shoulder. 'I'm not going anywhere.'

Kyin turned to Willow and Ashton. 'Was there anything else you needed?'

Willow blinked. 'No?'

'Then this has been lovely, and I'm sure we're all very grateful, and I'll start work on the damaged systems in, ah, approximately two hours. No, make that three,' Kyin said. He gestured towards the door. 'But our human needs a bath and several orgasms, and it has to happen *right now*.' He all but pushed the Tirians outside, his customary grin turned hungry. 'I'm sure you understand.'

'We're knocking on this door in an hour,' Ashton said over his shoulder. 'The King won't wait longer just so you can fuck.'

'He'll have to,' Kyin answered, and waved over the sensor to close the door behind them.

'Oh my *God*, Kyin,' Claire said. 'You can't *do* that.'

He grinned at her. 'I just did.' He picked her up and hoisted her over his shoulder as she laughed, protesting. 'Now, bath time.'

'You're super embarrassing, do you know that?'

'And you're going to be the happiest human in the universe,' he answered. '*Bath.*'

He carried her to the edge, then set her back on her feet, giving her a slow, soft kiss. He pulled the gloves from their hands, then unzipped her suit, rather than ripping it open. I was grateful – I wasn't sure how we'd replace Claire's suit if it were damaged. He did the same with the jumpsuit, stripping her to the waist and then dropping to his knees, taking a nipple immediately into his mouth. Claire closed her eyes, her head tipping back, arching into the sudden touch as if she'd been waiting for hours. Kyin swapped breasts, pulling her suits down as he did, until they pooled in bunches of silver at her feet. I drank her in, lingering on her fluttering eyelashes, her parted lips, the flush of her cheeks, the curves of her neck and waist. Claire might have been an artist, but she made a beautiful picture without doing any work at all; I could have looked at her forever.

Kyin tugged the suits from her feet then made short work of his own; when he was done, he stepped into the water and pulled Claire in afterwards. The sighing sound she made when her skin touched the water went straight to my cock and I growled, desire heating my limbs as Kyin arranged Claire on his lap.

'Are you waiting for a formal invitation?' he rumbled at Lanir and me, running his nose up her neck before nipping her ear. 'Get in the fucking water.'

Lanir had gathered his wits far more swiftly than I, placing a pile of soft towels at the side of the bath, then stripping off and joining them, his cock half-hard already. Mine wasn't in any better state; I didn't know which of them I wanted first, only that I wanted *all* of them. I stripped my suits off and palmed my cock as Lanir drew Kyin in for a slow, teasing kiss, pausing only to turn his attention to Claire, then back again.

'Fuck,' I breathed, watching them. My heart thumped wildly as I realised my entire world was in that bath, exchanging kisses that were somehow both filthily erotic and wrenchingly sweet; they were beautiful, each of them perfectly imperfect, each beyond compare.

And each of them was *mine*.

'Gyd,' Lanir murmured, his lips against Claire's neck. 'I'm saying this as a First Circle empath. Have your emotional revelation later.'

'You'll miss Claire's first orgasm if you don't hurry up,' Kyin agreed.

'I'm not that close – *oh*,' Claire squeaked, as Kyin did something under the water with his tail. 'Oh, *oh*, oh. Gydion, *hurry up*.'

I walked to them and slipped into the water, pausing to press my mouth to Kyin's, nipping at his bottom lip. His tongue touched my own, sending a wave of heat through me as I realised just how much I'd missed being close to him. I broke away, moving to claim Lanir's lips as Kyin spun Claire on his lap so her back pressed against him; her head fell to rest on his shoulder.

Lanir's fingers found me under the water, wrapping around my cock. I groaned into his mouth, cupping his nape before unwinding his hair from its braid; the silver waves fell to frame his face.

'Oh,' Claire breathed. 'God. You're so beautiful.'

I didn't know who she was talking to and it didn't matter. I took hold of Lanir, moving my hand up and down his cock until he was panting into my mouth and whispering pleas.

'Claire first, Gyd,' Kyin grated out.

I laughed and bit Lanir's lip. 'Apparently Kyin needs help making our human come.' I nudged Lanir towards Claire. 'Help him, won't you, my love?'

Lanir fell to his knees in the water, spreading Claire's thighs wide. She squeaked as his fingers found her entrance; she arched as he pushed inside. Kyin's tail was at her apex, the two tufts moving either side of her swollen bud as his hands gently kneaded her breasts.

Her eyes flickered to me; she licked her lips. 'Come here, Gydion,' she said softly.

I took the soft request as an order, sitting next to Kyin on the step and seizing her lips with mine. I could feel her shake, her entire body quivering under Kyin and Lanir's ministrations. I slipped a hand over her round stomach and between her legs, mapping out where Lanir's fingers were buried inside her, moving slowly in and out. I traced soft swirls over her swollen flesh, moving down to caress the sensitive skin between her entrance and her delectable ass. When I brushed lower, she tensed, crying out wordlessly before her climax crashed over her.

Kyin made a deep, satisfied sound, his tail stroking through her shudders. He brushed a line of kisses up her neck, his lips curving into a smug smile as she squirmed and whimpered. 'You're so beautiful, Claire,' he crooned.

'Perfect,' Lanir agreed softly, gently pulling his fingers from her body and bringing them to his lips, licking her release from his skin with his thick white tongue.

'Fuck,' Claire said breathlessly. 'That's … That's *unfair*, Lan.'

'That didn't even take the edge off, did it, *cora*?' Kyin gave a lazy grin, his fingers pushing inside where Lanir's had been, the heel of his hand pressing down on her clit. 'Do you want something different this time?' Through the rippling surface of the water, I watched him press a third finger into her, stretching her around him.

'Something different?' Claire turned her head to me, eyeing my cock through the water. 'Yes. Yes, I want that.'

'Good,' Kyin praised. 'Gydion?'

I reached across and took Claire's hips, pulling her to me. 'You're mine this time,' I growled, noting the way she melted against me. 'I'm going to fuck you, Claire. Not completely, not yet, not the way I want to. Not until you're stretched and dripping and begging for my tie – and then I'll show you exactly what it means to be a Kjidja's mate.' She made a tiny whimpering sound, her fingernails digging into my thighs. 'Today, I'll fuck you fast and shallow, and when you come around my cock, you'll say my name. And while I do that, you're going to use those lovely hands on Kyin, because Ky hasn't had Lan inside him for far too long, but someone has to make him come while that happens.'

Kyin groaned. '*That*. All of that. Please.'

'Claire?'

'Fuck, yes,' she breathed.

'Lan?'

Lanir swallowed. 'Yes,' he said, his voice strangled.

We'd last about six seconds – probably collectively – but I didn't care. I wrapped my arms around Claire, sucking softly on her neck, dragging my teeth over the soft skin. My instincts were pushing to the surface, demanding I bend my new mate over the side of the bath and fuck her until she couldn't see straight, tying her to make sure she stayed full of my release, so full it took hold and blossomed inside her. I closed my eyes and buried my face in her hair, trying to push the thought of Claire swollen with my cub away. She squirmed in my lap, lifting her hips until I could feel the heat of her core hovering over my aching head, and it took every ounce of self-control not to flex my hips and drive up into her until my fantasy became reality.

'Gydion,' she whispered.

'It's all yours, little one. Show me what you want.'

She gave a breathless moan, and lowered her hips, gripping my shaft with one small hand, rubbing her thumb over where my tie would swell.

Her heat – almost scalding – enveloped the tip of me, and slowly – so *slowly* – began to move down.

'God, Gyd,' she whimpered. 'That feels – that feels –'

A low rumble sounded from outside the room, and a moment later I caught Claire as we were all thrown sideways.

LANIR

Fear and panic swept through the city.

I strengthened my shield against it, my ears ringing, my head throbbing from the strength of emotion pouring from all sides. It battered me, fortified by grief and shock, and I began to sink beneath its heavy tide.

'Lan.'

I moaned against the onslaught, tears streaming down my cheeks as a spike of despair rammed straight into my chest. Pain radiated, so strong I curled into a ball, so strong I couldn't tell whether it was my body or my mind that was damaged.

'Lanir.'

The grief was so strong, so fresh; I caught a rare telepathic image of bloodstained hands and limbs askew, a pair of black eyes staring sightlessly, pearlescent skin charred by flame. I howled, sorrow piercing me, impaling me, tearing me into agonising pieces.

'*Lanir.*'

Hands tugged ruthlessly at my hair. Lips found mine and *bit*, so hard I tasted my own blood, metallic on my tongue. Another pair of arms circled my waist, holding me so tight it was almost painful. A third pair of hands – more tentative, softer – stroked my arm, my chest, my cheeks.

I inhaled desperately, then sought Gydion's lips, smearing them with my own blood. 'Gyd,' I croaked.

'We're here.' He stroked my face. 'We're here. We're always here.'

'Kyin,' I whispered. He'd been gone, left us, but I'd imagined he'd come back, that everything was the way it was supposed to be, but I couldn't tell whether that was real or just something I'd wished for, *dreamed* –

Kyin kissed my shoulder, his hair brushing my skin. 'Come back to us, Lan. What you're feeling isn't yours. Don't hold onto it.'

There was something else, some*one* else, our centre, our *soul*; new and bright, complex and *essential* … 'Claire,' I said desperately.

'Here, Lan,' she said softly, pressing my hand to her cheek.

I exhaled slowly, trying to let the emotion – the *devastation* – wash over me and away. Kyin was right; it wasn't mine, and I didn't have to hold it. It didn't mean I couldn't still *feel* it, but I forced myself to be passive under its waves, to let it pass by.

'What happened?' I groaned.

A flask was pressed against my lips; I swallowed gratefully.

'A pulse bomb, it felt like.' Gydion's voice was grim. 'Close. In the city, maybe. When you're ready, we'll go and find out. There'll be Roth needing help.'

I took another mouthful. 'You're all unharmed?'

'We're all fine.'

Claire looked up at me, her brown eyes worried; I bent and kissed her head. 'Will that happen often? You were in *pain*, Lanir.'

'I wasn't ready for it,' I said truthfully. I'd let my shield fall so I could soak up what they were feeling, and I'd been lost in the heady mix of desire and worship and *love*. I'd left myself vulnerable, so I'd been wide open to the devastation.

I'd need to be more careful next time.

'We better get dry,' Gydion said reluctantly. 'If we don't present ourselves to assist, I have a feeling that a Tirian guard will arrive to drag us there.'

Kyin took Claire's chin in his hand and nipped her bottom lip. 'It was still the best bath I've ever had, *cora*.'

She flushed a lovely pink, which was almost enough to make me feel better.

Almost.

We dried and got dressed again, all desire fled before the weight of what had just happened. Even so, Gydion and Kyin were careful to shower both Claire and I with affection, covering us with kisses and praise. I felt like a wound that was still open and weeping, as if every vulnerability was on show, so I let Gydion's whispers shiver across my skin, let him bandage me in words of love.

I was so wrapped up in Gydion's affection, so preoccupied with reinforcing my shields from the continuing onslaught of grief and shock, that I didn't feel the being behind the door, not until they gave an impatient knock.

It wasn't a surprise; I'd seen her coming. When other beings talked about the Illisae *seeing the future*, they often got angry that we didn't issue warnings. The thing was, though, that the future wasn't set in stone until it happened. What we *really* saw were possibilities, some more likely than others, and we could never know what would *actually* happen until it did. The possibilities were myriad – endless, even – every path branching with every possible action, every possible *choice*, like a tree that grew perpetually, its tangled mass of branches stretching into the forever of oblivion.

There was a reason most First-Circle seers went mad.

I wasn't a strong seer. I couldn't control it, and it happened so infrequently that I hadn't even bothered to tell the other First-Circle Mages that I had a shadow of the gift. My main gift was empathy; the visions were an occasional by-product of the *elya* swirling in and around me. But when I'd met Willow, I'd seen *this* moment, so likely it was almost inevitable, and I'd seen *her*.

'Do you know,' a voice drawled from behind the door, 'when Ash and Will said that the new human was called *Claire*, I thought there was no fucking *way* it could be the Claire that I knew. But then, the universe has been mother-licking *weird* lately, so if I open this door and it's you, I'm really not going to be that surprised.'

Claire paled, her lips parted in shock. 'Maeve?' she breathed, her eyes wide and wild.

The door slid open – without any of us activating the sensor – to reveal a tall, slender human with chestnut hair and a wide grin.

'Fuck me,' Claire whispered.

'Nah,' the human said, her grin widening. 'I've got three partners now, and it's more than enough.' Her eyes roamed over us; she laughed. 'Well, well, *well*. Ashton did mention something about your mates. Looks like that shit is *catching*.'

Claire sprinted towards her; the human caught her and hugged her close. 'Is *this* where you've been?' Claire demanded. 'Your email said you took a trip north. This is pretty far *north*, Maeve!'

The human – *Maeve* – laughed again. 'Fuck, Claire, I can't believe it's you. This is fucking *insane*.' She held Claire at arm's length, suddenly serious. 'You look tired. Are you alright?'

'I'm fine,' Claire answered. 'But Maeve – how the fuck are you here?'

'I went to find Tessa,' Maeve said, moving inside and sinking onto the edge of the bed, pulling Claire to sit with her. 'A Tirian saw one of my social media posts and thought she might know where Tessa was. I left Earth with her in a fucking *spaceship*.' She eyed Kyin. 'Well, I guess that's not so impressive; you've clearly been on one, too.'

Claire shook her head. 'I can't believe you went with an *alien* to find Tessa. Wait – *did you find her?*'

Maeve took Claire's hands. 'Yep. I found her. There's some stuff I've got to tell you real quick, and just ... try to breathe, yeah?'

Claire's eyes went wide, her emotions a mess of astonishment, anticipation, and love for her friend.

'Tessa went with her own mates – three males – to a planet called Natare. I found her there. She's pregnant – like, *imminently-giving-birth* kind of pregnant. But one of her males is a Prince and also a pretty impressive fighter, so they're here.'

'*Here?*' Claire squeaked. 'Like, *here*? On Scytha?'

'Well, more arriving at your door in like, five minutes or so kind of *here*,' Maeve answered. 'Obviously, I would have come to see you anyway, but we have a favour to ask. That strike just took out power to the rooms where Tessa was staying. She's fine,' she added swiftly, seeing Claire's brow furrow with concern, 'but she's asking for water. We're bringing her here – as in, next door.' Maeve studied Claire's face. 'You told me once that you were a birth partner for your ex. Would you ... That is ...' She took a deep breath. 'We have a doctor – Willow, obviously, you met him – and Tessa's partner Cy is also pretty handy with a scanner, but babies really aren't my thing, and Anna is pretty busy with the whole *war*, and –'

'*Anna?*' Claire interrupted, swaying.

'*Cora?*' Kyin said sharply, stepping forward. His fingers and tail twitched with the need to reach for her, but he held himself back with obvious difficulty.

'Um, obviously I don't want to make this any worse, but Anna is kind of the new Roth Queen?' Maeve said.

Claire closed her eyes.

Maeve patted her shoulder. 'I'll just give you a moment.' She eyed Kyin. 'Now is probably the time for a hug, or whatever.'

Kyin knelt by the bed, taking Claire's hands and pressing a line of kisses across her knuckles. Claire leaned forward, resting her forehead on his while she inhaled slowly. 'Do you need Lan?'

'Lan needs to rest,' Claire whispered. She glanced across at me. 'I can manage.'

My hearts ached. Gydion wrapped an arm around my waist, running his claws lightly over my stomach.

'Okay,' Claire said a moment later, sitting up straight, though she kept hold of Kyin's hands. 'You want me to be Tessa's birth partner? You know I don't have a background as a midwife, right? I was just ... *there* ... when Aimee gave birth?'

Maeve nodded. 'I think Tessa just needs a familiar face by her side. She likes Willow and adores her partners, but she wants a human woman with her.' She paused. 'She's putting on a brave face, but I think she's scared.'

I could feel Claire's fear and insecurity, pressing against my shield, more immediate than the chaos still emanating from further away. She was trying to breathe through it, to ride the wave, to acknowledge it and move past it. My hearts swelled with admiration for her, and I pushed the feeling towards her, hoping she'd understand how proud I was, how strong *she* was.

She glanced at me, giving me a small, private smile. She was so beautiful that my breath caught; for a moment, I had a hard time believing that we were here, in this room in the Spire in Scytha City, and she was ours.

'I'll do it,' she said quietly. 'I'll be with Tessa for as long as she needs.'

Maeve tipped her head back in relief. 'Thank fuck,' she said. 'Because I *really* wouldn't have been any help.'

I bit my lip to hide a smile. Almost all of Willow's paths converged into the same future, and in it, I'd seen Maeve helping to deliver both her daughters.

She'd have a lot to learn between now and then.

I felt a glimmer of emotion outside; the door slid open a moment later. '*Karia*,' Ashton said. 'They're bringing Tessa now. And Alcide has asked us to join him in the city.' His eyes flickered to us. 'He could use some extra help down there. And some assistance in fixing the systems,' he added pointedly to Kyin.

'Fine, but he owes us another bath when we're done,' Kyin said ungraciously. 'You can tell him that his war is superbly inconvenient. Claire barely even –'

'*Kyin*,' Claire hissed, flushing.

Kyin grinned at her, unperturbed. 'What?' He surged up and kissed her, briefly but thoroughly. 'Bye, *cora*. I assume humans give birth like Darnagh do, so have fun with the pushing and the swearing.'

He got up and strode into the corridor, shouting for someone to show him the control room. I felt a few startled reactions from further away; knowing Kyin, he'd be settled where he needed to be with a mug of *limere* in hand before Gydion and I even left the room.

'I'll take you to Tessa,' Maeve said, standing. She stepped to Ashton's side, curling her arm around his waist. 'Where's El?'

'She went back up to the ship,' Ashton answered, dipping his head to press a kiss to Maeve's cheek. 'She said she wouldn't be long. We should go and get suited up.'

Maeve nodded. 'You take them, I'll get Claire settled and join you.' She cupped the big Tirian's cheek. 'Be careful.'

'Always.' He turned to us. 'Come on. We'll go to the armoury, then find the King.'

Gydion moved towards him, but I paused. It was our first time being separated from Claire, and it was making something in my stomach twist. The notion of walking away from her felt wrong.

She noticed my indecision, standing to wind her arms around my waist. 'It will be fine, Lan,' she whispered.

I pressed a kiss to her hair. 'I know,' I murmured. I gently took her chin in my fingers and tilted her face up, studying her wide brown eyes, her sharp chin, her beautiful lips. She was so lovely it was almost painful. 'We'll see you soon.'

A low snarl ripped through the corridor outside.

Maeve ran a hand through her hair. 'I really hate to ruin the moment, but that's Morgan, and he's only going to get growlier.'

I let Claire go; she followed Maeve from the room with a lingering glance back at Gydion and I.

Ashton sighed and rubbed his chest. 'Green gods, your *faces*. Don't worry; I'm fairly sure Willow and I looked like that for weeks before Maeve came around. It will all come good in the end.'

# CLAIRE

'MOTHERFUCKING *BASTARD*.'

I glanced at Maeve, startled.

'Turns out Tessa's allergic to the painkiller Cy and Willow made for her,' Maeve said, biting her lip. 'She was planning on just riding the high through the whole thing. She's not impressed that her plans have changed. And that blast didn't help.'

'Has that happened before?' I said, meaning the bomb.

'Yep. Often. But that's the closest it's come to the Spire.' Maeve flashed me a sympathetic smile. 'You arrived just in time. Or too soon, whichever way you want to look at it.'

'Would you like some water, Tessa?' Willow's voice coaxed from inside the room.

'Last time I had water, I vomited it all over my feet,' Tessa answered crossly. 'And if you suggest food again, Morgan, I will eat *you*.'

'Tessa, beautiful, do you want to sit down? Cy made one of the giant balls you asked for,' said an unfamiliar voice.

'Stop *coaxing* me, Aster. I'm *having* a child, not turning into one.'

Maeve laughed softly. 'Fucking hell, she is *cranky*.' Maeve waved her hand over the door sensor. 'Not gonna lie, I'm kind of sad that I'm missing this now.'

'That better be Maeve, or – *oh*,' said Tessa, her green eyes widening in surprise. 'Oh, *Claire*.' She stared at me for a moment, and then burst into tears.

I ran to her, wrapping my arms around her shoulders from the side, careful to avoid her swollen stomach. She looked beautiful, though her face was pale with exhaustion and there were dark smudges under her eyes. 'Hey, Tessa.'

'When Maeve told me you were here I almost *died*,' Tessa sobbed. 'Like, *what the fuck*, Claire.'

'Wild, huh,' I said, because what else could I say? 'And apparently you're pregnant or something?'

She hiccupped a laugh and sniffed. 'I didn't even get the full nine months. The pregnancy was normal until the fifth month, and then *this* happened.' She rubbed her stomach. 'The baby is fine, as far as Cy and Willow can tell. It just ... *accelerated*. Enterocti pregnancies are only four months, so I suppose it makes a weird kind of sense.'

'Enterocti?'

Tessa gestured to a towering blonde male hovering anxiously between the huge bed and deep, pool-like bath. 'That one.'

I studied him, startled. He looked exactly like a human to me.

A male with black curling hair and glowing golden eyes grinned. 'Hullo, Claire. That's Morgan, I'm Aster, and behind you is Cy. We're very happy to meet you.'

I turned in time to see a beautiful redhead walk through the door, carrying a tablet, a phone, and – for some unknown reason – a pile of CDs. 'I didn't know which one, so I brought them all,' he said. He stopped still and stared at me. 'Another human?'

'The one I told you about,' Maeve said. 'Claire. She's going to stay with Tessa.'

'Oh.' He gave me a distracted smile. 'Sorry. I remember now.' He rubbed a temple. 'I feel like my circuits are fried.'

Tessa stiffened; I dropped my arms and watched her stomach tighten beneath her shirt. She didn't make any noise, just took a series of deep breaths through her nose. Every eye in the room was on her: Morgan was wary; Aster, excited; Cy was worried; and Willow was assessing.

Maeve frowned.

When Tessa straightened, the contraction clearly passed, Maeve cleared her throat. 'Yep, this is really not my scene. Love you, Tessa. Elswyth said she'd come by later, if you wanted her to. Otherwise ...' She pulled me into a hug. 'I'm very glad you're here, for totally unselfish reasons.'

I snorted and waved as she walked from the room, calling *good luck!* to Tessa over her shoulder.

Tessa took my hand. 'I have no idea what I'm doing,' she said desperately. 'We haven't watched any birth stuff because we thought we still had *months* to get across it. I read a chapter of a book on birth and oh my *god*, Claire, it was *heinous*. And when it wasn't heinous, it also wasn't *helpful*. Like, what the fuck is *tearing*? Is that *actually* a thing? How do I *not do that*? And like, abdominal massage?' She flicked a glance at Willow. 'I trust you, Willow, really, I do, but like ... You guys are part *tree*. What if something goes wrong and you can't help me?'

I took Tessa's hands; they were cold. 'Tessa, you're doing *amazingly*. Whatever happens, you're incredible. You've just grown a *baby*, for fuck's sake. You're a goddess. Like, *literally*.' I squeezed her fingers gently. 'Tearing is a thing that can happen. It happened to Aimee, when I was her birth partner. There are different degrees, depending on where you tear and how badly. Aimee had second degree tearing, which is where you tear into the perineum. The doctor sewed her up and gave her some painkillers. It took about a month to heal. And abdominal massage after the birth helps the uterus contract so that you stop bleeding. I'm not going to lie, it looked awful. But midwives do it so there's less chance of haemorrhage.'

Tessa stared at me. 'Okay.' She took a deep breath. 'Okay.'

'I'm in the files of a maternity hospital,' Cy muttered, his fingers flicking furiously over the tablet screen. 'Where is the training material – ah! Found it.' He looked up at Willow. 'I've just sent you everything. I'll look for more.'

Willow was frowning down at his own screen. 'Honestly, I think the healing wand or moss bandage would be better for that kind of injury,' he murmured to Cy. 'And I can use both a topical painkiller we made for Maeve, with the blackbark mixture. We can't give it to Tessa now, because we're not sure what effect it will have on the baby,' he explained, seeing my frown. 'But I'll have some ready for afterwards. The chemical compounds are similar enough to your own painkillers, though we should think about whether transmission via breastmilk will be an issue ...' He trailed off, seeing Tessa's expression.

'Claire,' she said, horrified. 'How the *fuck* do I breastfeed?'

'Hey,' I said gently. 'Cy and Willow will find every video they can, and we'll work it out. You're going to be fine, Tessa. Your *baby* is going to be fine.'

She exhaled. 'Fuck, I'm glad you're here.'

I decided to push my luck, grabbing the flask Aster was surreptitiously offering and giving it to Tessa. She grumbled but drank, pausing afterwards as another contraction took her.

'Aimee took these classes,' I said, once the contraction had passed, 'that taught her how to breathe through the sensations. You're doing it just like she was. You're a natural, Tessa.'

She immediately glared at Aster. 'Not a fucking *word*.'

He held his hands up, grinning once more. 'Quiet as the vacuum, starlight.'

'Aster wants a *turn*,' she said to me, still glaring. 'As if his dick is getting within a galaxy radius of my body after this.'

'A turn? At making a *baby*?' My stomach churned. 'Fuck. I hadn't even thought of that.'

Tessa chuckled. 'Maeve told me you'd found three of your own. Seems like it's our lucky number.' Her eyes roved over her partners, suddenly soft. 'We didn't mean for this to happen. The opposite, actually. But I can't say I'm sorry.' She winced as the next contraction made her body tense. 'At least, not yet.'

One of the things that people don't tell you about birth is that it can be *long*. Aimee laboured for sixteen hours before she entered the active phase; it took Tessa ten. During those hours, Tessa slipped further and further inside herself, her body becoming her world. Cy had found some birth meditation affirmations and played them in a soft loop in the background, Tessa matching her breathing to the gentle voice of the instructor. At some stage, she decided she wanted the bath, and she slipped into the water with Morgan, his legs changing into eight sucker-lined tentacle limbs. I bit my lip, trying not to exclaim in surprise or stare. After a while, Tessa grudgingly allowed him to rub her back, propping her head on her arms on the side of the pool while his limbs slid gently over her.

It was beautiful, actually.

I'd been Aimee's birth partner because she didn't have one. We'd dated in our first year of art school, broken up in the second, and were friends again by the third. She'd gotten pregnant by another artist during a hookup just before our Honours graduation. Afterwards, Aimee found out that not only was he married, but his wife was *also* pregnant. As he declined to have any involvement in his child's life, Aimee did it all herself, with the help of her family and some friends.

Watching a birth with *three* partners present, all of whom clearly adored Tessa, was a very different vibe.

By the time things were getting intense, all of them were in the water with her: Morgan continued his gentle massage while Aster and Cy held her hands, helping her stand away from the side of the pool.

'I think,' Tessa gasped, 'I think – it feels – *different.*'

'The midwives had a mirror they could use to check how dilated Aimee was without touching her,' I murmured to Willow.

'On it.' He pulled a mirror from his medical bag, then handed it to Cy.

'Can I check, *elyn*?' Cy asked quietly.

A moment later, it was done; Cy had paled slightly. 'It looks like the diagrams,' he said. 'I think you can push now, beautiful. If you want to.'

Television and films would have people believe that this part of labour was always over in a matter of minutes – a few pushes and the baby arrives; the mother is still perfectly made up, every hair in place, ready for visitors. After an hour of Tessa's body working hard, and constant gentle encouragement from her males, her daughter came into the world. Her head was covered in blonde fuzz, and her tiny body was immediately cradled by a thick, sucker-lined limb. Tessa looked ready to fall over, her face red and her hair damp with sweat; she, too, was wrapped in one of Morgan's limbs, which looked to be half holding her up as Aster gently took their baby from Morgan and nestled her in Tessa's arms.

Tessa was crying as she held her, but she wasn't the only one. Glowing tears were streaming down Aster's face and Morgan's eyes looked suspiciously shiny. I retreated as far as I could, fussing with the bed and unfolding and folding a stack of towels, letting them have their moment before the realities of the placenta delivery took them all back down to earth again.

It was only because I was concentrating on something else that I felt it: a soft rumble through the floor.

I looked up and caught Willow's gaze. Wordlessly, he moved away from the pool, turning his back to check his wrist screen.

'Fuck,' he whispered, looking up at me. 'There's an alert. The Roth rebels are here.'

I SPUN THE ENGINEER'S chair in a circle.

The giant Roth didn't look happy about it, but if he didn't want me to do it, then maybe he should have been better at his job and not needed my help in the first place. His name was Bryn, and he protested that he was a ship's engineer, that everything was completely different on terra, and he couldn't reasonably be expected to know how to fix *every* system in the galaxy.

He was grouchy and growly and muttered a lot of things under his breath, but he made excellent *limere*.

It had taken me most of the day, but I had the communications systems back up and running, and had hooked up all available livestreams to the Spire. It was almost alarming how many streams the old King had used: he'd had eyes all over Scytha.

All the better to keep his subjects living in fear, I supposed. There was no way a being would resist his rule if there was a ninety-eight percent chance someone would catch them at it.

I'd run a diagnostic on the water systems; unfortunately, there was physical damage to the pipes and pumps used by the underground treatment facility, and I couldn't do a thing until they were fixed. There was a team of beings on it now – Roth and Tirian, along with some Luncest engineers sent from the Intergalactic Council – but they were taking their sweet time. As the climate systems relied on treated water for cooling regulation, I couldn't do anything about them yet, either.

I spun around once more. Bryn gave me a half-hearted glower, then turned his attention back to his screen, watching as a broad-shouldered Roth banged a pipe with a metal tool.

At least, that's what it seemed like he was doing.

I turned back to the comm system. There were livestreams from all through the Spire – from the empty halls, the corridors, the stairwells. There was also one from the King's own suite, which I made a mental note to tell him about; I was fairly certain he wouldn't want his private moments captured for all of Scytha – well, for Bryn, at least – to see. I trawled through the external feeds; some captured the sides of the Spire – *why* – while others looked out over the city.

I caught movement on one, and paused.

Other than the Spire, Scytha City was subterra. Temperatures during the day were too hot even for the Roth, who generally came across as the kind of beings who could live wherever they fucking wanted. Several generations ago, they'd started to dig down, dismantling the buildings above ground. Everything was below – their houses, their shops, their gathering places. From above, all you could see were ripples of red, stretching for miles where the ground had been displaced by the structures beneath it.

But there was *movement* at the edge of the city.

'Fuck,' I breathed, zooming in. '*Fuck*. Bryn. Is that what I think it is?'

The Roth peered at the screen, then blanched. He tapped his wrist screen. 'Uh, Majesty? We have a problem. Rebel forces approaching from the west.' He swallowed. 'Lots of them. I'm sending the visuals now.'

'How are the water systems going?' came a voice from his wrist.

'There's a team working to repair the damage now. Kyin says that he can't do anything about the system failure until the pipes are fixed.'

'And the comm system?'

'Fixed,' I called. 'Did you know there's a livestream of your bedroom?'

'There's a fucking *what*?' came a different voice. It was softer, as if further away.

'Shh, Cal,' the King said. 'Ah. Can we stop that one?'

'Yep,' I said cheerfully. 'And I promise I won't even look through the past feeds.'

'Good?' The King paused. 'Do you think you could wipe them while you're at it? Permanently?'

'It will be done, Highness,' Bryn said gruffly.

'We'll head out. Bryn, Vesper will bring Anna back to the Spire. She's asking for a livestream of our forces.'

Bryn frowned. 'Is she sure?'

The King sighed. 'Very sure, Bryn. And for my own safety, I'd prefer not to ask her again.'

'We'll arrange one, then.'

'My thanks. Remind me to give you a pay rise if I survive.'

'That's three now, Majesty,' Bryn said lightly. 'You'd better live. Dread gods be with you.'

'And with you.'

The comm cut out, and I side-eyed Bryn. 'Are you and the King ... close?'

Bryn snorted. 'He's a King. That wouldn't be at all proper.'

'It *sounds* like you're friends.'

There was a short silence. 'He's a good male,' Bryn said. 'He cares.' He fiddled with his wrist screen. 'I was with him when his father attacked his ship. I was with him when his father's orb fell to pieces in the black. I was with him when he married his loves. I was with him when he went to Natare to beg for the Council's help. I was with him when he landed here, when Fiach Redhand's forces tried to shoot us down. I was with him when his forces took Scytha City, and when the rebels tried to steal a weapons cache and his husband Callan almost died. I was with him when the Dread Order welcomed us into the Spire. I've been with him for every battle, watching from afar. And if he goes down?' Bryn shrugged. 'I'll keep fighting for him, and for what he believes in.'

'And what does he believe in?' I said softly.

'A better life,' Bryn answered. He glanced at me. 'The Queen will want to watch with all of us. Can you set up a stream of the King's forces to the Great Hall?'

I nodded, and a few moments later, it was done. I'd streamed a number of feeds to the main screen, giving whoever was watching multiple viewpoints of the conflict.

'Are we sure we're safe here?'

'In the Spire? It's the safest place on the entire planet – unless Alcide dies and Redhands storms it,' Bryn answered matter-of-factly. He gestured to a screen, showing a large hall where beings were starting to gather. 'See those Roth with the gilt stripes on their horns? They belong to our Dread Order. No Roth on Scytha is going to risk the dread gods' wrath by harming their priests.'

I peered at the screen. It wasn't just priests in the room, but other beings, too: Tirians, cephalopods, Darnagh, Zeddik, Sverns. As I watched, light swirled in one corner, momentarily blinding; a heartbeat later, a dark-haired humanoid male and a blonde humanoid female stood, the female with her hand over her mouth.

'That's our Queen,' Bryn said proudly. 'And Vesper, one of her husbands.'

I blinked. 'A starling?'

Bryn nodded. 'Twin to Aster, the Prince of Natare's consort.'

'Small fucking universe,' I muttered, my eyes going back to the approaching rebel army. There was nowhere to hide, so they didn't bother.

Even from a distance, I could see their shiny new guns.

I swore under my breath. 'Can you open a feed to a Tirian Captain named Peony? Her ship's name is *Forest Souls.*'

Bryn nodded, tapping at his hand screen to open a comm channel.

She took a few moments to answer. 'Bryn? Ah, Kyin Crace. I am happy to see you off that ship.'

'Me too, Captain. That thing we talked about? The selling to both sides?' I tapped to connect her to the livestream of the city. 'Those guns look *very* new.'

'And exactly the same as the design offered to the Allied forces,' the Captain muttered. 'Thank you, Crace. The Tirian

Grove has been appraised of the situation and has passed the information onto the Intergalactic Council. We'll add this to the evidence.' She paused. 'Crace, I can't guarantee you won't be pulled into this.'

'I know,' I said. 'But my mates *can't* be. Any consequences will be entirely mine, Captain. They are bystanders and have done nothing wrong.'

'I understand.' She looked aside. 'I need to go. My guards are marching to battle. May the stars watch over you, Crace.'

'May the stars watch you, too, Captain.'

'That sounded serious,' Bryn said, when I cut off the comm.

'Just trying to get my father what he deserves,' I muttered.

'Xanthin Crace? I've heard of him. In my experience, that type of being *never* get what they *really* deserve,' Bryn answered. 'Look at Alcide's father. He *deserved* to have the years of pain he'd inflicted on others given back to him. What he got was instant death with a crown still firmly on his head.'

'At least he's gone.' I stared at the livestream to the Great Hall, where the priests were flocking around their small human Queen. 'I'd settle for that, I think.'

Bryn leaned forward. 'Alcide's in the field,' he said tightly, gesturing.

I watched as the Roth King's troops spilled from a subterra gate, hidden behind one of the city's ripples. Like the rebels, they weren't trying to hide; their horns caught the sun's harsh light, spattered with the King's signature gold. Alcide stood out, his horns entirely gilded, his red hair gleaming, a circlet nestled amongst the auburn waves. He was shadowed by a huge Roth male with black hair falling almost to his shoulders and gilt spirals climbing his horns. One was broken, its edge ragged, but the other curved back proudly.

'That's Callan,' Bryn said. 'The King and Queen's other husband.'

'Four *is* an excellent number,' I muttered, catching sight of a contingent of Tirians, all wearing matching bark armour – except for the chestnut-haired human amongst them, who wore a suit like the ones we'd worn in the desert. 'Fuck,' I said. 'That's Claire's friend. Maeve. They let her on the field?'

Bryn snorted. '*Let* her? Have you met her? No one *lets* that female do anything; she does whatever she gods-well pleases. Besides, Anna said she passed all the Tirian entrance tests a month ago. She earned her place there.'

Twin points of light glimmered in the corner of the screen; I peered closer as two black-haired starlings materialised, one with his hand curled around the waist of a broad-shouldered Enterocti male, his tentacles a wary orange.

'Vesper again,' Bryn said, pointing, 'and his twin, Aster. Aster's mate, Morgan, Prince of Natare.'

'How the fuck can you tell the starlings apart?'

Bryn gave a one-shouldered shrug. 'Vesper's prettier.'

I frowned at the screen. 'The rebels have more soldiers than we do.'

'Yes,' Bryn said quietly. 'Not only that, Alcide has ordered that only non-lethal force be used.'

I stared at the big engineer. 'Uh – he *what*?'

'His forces don't kill. Stun, yes, but they won't kill. Alcide says that there's no use in being victorious over an empty planet.'

'That is the most unhinged thing I've heard in – well, *today*, at least,' I said. 'But what about the other side?'

Bryn's black lips twisted. 'They are not playing by the same rules.'

'By the stars,' I muttered. My eyes caught a glimmer of familiar blue; I peered closer. 'No,' I said. '*No.*'

'What's wrong?'

'My mate is down there. Though Gydion would *never* leave Lan to do this on his own, which means my *mates* are down there.' I caught sight of Gydion's dark head. 'No, no, *no*. Why the *fuck* are they on the front line?'

I stood up.

'What are you doing?' Bryn said warily.

'Going down there.'

He caught my arm. 'Kyin. They've spent the entire day being briefed. They're armed. Your mates are surrounded by Tirians and Roth. They're probably just as safe as you are. In fact, you going down there will probably put them in *more* danger.'

'The human helping the one giving birth,' I said, ignoring him. 'Claire. She's our mate. Will you make sure she's safe?'

Bryn sighed and tapped on his wrist screen. 'Darius? I know I said I wasn't fighting today, but something's changed. There are two humans in the guest wing – Tessa, the Enterocti Prince's mate, and Claire, Kyin Crace's. Will you watch them?'

'Bryn,' came a growling voice over his wrist screen. 'What –'

'Please?'

There was a sigh. 'Fine,' Darius grumbled. 'But you owe me for breaking that promise. May the dread gods be with you.'

'And with you, love.'

Bryn cut off the comm and stood. 'My claimed will watch the humans. Come on. Let's get armed.'

GYDION

I COULD FEEL THE tension in the air around me, even without Lanir's gifts.

Fiach Redhand's forces were streaming in from the western side of the city, armed to the horns. Their progress was slowed by a search for civilians, one that was – thank the Goddess – unsuccessful. The Roth had been evacuated to the Spire as soon as the rebel troops were spotted.

'They're desperate,' Lanir murmured to me. 'It's pouring off them.' His eyes unfocused as his veins began to glow beneath his skin; I took his arm so he wouldn't stumble as we moved forward. 'They can feel that it's hopeless.' He blinked, his gaze clearing. 'They think the King is winning. They think this is their last chance.'

I tapped my claws on my thigh. That was both good and bad. Desperate soldiers were more apt to be careless; they were more likely to be ruthless, too, in a last frantic grab for victory.

The King was leading the way forward, with his husbands – the Roth, Callan, and Vesper the starling – by his side. He'd made himself conspicuous with his golden horns and uncovered hair; I admired his courage as much as it perturbed me. It was brave, but stupid, too; while every gilded glance of him would give hope to his troops, it also gave his enemy a clear target.

On Kjid, we flit through the forest like shadows. It went against my every instinct to fight like this, out in the open air.

'They're going to try to kill us,' Lanir said evenly.

'Yes.'

'I hope Claire is all right.'

'Claire will be better if you get back alive,' I answered. 'One thing at a time, my love.'

Lanir nodded, his hand going to the sword at his hip. There were two more strapped across his back, and two stun guns lining his thighs. I swallowed and looked away; I'd do everything in my power to make sure he didn't need to use any of them.

I'd tried to convince him to stay. It was one thing for me to fight – I was a guard, it was what I *did* – but quite another for Lanir to come with me. He was perfectly capable of holding his own, I knew that, but his gifts made him vulnerable on the battlefield. The heightened emotions of conflict would surge around him, and beings would desperately grab for life before they fell into the Goddess' arms.

I know it will be hard, Gyd, he'd said. *But I* want *to do this. I can make a difference, I know it.*

Lanir was a good warrior, and I knew he *could* make a difference, but his life was everything. I'd give mine to make sure he lived unscarred. And he couldn't do that with death on his hands; as an empath, if he killed, he'd feel every moment of pain and realisation and grief, and he'd know that *he* was the one who'd caused it. He'd remember it forever.

I wouldn't let that happen.

The Tirians around us were silent; the only sound was the rhythmic thump of their feet. They didn't walk so much as march in unison, another thing foreign to me. The Kjidja fought alone, not in units. Even as a Divine Guard, I trained *against* my fellow warriors, not *with* them, as we were each assigned a Priestess whose life became our own.

My fingers curled tighter around my staff.

I could see Ashton ahead of me, holding a staff of his own. Maeve was by his side, one hand wrapped loosely around a stun gun. They walked as one, moved as one, and my heart constricted as I thought of Claire's lessons in the simulation room – lessons I was glad she hadn't needed.

We were halfway through the city when the first shot rang out; ahead of us, a Roth soldier fell to the ground.

Even from a distance I could see the blue blood pool on the red clay. Lanir stiffened as he felt the soldier's death.

'Shields,' Alcide said calmly over our comms. 'And remember, soldiers: guns set to stun only. Spare every life you can. Except for Fiach Redhands.' His voice dropped. 'Redhands is *mine*.'

I forced my fingers to hold my staff loosely. Beside me, Lanir calmly activated his bodyshield and unholstered his guns.

'Love you, Lan,' I said quietly.

He moved to stand with me, shoulder-to-shoulder. 'Love you, Gyd.'

I raised my chin. 'Let's do this.'

CLAIRE

WHEN TESSA WAS SAFELY tucked into bed, Aster and Morgan left to join the Roth King's troops. Tessa kissed her males goodbye with enviable composure, though she cried once the door closed behind them. Cy held her tight, murmuring to her as she rocked their newborn daughter. I'd never seen her look so tired; she was asleep before we'd even left the room, Cy carefully taking the tiny baby into one arm while supporting Tessa with the other.

'He'll let us know if she needs anything,' Willow said quietly, once we were outside. 'His irises contain scanners that will pick up issues sooner than I could. I'll come back to check on her again in a few hours anyway, but if she can sleep now, she should.'

'You seem ... tense,' I said cautiously.

He gave me a tight smile. 'Ashton and Maeve are with the Roth King. Elswyth is still up on the ship with her heartree.

I don't like being away from them. Especially not while Ash and Maeve are about to be in active conflict.' He looked away. 'Usually, I'd be with them. Not on the front line, of course; I'd follow with the other medics. But Maeve asked me to stay with Tessa, and when Maeve asks, rather than *tells* ... Well. She's impossible to refuse, either way.'

'You love her,' I said with a slight smile.

'Entirely. Desperately. Blindly. Possibly even stupidly.'

'I'm glad. I've never known Maeve to ... well, commit.'

I regretted the comment as soon as it passed my lips; what if it made Willow feel uncomfortable, or sounded as if I were judging Maeve? In my opinion, Maeve simply had high standards and loved her freedom, and her commitment to her Tirians reflected how amazing she thought they were. But Willow didn't seem offended, simply smiling the smile of someone entirely sure of his partner, someone entirely sure that he was loved in the same way he himself loved.

'Yes, she told us. But Elswyth wore her down, and Ash and I reaped the benefits.' He gave me another smile. 'What about you? How did you meet your family?'

My family.

The word struck a chord within me, somewhere deep and secret. Because it was clear that whatever I had with my males, it was more than just sex. It had only been a matter of hours, but I was missing them in the same way I missed my tablet and stylus – like I *needed* them close to me, in the same way I needed air and water and food. I ached when they were gone, as though they were necessary to my existence. But not just *necessary* – like art, they made my life *better*.

'It was an accident,' I said. 'They didn't mean to abduct me. But now ... Now, I think I'm glad they did.'

'It sounds as if you've had quite an adventure.' Willow led me down a corridor lit with oil lamps rather than floor lights; they flickered as we passed. 'It must have been very stressful, leaving your home in that way. It must be stressful *now*, having flown into a warzone on a planet you didn't know existed a few weeks ago.' He reached out and waved his hand over a scanner; a door opened before us. 'I think you're very brave, Claire.'

I choked a laugh. 'Lanir spent half the journey keeping me calm. I don't think that qualifies as *brave*.'

'Of course it does.' The door slid closed behind us. 'You think Ashton isn't afraid right now? He's terrified. He knows exactly what he's facing; he knows every time. But that's the difference between bravery and fear; he knows, and he still stands tall. It doesn't mean it doesn't get to him; it does. But he wakes up the next morning and does it all over again.' He glanced at me. 'You're standing here, which means you did the same thing, Claire. You were stolen from your planet, and instead of succumbing to fear, you got to your feet the next morning and faced it. *And* you found something special along the way.' He paused. 'They love you. Just in case you were wondering. I can see it.'

I swallowed. 'Yes. I think they do.'

'And you?'

I exhaled. 'I'm ... Everything has happened so swiftly. I don't know if I have a word for what I am. But I know that I want to find out.'

Willow nodded, then waved open another door. 'I'm glad. It's ... rare ... for Illisae to love. Their magic – their *elya* – becomes everything to them. The Mages' Circle sees love – true connection, whichever form it takes – as a distraction from what really matters, and so they discourage relationships of all kinds. Or so my mother told me.' He cleared his throat. 'It's ... nice ... to know that my mother wasn't the only one who felt that was wrong. That she wasn't the only one willing to sacrifice everything she knew for her heart. It makes me feel ...' He inhaled. 'It makes me feel less lonely.'

I touched his shoulder. 'I don't know what will happen when this is over. But you should keep in touch with Lan.' I smiled. 'Your daughter will have Illisae heritage, too.'

He coughed. 'Green gods, don't tell Maeve. She's stuck on all the ways birth can go wrong, all the ways it could cause harm. Which is understandable, but she's pushing aside the joy it can bring.'

I laughed. 'A few months ago, Maeve wouldn't have even had that conversation. She's ...' I cast about for the right words. 'She's fiercer and softer, all at once. Stronger and gentler. And Tessa ... I can't believe she's a mother now. And those three males ... I think they'd jump off a cliff if she asked them to.'

'And more. They adore her.' He waved his hand over yet another scanner with a grin. 'And then there's Anna, of course.'

The door opened into a huge hall. Like the other one we'd seen, its walls were covered in beautiful frescoes, their colour faded and their scenes an echo of what they once were. Unlike the other hall, this one had several screens on its walls, all showing beings marching through the odd, rippled landscape of the city, red clay beneath their feet and the smudge of pollution above their heads. There were a number of Roth sitting in the middle of the hall, their horns painted with gilt; amongst them, ringed by Roth as if in protection, sat a small, delicate blonde woman, a golden circlet nestled in her elegant chignon.

'Anna?' I breathed.

She glanced across; when our eyes met, her lips parted. 'Claire!' she shrieked. The Roth around her murmured, startled, then moved aside as she scrambled to her feet and ran through them.

I wrapped my arms around her, laughing as the huge Roth watched their little human Queen start to bawl, and just like that, all the hurt, resentment, and inadequacy I'd felt when I'd thought she'd abandoned me just ... disappeared.

Let's talk about those thoughts, my counsellor said in my memory, her voice gentle. *What evidence do you have to support them?*

Of course Anna wouldn't have gone without a good reason. *Of course* she wouldn't have left without telling me if she'd had a choice in the matter. But I'd talked myself into something negative, and doubled down until I couldn't find my way out of it.

I buried my face in her shoulder.

'God, I missed you so much,' she sobbed. 'When Maeve said you were here, I almost had a heart attack. What the actual *heck*, Claire?' She sniffed. 'Maeve said you'd been abducted?'

'Accidentally,' I said, wiping my own tears away.

Anna snorted. 'Nice. I got abducted *on purpose*.'

'But it turned out okay in the end?'

She gave a watery smile. 'More than okay. At least, I hope it will be.' She gestured at the screens. 'Alcide and I argued about the livefeeds for like, a full hour. But I told him that not knowing what was happening would be worse than watching, and I talked Vesper and Cal around, and *voila*.' She frowned at me. 'Where are your mates? Maeve said you had three?'

I swallowed. 'I think two of them are there.' I searched the screens, finally fixing on a glimmer of blue. 'Yes. There.'

'There's Ash and Maeve,' Willow said softly. 'Just ahead of Lanir.'

'Do you want to watch?' Anna asked gently.

'I –' I bit my lip. I honestly didn't know. Which was worse – watching, and seeing something happen that I could do nothing about? Or not watching, and thinking the worst? 'Okay,' I said at last. 'Can I sit with you? Or will the golden-horned guys freak out?'

Anna smiled. 'The priests think I am the Sun Queen come again, despite her being Roth, twice my height, and having pitch-black hair. I think they'll let me bring a few friends.'

I followed her back to the centre of the room, trying to ignore the stares. Anna drew the eye here in a different way to Earth; she walked with her shoulders back and her chin high, self-possessed and calm. It wasn't just her prettiness that you wanted to see; you wanted her to notice you, to grace you with a smile.

'This suits you, Anna,' I said.

There were no chairs, so she settled on the floor – still practical Anna, despite everything. 'It's been a steep learning curve.' She leaned forward to whisper to me and Willow. 'I'm faking it.'

There was a murmur as one of the screens focused on the Roth King. He was handsome, with auburn hair and graceful horns, his black eyes stark against his pearlescent scaled skin, his eyelids and lips painted gold to match his horns. Anna stiffened; she reached out and took my hand.

'Shields.' His voice wove through the hall, smooth and deep. 'And remember, soldiers: guns set to stun only. Spare every life you can. Except for Fiach Redhands. Redhands is *mine*.'

Anna's fingers tightened.

I glanced at another screen, searching desperately for Lanir and Gydion, just as shots started to echo around us, coming loud and sharp over the speaker before Alcide cut his comm. A few Roth in the front lines fell to gasps of concern through the hall, their personal shields not activated in time, but when I found Lanir and Gydion I could see a slight shimmer in the air around them and I breathed a sigh of relief. Ahead of them, I saw the same shimmer around Maeve and Ashton; Willow worried at his bottom lip as Ashton began to swing his staff.

'Sorry,' he said, getting to his feet. 'I'm not sure I can watch. Having one mate fighting was bad enough, but two ... I'll go and make Cy and Tessa some food. Will you ...?'

'Of course,' Anna said immediately. 'I'll let you know if anything happens.'

He gave me a worried half-smile, and squeezed through the circle of priests.

'I know it's probably weird,' Anna said. 'But I just have this thing that if I don't take my eyes off them, then they can't get hurt.'

'Was it the King who took you from Earth?'

Anna shook her head. 'Callan. That one.' She pointed to a huge Roth standing in front of the King, a stun gun in both hands, one horn with a broken, jagged edge. 'He, um, said he caught my scent, and he couldn't leave me there, and then afterwards he couldn't make himself bring me back.'

'Finders keepers?'

Anna coughed a laugh. 'Something like that. Luckily, it turned out that I didn't mind. They had to put me in a cell with Vesper –'

'Um, what the *fuck*?' I interrupted. 'A *cell*? Like, a *jail*?'

'I know, I know, it sounds so bad, but the alternative was me roaming a ship full of Roth males who would have very definitely done something much worse than keep me caged,' she went on, matter-of-factly. 'It was less a keeping-*me*-inside and more a keeping-them-away type thing. When Alcide destroyed the old King's ship, they gave me a choice of where to be, and the second they let Vesper out of his chains he brought me to Earth. I chose to go back to Alcide and Callan. And there's been no cells since,' she added, her lips curving into a tiny, secret smile. 'There have been restraints, but it hasn't been *me* wearing them. I think Vesper likes the irony of it.'

'You're happy,' I said. 'Even with all this.' I gestured to the screens, where it seemed as if a tense stand-off was taking place.

'Yes,' Anna said. 'I didn't think I could feel this much joy. And I definitely didn't think I would ever have this much love to give. Sometimes, I don't know what to do with it all.'

I glanced at the priests around us. 'You give it to the Roth,' I realised. 'That's why they accepted you so quickly. That's why the priests protect you.'

'I think so.' She shrugged. 'I'm not doing it to look good, or to try to sway hearts. It just ... It just feels *right*.'

'Move forward!' Alcide roared suddenly, making everyone in the hall jump.

'Urgh,' Anna muttered, closing her eyes. She inhaled, then exhaled slowly. 'Okay. I can do this. Vesper is with them. He's not going to let anyone hurt them. He promised.' She opened her eyes and fixed them on the screen.

'Anna?' The voice came from her wrist.

'Alcide?' Anna answered tightly.

'I love you.' On the screen, the King's lips moved, but no sound came from the speakers in the hall.

'I love you too, but don't you *dare* think you're saying that *just in case*.'

A chuckle sounded. 'Told you.'

'Love you, Callan,' Anna said. 'I know Vesper is there. Tell him that he's tolerable.'

The voice came from further away. 'Tell her that she's much handsomer than Mr Bingley.'

Anna snorted. 'I ... Come back, okay?'

'You know what to do if we don't.' Shots rang out, muffled slightly by the smaller speaker. 'Oof. That was close.'

Anna closed her eyes again. 'I'm cutting the comm. I love you all. Please don't die.'

'Was Vesper quoting Austen?' I said, when I'd given her a moment – or several – to compose herself.

She forced a smile. 'I'm making him read all her novels. He likes them. *Northanger Abbey* is his favourite so far. And he has an uncanny memory for quotes. I think I'll make him try Elizabeth Gaskell next.'

On the screens, the King's soldiers were moving forward. Their shields lit with every hit, making the air around them a constant wave of movement and colour. Anna gave a soft moan; the hits were concentrated around the King, his shield a shimmer of white. Alcide looked serious but determined; he raised his chin against the onslaught, returning fire calmly.

I searched the other screens until I found Lanir and Gydion again. They were moving concerningly close to the front line; Gydion looked as if he were barely holding himself back, his body coiled as if he were waiting to spring. Lanir's forehead was creased in concentration. My stomach churned at his expression; I wondered if he was trying to fight against the emotions circling around him, and how much it would cost him.

A bronze shadow moved through the soldiers; I gasped and scrambled to my feet, moving closer to the screen, ignoring the grumbles of the priests as I pushed my way forwards.

'Kyin, what the *fuck*,' I cried.

Kyin was weaving through the Tirian soldiers, making his way towards Lanir and Gydion. That Gydion and Lanir were out there was bad enough; the notion that *all three* of them were in danger made me breathless with fear. Kyin was supposed to be safe in a control room with a cup of *limere*, not pushing his way towards a line of soldiers who would happily *kill* him.

I clenched my fingers into fists.

The air lit up around Gydion and Lanir; Lanir returned fire, while Gydion's patience evidently snapped. He sprinted forward, sweeping his staff out as he did so, catching one Roth fighter – his horns stained red in honour of his leader – under the chin with a force that made me wince. The Roth dropped like a sack of bricks; Lanir shot him with a stun gun for good measure.

They moved forward that way – Gydion toppling Roth soldiers like he did it every day before breakfast, Lanir incapacitating them to ensure they couldn't keep fighting back – until they were all but surrounded by Roth rebel soldiers. My hand was at my mouth and my heart was pounding in my ears. I realised just how easy Gydion had gone on me during my lessons: he was made of lethal grace, his movements so fast and so smooth that even the Roth couldn't fight back in time. Lanir wasn't exactly overshadowed, either; when a soldier came directly at him, the Illisae took him down with two calculated blows, even though the Roth was broader and taller than him.

They were so beautiful, and so devastating.

I hated to admit it, but it was so *hot*. Just hours ago, they'd been naked in a bath – with *me*. I'd *almost* had Gydion's cock inside me. The hands that were holding weapons had been on my skin, in my body, holding me. And they'd been gentle, reverent.

That they were capable of causing harm should have scared me. Instead, it just made me want them more. I might have been afraid about leaving Earth, might have been afraid of flying across galaxies – but I'd never been afraid of *them*.

There was a blur of movement as Kyin fought his way through. He had a stun gun in one hand and a sword in the other, and his movements were smooth and precise: cut, stun, cut, stun. His tail – the tail he'd used to make me come – whipped across a Roth warrior's cheek as Kyin spun, leaving an immediate blue bruise in its wake beneath the soldier's pearlescent scales.

For a moment, I wished I was more like Maeve, that I could be out there with them, fighting by their side. In the next heartbeat, I realised that I couldn't do what she was doing, even if I had the skill; I simply didn't have the instincts. My strength was different to Maeve's, different to Tessa's, different to Anna's, even. Maeve was brave and brash and confident; Tessa was self-assured and generous and open; Anna was poised and graceful and kind.

I wasn't any of those things, but I was resilient, and I was stubborn, and I could see beauty wherever it existed around me. I saw it in the savageness of my males, in the controlled power of their movements, in the way they bared their teeth and extended their claws. I'd never forget that this side of them existed.

My heart ached. I made my way back to Anna, stepping more carefully through the ring of priests this time. Anna reach out and took my hand; I wasn't sure whether it was for my comfort, or hers.

'The body shields won't hold much longer,' she said tightly. 'They have a finite power reserve and fail after a certain number of hits.' She blew out a breath. 'The shields came from the Allied forces, and Fiach's soldiers don't have them, but they're using lethal force, instead. At the moment, the battle is balanced. Once the shields fail ...'

'They have to do something now,' I realised.

'They are.' Anna nodded to a screen to the left, where we could see several of the King's soldiers working on something, surrounded by a wall of gilded Roth protectors. 'Modified cluster bombs, with an energy pulse that causes unconsciousness. Alcide is hoping to thin their numbers.'

'I thought this war would be different,' I said, watching the screens. 'They can fly through fucking *space*. But even with all this complex tech, they're still just shooting at each other across a field.'

'The stakes are different in this war.' Anna touched her hair nervously with her free hand. 'Usually, the Roth would use weapons from space, and never even come close to those they were attacking. But Alcide has refused to do that. He says there's no point in ruling over an empty planet, and if he kept fighting the way his father had, then he would be no better than any of the other Roth Kings. Cy and Vesper have been creating a propaganda campaign, talking about how Alcide wanted to keep the civilian Roth safe and would only fight in a way that minimised civilian casualties. It's been so successful that Fiach was forced to change his tactics and fight by Alcide's rules. Well, almost by his rules,' she added, her eyes fixed to the screens. 'It was really clever. Alcide reframed everything so it benefited the

Roth as a species, talking about how he wanted to clean the water and nourish the earth and rebuild Scytha's glory days. Vesper dressed him like one of their famous Kings, and it snowballed. Cide's grandmother led a resistance network when she was still alive, and many of the Roth who knew her offered to fight for Alcide. After that, civilian Roth began to join Alcide, too. That, with the support of the Dread Order, is everything,' she went on. 'The priests' support means that some of the Roth believe that Alcide is half-divine. Many of the civilians had no appetite for what Alcide's father was doing – they don't care about expansion and taking over planets they'll never get to see. They want to live a full life and know that their loved ones will be safe. And they know that Alcide will help them do that.'

'Dread gods be with him,' the priest closest to us said.

'And with you,' Anna returned.

'It doesn't matter that you're human?' I said quietly.

Anna shook her head, her expression sad. 'There are very few female Roth left,' she said softly. 'And most are past the years they could bear younglings. Alcide would always have had to marry outside his own kind. But honestly, marrying Callan has helped. We never expected that.'

'What do you mean?'

'We thought there'd be repercussions for us being what we are – the four of us being together, I mean. The old King was hateful and intolerant, and he encouraged his supporters to be the same. But Alcide decided to be honest about it, and it was one of the first things he told the Roth, before we even arrived on the planet. He was very clear that he had three consorts, two of them male. It didn't happen immediately, but now Callan is almost as popular as Alcide.' Her lips twitched into a smile. 'He's everything the young Roth want to be – strong and intelligent and daring, a pilot and a soldier, loyal to his King, and comfortable in his own skin. They're warier about Vesper, but honestly, that's just smart.'

'I'm looking forward to meeting them.'

Anna squeezed my hand. 'Oh, look, the front line is backing off,' she said softly. 'They're about to launch the cluster bombs.'

Even though I knew they wouldn't kill anyone, I still couldn't watch. I heard it, though; a whine as they went up through the air, an eerie silence just before they landed, then the deep *boom* as they went off.

Anna exhaled shakily. 'That's good,' she muttered. 'That's good.'

I looked back up to see a significant number of enemy Roth on the ground, motionless. Some were staggering behind them, shaking their heads against the force of the blow, disoriented.

But there were still lines of soldiers behind *them*, standing upright and alert.

'There's Redhands,' Anna said tightly. She pointed to a Roth as big as Callan with two red handprints on the front of his armour.

I hoped they were made from paint.

'Coward,' the priest closest to us said angrily. 'Our King is on the front line, and Fiach hides behind the bodies of civilian Roth.' He tapped on his wrist screen. 'I want that livecast,' he said to whoever was listening on the other end. 'All of Scytha needs to know that Fiach hid while our King faced battle with courage.'

Anna's lips twisted. I had a feeling that she would have preferred Alcide standing behind rows of soldiers, but she didn't say anything.

My gaze strayed across the screens, finding one where the camera – or whatever the device was – had panned out. On it, the forces on the battlefield became a shadow across the red clay, an echo of the city's rippling circles. *It would be a beautiful photo*, I thought absently; a landscape made entirely of shades of red.

My eyes caught on something.

'What is that?' I breathed, frowning at the screen.

'What?' Anna said absently, her focus on Alcide.

'That, there.' I pointed to where I could see an odd shift in the colour of the clay, some distance from the shadow of the armies. It wasn't from one of the city's ripples, wasn't from Alcide or Fiach Redhand's forces. It wasn't a shadow; rather, it was lighter, and it was –

Moving.

'There,' I said again. 'That patch where the clay is lighter. What *is* that?'

'I can't –' Anna started. She frowned, then got to her feet, moving closer to the screen. 'Oh my god, I see it. Callan!' she cried, pressing her wrist screen. 'The missing burrower! It's coming straight for you from the south-east. You need to get it before –'

'On it,' came a grim voice from her wrist. 'Vesper, can you –'

Callan's voice cut off; I wrenched my attention back to the main screen, where Vesper disappeared in a swirl of darkness.

'What's a burrower?' I asked breathlessly.

'A machine used to make the tunnels the Roth build into,' Anna explained tightly. 'Just after Alcide took Scytha City, a group of rebels attacked a weapons cache near the outskirts. They took most of the weapons, and stole a burrower stationed nearby to help make escape tunnels.' She swallowed. 'It's how

Callan was injured. He was underground, in the city, doing a sweep with some of the soldiers. The alarm on the cache was triggered and they went to investigate. The rebels had left a timed bomb, and when it detonated ...' She exhaled. 'The cache and the corridor collapsed. Callan was caught by it, trapped underground. He was down there for hours.' Anna's fingers balled into fists. 'I've never been so scared. Not until today, at least.'

'So the missing burrower could be full of stolen weapons?'

'It's likely,' Anna answered. 'But now they know it's there. And the design allows only two Roth inside it at a time. Vesper will handle them. We knew the rebels wouldn't take the burrower if they didn't plan to use it. We planned for this.'

'Vesper will ...' I trailed off as the moving shift in colour stopped. A moment later, the clay trembled. I held my breath as the surface around it collapsed, slowly at first, then all at once, until there was a crater in the city's outskirts. 'Fuck. Vesper will handle it. Just like that.'

Anna gave a tight nod. 'Just like that,' she echoed. She glanced at me. 'You just saved lives.'

I shook my head. 'Someone else would have noticed. And Vesper did the actual work.'

'They wouldn't have seen it as quickly as you did.' Anna pointed to the screen. 'Look at how big that crater is, compared to the armies. So many could have died.'

She was right; the crater was half the size of the shadow of the armies. *It would have taken out hundreds of beings*, I realised, shivering.

'Between you and Kyin, we're so lucky that you're here, Claire.' Anna's attention went back to where her partners were fighting on the red clay.

I realised that she wasn't letting herself dwell on what a close call that had been because she *couldn't*. She didn't have the time or space to digest it, to wonder what happened to the burrower's driver, to wonder what Vesper had done. I had no doubt it would come back to her later, but right now, her priority was her mates.

I wrapped my arms around myself, wishing I could bury my face in Lanir's neck, feel Kyin's tail wrap around me, hear Gydion's steady voice. I wondered if they'd even noticed anything had happened.

My eyes searched for them. My males were standing tense and ready, waiting for their next instruction. Gydion and Lanir had clearly noticed that Kyin had joined them; they stood shoulder-to-shoulder in front of him in a wall of protection. Kyin evidently wasn't impressed at them doing so; his tail whipped from side to side in agitation.

'Fiach Redhands!' Alcide shouted suddenly, startling every being in the hall. 'We can end this, you and me! Face me like the King you want to be, cousin!'

Anna whimpered; I reached to take her hand once more. On the screen, Vesper reappeared at Alcide's side, his expression grim.

The huge, red-horned Roth stepped forward. 'Come then, pretender,' he sneered. 'Come, and meet your fate.'

Alcide squared his shoulders and strode towards him, his golden armour glittering against the backdrop of the unforgiving red clay.

LANIR

A mix of trepidation and excitement flowed over me, so strong I could barely keep it at bay. It was undercut with bloodlust and exhaustion, with fear and savagery.

I was already tired, and the emotional cascade caused by Alcide's challenge threatened to floor me completely. I scrubbed my face with my free hand, trying to regain control.

'Lan,' Kyin rumbled behind me, concern lacing his voice.

'I'm all right,' I muttered.

I wasn't all right, not even close to it. I had expected the toll that every death would take, but I wasn't prepared for it, for the awful way the final, desperate grabs for life assaulted my mental shield and shook me to my very core. My body was trembling with second-hand grief, shock, anger, sadness and despair. I wanted nothing more than to turn away from it, to head back to the Spire and find Claire and bury my face in her lap; to breathe her in and wrap myself in the warmth of her affection, to make sure that Gydion and Kyin were with us, safe and loved, as they should be.

Instead, we were covered in sweat and red dust, and Alcide was striding forward to change the history of his planet forever.

Callan and Vesper shadowed him, mirroring two of Fiach Redhand's soldiers, all ready to act as seconds if their commander fell. Callan's face was grim, and Vesper's twisted with worry, but Alcide's face was disarmingly open, as if he welcomed the moment.

'Fuck,' Gydion breathed, his fingers tightening on his staff.

Gydion's armoured suit was torn along the calf; a Roth had gotten past his shield and slashed at him with a knife before I'd stunned him. The red of his drying blood was visible through the rent material; no matter where I looked, I couldn't help but see it from the corner of my eye.

I swallowed, trying to concentrate.

Fiach stopped a few metres back from Alcide, sneering at the shorter, more slender Roth. Alcide was all self-possession and elegance to Fiach's brute strength; looking at them, it didn't seem like a fair battle, but Alcide did not seem afraid. He drew his sword from the scabbard at his back, his posture loose, waiting. Light gleamed off his odd, rippled blade. Its pommel was covered in fading fabric, as if it were an antique, just for show.

'They're Roth scales,' Gydion said under his breath. 'The blade. It's made of Roth scales.'

Fiach laughed. 'You're going to fight with *that*?' He drew his own sword, its blade unmarked and so sharp that the air itself shimmered around it. 'You'll be history, *Cide*. Just like your sword.'

Alcide gave him a beatific smile. 'Perhaps,' he said. 'Either way, aren't you tired of waiting?'

Fiach sprang forward without warning, and chaos broke out on the red clay.

The rebel leader swept a savage stroke upwards, a stroke which would have cleaved Alcide's face in two – had he not parried with a shocking swiftness, stepping to the side and catching Fiach's sword with his own. His cousin had a moment to look surprised that Alcide's ancient sword was capable of such a thing before he began desperately blocking Alcide's flurry of return strikes, his eyes narrowing in concentration.

Fiach's seconds slid forward to engage Callan and Vesper; Callan calmly shot them with his stun gun before turning his attention to Fiach's approaching front line. He and Vesper exchanged a glance, clearly unwilling to leave Alcide; a moment later, Vesper's twin materialised by his side, his arm curled around the waist of the huge Enterocti Prince who unleashed a wordless snarl and sprinted forward, Aster following close behind. The starling was devastating, materialising next to Roth and taking them down in a moment, only to disappear and move on to the next one, always tracking his cephalopod mate.

'Lan,' Gydion said sharply. 'Eyes on your own battles.'

I shook myself and followed him forward, Kyin in step beside me.

Every sharp shock of pain battered my shield as I moved, becoming stronger each time it was *me* who dealt the blow. It wasn't physical pain, not exactly, but rather the emotional reactions *to* the pain: shock, confusion, anger, terror, desperation. There were flickers of surprise around us as personal shields began to fail, and the opposing Roth's weapons began to carve paths through our ranks. A Roth ran at me, snarling; the air shimmered weakly, telling me I had only a few more blows before I'd be fighting for real. He shot twice at Kyin before I tripped him and gave a hard blow to his head, wincing at his shock – and fear – before he blacked out.

'Lan,' Kyin said warningly, as more soldiers sprinted across the clay towards us. He stepped forward, level with Gydion, shooting steadily into the opposing ranks as Gydion spun his staff.

'*Morgan!*'

The shout came from close by, full of panic. I glanced sideways to see the Enterocti Prince stagger, holding his shoulder, blood trickling through his fingers. His form flickered as he shifted from humanoid to his trueform, his eight strong limbs an outraged red as he ripped Tirian heartmoss from his belt and stuffed it over the wound.

'*You're dead.*'

Aster's voice was cold and full of caverns; his glowing eyes fixed on the Roth who'd shot the Prince. He disappeared; a moment later, the Roth was nothing but a pile of ash, and Aster gave a wild smile to the Roth rushing forward to circle him. 'Go on,' he taunted. '*Try me.*'

'Fuck,' Gydion muttered.

'Aster!' Maeve shouted, startling me with her closeness. 'Get the *fuck* back!' She spun, disarming a Roth whose eyes had fixed on Ashton. 'Take Morgan to the medic, you dick, or Tessa will gut you!'

Aster grimaced, but a moment later, he and Morgan were shimmers of darklight, and they disappeared from the field.

'This is not good,' Ashton grated out, stepping in front of Maeve and into the melee. 'I've got two more hits before my shield fails.'

'Then let me go ahead, you oak-brained pillock,' Maeve snarled, shooting two Roth neatly after Ashton took them down.

'With all due love and respect, *karia*,' Ashton answered calmly, 'you can fuck right off.'

Maeve muttered something under her breath, then glanced wide-eyed at me. '*Lanir*! To your right!'

I turned, raising my arm just in time. A Roth had slipped past Gydion and Kyin, both engaged with other Roth, and loosed two shots at me. The air glowed blue as my shield failed; I returned fire, but not before he shot again.

At Kyin.

Whose shield didn't glimmer.

It will be fine, I thought. He still had his ring with its personal shield, and –

And he'd given it to Claire.

The shot took him in the lower back. Everything around me froze as he fell with excruciating slowness, crumpling on the red clay.

My ears began to ring.

'*Kyin!*' Gydion roared, falling to his knees. '*No, no, Ky, no.* Vesper! Kyin needs a medic, now! Goddess damn it, *Vesper!*'

I glanced across the field. Alcide and Fiach were still fighting, their swords ringing through the battle. Alcide's expression was blank, but his auburn hair was damp with exertion. Fiach's face was weary, but his blows remained strong, while Alcide was clearly starting to falter. Vesper met my eyes, his expression full of sorrow.

I hated him in that moment, but I understood. He wasn't leaving Alcide's side. Not for Kyin, and not for *anyone*.

'No, no, *no*, Ky,' Gydion was pleading, trying to find Kyin's pulse, to shake him back awake, to cover the wound on his back, which was open and leaking and everything wrong. Tears were pouring down Maeve's face, and she and Ashton stood in front of them, protecting Gydion from the oncoming Roth line.

They wouldn't last forever. Even as I watched, Ashton's shield glowed blue.

'Love you, Maeve,' he said calmly.

'*Fuck you*, Ashton,' Maeve snarled back. 'Don't you *dare* think –'

I saw a red-horned Roth step forward and raise his gun.

I inhaled slowly, then threw my arms out, dropping my weapons. My skin flared, glowing iridescent, as the *elya* around me – inside me – answered my call.

My love was on the clay, but I wouldn't let anyone else join him.

My head tipped back towards the polluted sky as I drew the *elya* in. Usually, I had no need to call it to me in such a way, but today wasn't a *usual* day.

I drew in all the pain, all the fear, all the exhaustion and suffering and rage. I drew it in, and I held it, pulling it all into a ball inside me, everything that I could feel from the beings around me. I held it, and I added to it, layering my own terror and rage over the emotion from the battlefield, binding it together with my devastation at the sight of Kyin lying on the clay, my soul-shattering heartbreak at seeing my love's blood running from his terrible wound. I layered and I layered, and I packed it all together tight.

For a moment, the air itself trembled, the *elya* around me blindingly white.

I exhaled, and I let go.

The rippling flow of power smashed outwards, throwing every being in its wake backwards. They shrieked and shouted and screamed and sobbed as the emotions from the battlefield tore through them, slamming them into the ground, the overwhelming mess of sensation keeping them there.

And then, without mercy, I followed that terror and rage and hatred and suffering with a wild wave of my own grief, fresh and devastating and rending, as if my heart had been torn in two then pulled from my chest still beating.

Maeve screamed, the sound almost animal in its desperation, tearing from her throat as she lay on the sand, frantically reaching for Ashton. It brought me back to myself and I dropped my arms abruptly.

I was the only being on the field still standing.

And the only one still with their wits – apart from Alcide.

The Roth King stumbled to his feet, his sword in his shaking hand, and he drove it straight through the chest of Fiach Redhands.

The rebel's dying gasp echoed across the field, and an eerie silence fell.

I crumpled to my knees, reaching for Kyin and Gydion, but the world went black before I could touch them.

GYDION

I DRAGGED MYSELF UPRIGHT. Every muscle hurt, and my entire body was trembling from the wave of emotion that Lanir had sent across the field. I glanced across at him; he was curled on his side, entirely still.

Too still.

'*No,*' I whispered. *No. Not both of them. The Goddess could never be so cruel –*

The air glowed, and Aster materialised a moment later, leaning down next to Kyin. 'Fuck,' he swore. 'Their light is ... Come on,' he said to me. 'You'll need to touch me so I can take all three of you.'

I reached out and touched his arm.

Kjidja, it turned out, had an odd reaction to starlings' mode of transport: everything went white, and all sensation disappeared. When the world materialised once more – or I materialised within it, either one – Morgan shoved a bucket under my chin, clearly expecting something. I straightened and blinked at him; he raised an eyebrow.

'All right then,' he said.

His shoulder was bandaged and he looked pale, as if he'd lost too much blood. There was a rumpled cot behind him where I suspected he should have been lying down, if Willow's exasperated sigh was anything to go by. Rows of cots stretched behind him to either side of the narrow tent; Aster had brought us to the field medics. I'd been under the impression that Willow was going to stay in the Spire, but he must have rushed to the field after Morgan's injury.

'This one's an emergency,' Aster said grimly, laying Kyin gently on a free bed. 'That one ...' He glanced at me, then at the cot where Lanir lay prone. 'That one, I don't know what's happened. I can't feel him at all.'

I swallowed. 'Please, I –' My knees abruptly gave out and I folded to the floor. 'Please.'

Willow immediately went to work on Kyin, examining his wound before running a scanner over the damaged flesh. I swallowed, noticing what was clearly bone beneath the mess of flesh and red pool of blood. Another medic hovered over Lanir, frowning at the readings on his hand scanner.

'Nothing,' the medic murmured, his frown deepening. 'The scanner isn't even ...' He smacked the scanner against his thigh, then examined Lanir's eyes, then tried to find his pulse. 'There's no response.'

I cradled my head in my hands.

There was a flare of darklight as Aster disappeared. A few moments later he was back, and a warm hand slid over my shoulders. 'Gyd,' Claire choked. 'Oh, Gydion.'

I turned to her, letting her take me in her arms, and I keened.

She rocked me like a child, her tears falling on my neck. She would have seen everything, I realised. She would have watched the livecast on a screen, watched as Kyin fell and Lanir levelled the battlefield. I replayed it in my mind, the moment I'd failed to protect Kyin, the moment Lanir let his grief tear him apart.

I would have given anything not to carry that memory, and to take it from Claire.

'It's damaged his spine,' Willow murmured to another Tirian medic. 'See the vertebrae here? The two cracks and –'

I put my hands over my ears.

'Gyd,' Claire said gently, prying them away. She took my chin in her hand and forced my eyes to hers. 'Gyd. Kyin's still alive. If he's breathing, there's hope.' She searched my face, her lovely eyes red and shining with tears. 'You need to stay strong for him. We can't expect him to fight if we don't.'

'Lan is gone,' I said flatly.

Water spilled down her cheeks, but she held my gaze. 'Maybe they're wrong,' she said, her voice fierce. 'Maybe there's something –'

White light flared in the tent.

'That's my trick,' Aster said.

'El?' I looked up to see Willow's eyes go wide with shock. 'El, beautiful, what are you –'

A silver-haired Tirian female gave him a sweet kiss on the cheek. 'Sorry I'm late,' she said, her hair and skin lit from within with a white glow so strong it hurt to look at.

'*Late*? El, you're not supposed to be here.'

The female settled next to Lanir's bed, ignoring Willow. 'Oh, you've been careless, haven't you?' she chided gently, looking down at my mate. 'You gave all of your *elya* away.'

'Elswyth ...' Willow trailed off as she took Lanir's hand. 'My love, what –'

'The heartree told me I'd need extra today,' she said. 'That's why I was late. *Not enough*, she kept saying. *Not enough*. Now I understand.' She looked across at me and Claire, her eyes soft with compassion. 'I saw what he did. It's the bravest thing a being can do, to release their *elya* like that. It's like offering your beating heart on a platter.' She stroked Lanir's hair back from his face, wiping the red dust from his cheeks. He didn't stir. 'Luckily, I can help.'

Her glow brightened, so much my head began to throb with pain. All the beings in the tent shielded their eyes but Aster, who watched interestedly, his head slightly cocked to the side.

'You can have some of mine,' Elswyth whispered, and the tent went white.

Claire cried out, pressing her face into my chest. I held her tightly, praying.

When the light faded, Elswyth swayed, the glow beneath her skin gone. Willow caught her and lifted her into his arms. 'El?' he said anxiously.

She patted his face. 'I'm fine, Will. I've just never done that before.' She seemed to notice she had an audience, and flushed a deep green. 'Um. Where are Maeve and Ashton?'

'Still on the field,' Willow answered, glancing at a screen on the tent wall. 'But their readings are normal, so I'm assuming they're unharmed.'

Elswyth nodded. 'Oh! Look. He's back.'

A moment later, Lanir stirred, groaning.

My heart leapt up my throat.

Willow put Elswyth gently aside, then swiftly moved to Lanir, studying his scanner. 'Organ failure,' he muttered. 'His hearts. Cedar!' he shouted; a moment later, another Tirian medic appeared. 'Oxygen, fluids for Type 3 humanoid, and the cardiac scanner – oh.' He blinked at his scanner. 'Ah. He's … He's stabilising?' He turned to Elswyth. 'My love –'

'He just needed a moment,' Elswyth said, smiling. 'His hearts are strong. The fluids probably won't hurt, though, Cedar.'

The medic nodded and left, reappearing a few moments later with a needle stamp. Lanir's body contained far less water than mine and Kyin's, and he'd get what he needed by a small injection of minerals and salts. The medic – Cedar – pressed the stamp gently into Lanir's wrist then stepped back to watch the progress on their scanner.

'Kyin –' Lanir groaned.

'Be still,' Cedar said gently. 'Your mate is stable, but needs surgery. They're prepping the machines now.'

'Gyd –'

'I'm here, Lan.' I got to my feet, holding Claire to my chest – I didn't want to let her go – and moved closer, to where Lanir could see us. 'We thought – we thought –'

'You went away for a moment,' Claire said thickly, when I couldn't continue.

'I'm back now,' Lanir whispered, then gave a wordless moan. 'My *everything* hurts.'

'Your hearts were failing,' Willow said. 'It's to be expected. Probably. I've never treated an Illisae before.' He moved out of the way as two more Tirians came to fuss with Kyin's bed.

'We'll take him now,' one said quietly to Willow.

'We want to be there,' I said, suddenly panicked. *What if something went wrong?*

'No,' Willow said gently. 'I understand – I really do – but you'll distract the doctors, which Kyin doesn't need. Better to stay with Lanir.'

'But –'

'Gydion.' Claire touched my face. 'Someone else has to look after Kyin, just for a little while. We can wait.'

I looked down at her, her big brown eyes worried. I dipped my head and buried my face in her neck, overwhelmed. She stroked my hair, and after a moment, I felt another warm hand on my back as Lanir reached out to touch me.

I sat on the floor with Claire on my lap, and we waited.

KYIN

I WOKE UP IN a tent, surrounded by strange sounds, strange smells, and strange males.

I was lying on my stomach, my head propped uncomfortably on a hard pillow. I went to roll over, and found myself held still by stretches of moss bandage. Irritated, I reached down to tear it away; my hand was caught by another.

'Don't do that,' Willow said firmly. 'You can't move yet, Kyin. The doctors repaired your vertebrae, but the healing is still fragile, and they need to work on it again tomorrow. There were too many other emergencies today for them to finish.'

'Emergencies?' I croaked.

'Mmm. Alcide managed to kill Fiach Redhands, but some of his followers weren't interested in surrender.'

'Gyd and Lan?'

I heard Willow's scanner beep. 'Both fine. Both sleeping next door. Gydion was unharmed, and ...' He trailed off. 'Well, I don't really know what Lanir was, only that he stopped the battle after you were wounded, and that gave Alcide the opportunity to finish Fiach. Elswyth said that he'd used too much *elya*.'

I frowned, and moved my arm, then yelped as pain shot down my back.

'Don't do that, Kyin,' Willow said, exasperated. 'You need to stay as still as possible.'

'Claire? Is Claire all right? Did the other human ... spawn?'

'Tessa gave birth, yes.' Willow moved into my line of sight; his lips quirked in a slight smile. 'And Claire is fine. She was worried about you and Lanir, but she's well.'

'Willow,' I said anxiously, 'where *exactly* is my injury?'

'Your tail is also fine,' Willow said, checking my eyes with a small light. 'It had to be numbed with a local anaesthesia because it's close to the wound, and it's in a sling right now. If you're still and the surgery goes well again tomorrow, you'll make a full recovery.'

I sighed with relief, because I didn't know what I'd do without my tail. Claire liked it, and I liked it on her, and *in* her, and wrapped around her, and I'd miss all those things and more if I couldn't use it.

'Willow,' I said a moment later. 'I'm *very* bored.'

Willow cleared his throat. 'Well, I'm very busy, so you'll need to work that one out for yourself. I'll send Claire and Gydion in when they wake up, but they need rest. Don't move or I'll sedate you again,' he warned, seeing me twitch my fingers. 'I'll be back in half an hour to check on you.'

With that, I was left alone – from what I could tell, anyway.

I hummed to myself for a bit, then recited the schematic from my favourite system circuit, then told myself all the things I was going to do to Gydion, Lanir, and Claire when I could move again, then counted the stitches I could see in the pillow near my face.

'Willow,' I moaned when I was done. 'I'm so *bored*.'

The light in the room flared; I blinked against it.

A dark-haired starling frowned at me, surprised. 'Why are you in our supply cupboard?'

The Roth behind him studied me. 'This isn't the cupboard, Vesper.'

'Well, it's unconscionably rude either way,' the starling – Vesper – said, waving a hand at me. 'Beings just lying about in private places. It's –'

'You're Kyin Crace,' the Roth interrupted. He was huge, looming in the small room, and one of his horns was broken at the half-way point of its backwards curve.

'Why does that matter?' Vesper demanded. 'He's interrupting our make up time.'

I frowned. 'Make up time? Claire says it make *out*.'

'No, make *up*. We had a fight, oh, ages ago now.' Vesper waved his hand again. 'And Anna told us to make *up*. So we have been. Often, ever since then. In cupboards, especially. Don't you think they're lovely?'

'Cupboards? They're ... all right?' I said cautiously, realising they were the Roth King's consorts.

Vesper gave a slightly unhinged smile. 'I like knocking all the things off the shelves.'

The Roth flushed, then cleared his throat. If the starling was Vesper, then the Roth's name had to be Callan. 'You fixed the comm systems,' he said to me.

'Yes?'

'Thank you,' he said. 'If you hadn't done that, we wouldn't have proof of Fiach's death. The priests broadcast it across the entire planet.'

'It was nothing,' I said dismissively, because it really hadn't been very difficult. 'Are the water pipes fixed yet?'

He shook his head. 'The pipes themselves, yes. The systems, no.'

'Oh,' I said, chastened. 'I forgot about Bryn.'

'He's fine,' Callan said, amused. 'He was complaining be-cause he arrived late to battle and only got to face three of the rebel soldiers. There's not so much as a scratch on him.'

'How lovely for him,' I said sourly.

Vesper drifted closer. 'That looks absolutely disgusting,' he said, studying my back. 'Why must organics be so very *messy*?'

'You like us messy,' Callan said.

'*You*, yes.' Vesper waved an encompassing hand at me. 'This nonsense is all very unpleasant.'

'I'll try not to get shot in the back next time,' I said.

'That would be for the best, I think.' The starling turned to Callan. 'I'd like to find a different cupboard now, Cal.'

Callan flushed again, then shot me an apologetic look; a mo-ment later, they were gone in a flash of darklight.

I sighed. Vesper wasn't boring, but I couldn't begrudge them making *up* time. And a little while later, Bryn poked his head into the room with a screen in hand, and I spent the next few hours with the big, gruff Roth, fixing the water systems.

'I want to walk.'

'You can't walk, Kyin.'

'Well, I want to sit up.'

'And how the fuck do you think you're going to manage that?' Ashton said, amused. 'You had a *hole* in your back, Crace.'

'So everyone keeps saying,' I said crossly.

'Kyin,' Claire soothed. 'It's just for a few more days. You can wait a few days.'

'You're being a giant child,' Maeve said bluntly. 'You nearly died. Stop being an infant. You're worse than Ash was.'

'Like you'd be any better in my place,' I shot back. 'You're only down here because you're bored, too.'

Maeve crossed her arms and glared at me.

I liked all of Claire's friends – they'd all visited over the last few days, even Tessa, with her tiny spawn in her arms – but Maeve was particularly fun to rile.

They'd moved Lanir into the same room as me, which made the view *much* better. He reached out and stroked my cheek. He was still pale, his cheeks stained pastel, and he seemed to move more slowly than usual, though both he and Elswyth assured us it would get better as his body recovered. 'Stop that,' he said mildly. 'They're down here to visit you. Stop baiting them.'

I kissed his palm and grinned.

The entire Spire seemed to have an odd vibe, as if everyone was holding their breath. Alcide's forces were busy rounding up the last of Fiach's soldiers, which meant the Tirians were sticking around in case they were needed, but they didn't have much to do. They were busying themselves with repairs and generally getting beneath the Roths' huge feet while Alcide dealt with the business of – well, actually becoming King.

'Tessa lent me her eReader,' Claire said. 'If you stop moaning, I'll read something to you.'

'Only if it's dirty.'

Claire's lips twitched. 'Oh, it'll definitely be dirty. It might even have tails.'

I pretended to consider it. 'That. I want dirty. I want tails.'

'Ashton?'

The voice came from his wrist screen. 'Captain?' Ashton answered, his brow furrowing.

'You're with Kyin Crace?'

It was a question that wasn't quite a question. 'Yes, Captain,' Ashton said warily.

Captain Peony sighed. 'Crace, we have to arrest you,' she said tiredly. 'I'm sorry.'

Claire made a small noise of surprise.

I swallowed. 'I understand.' I wasn't lying; it had always been a possibility – a *probability* – that the Intergalactic Council would assume I was my father's accomplice. 'But *just* me – right, Captain?'

'Just you, Crace. We managed that much at least.'

Relief coursed through me; at least Lanir and Gydion were safe. I glanced across at them. Lanir's expression was understanding, but Gydion was glowering – both at Ashton, and at me – as his claws extended and pricked his thighs.

'He can't be moved, Captain,' Willow said, taking Ashton's wrist so he was speaking to her directly. 'That is my medical opinion, recorded prior to this conversation, signed off by three other medics.'

'I know, Doctor. I've seen the notes. But he will have to be isolated, and access to him will be both restricted and monitored.'

I groaned. I was already going slightly mad. 'For how long?'

'Until the Council decides otherwise.'

'I don't understand,' Claire said tightly.

She was sitting close enough to touch, so I took a lock of her hair between my fingers, knowing it might be the last time for a while. 'My father. That ore he took from Earth? Not only was it an unsanctioned purchase, but he forged the permissions *and* sold the ore to both sides during a civil conflict.'

'But that's not *your* fault.'

'No. But I collected the ore and transported it for him. And I doubt –' I took a deep breath '– I doubt it's the first time he's broken multiple laws, and I doubt it's the first time he's used me like that.'

'The Council have files on forty-three infractions,' Peony said softly. 'Your name is in eleven of them, Crace.'

I closed my eyes. That was worse than I thought, and it was doubtful that *any* reasonable being would believe I'd been unaware of my father's actions – *eleven times.*

Stupid, I thought to myself. *So stupid.* I'd always known what he was – a sorry waste of stardust with a knack for filling other beings' needs – but I'd never thought he'd be *that* bad a father.

'At least there's a chance he'll get what he deserves, I guess,' I said lightly.

'If it means anything,' Captain Peony said slowly, 'I vouched for you, Crace. And I think I talked some of the Council members around by telling them that *you* started this investigation. It might be helpful,' she went on, 'if you had some other Council members supporting you. Even some dignitaries outside the Council itself.'

I had a feeling she was trying to tell me something, but I was too frustrated – and addled by painkillers – to work it out. 'Thank you, Captain,' was all I said.

Maeve frowned at me, then tugged on Claire's arm. 'Come on,' she said abruptly.

Claire blinked at her. 'What? No, we have to do something! Kyin can't stay here by himse –'

'He has to,' Maeve interrupted. 'Say goodbye, then come with me.'

'Gods, Maeve, I thought we were ... Well, I didn't think we were *enemies*,' I muttered.

She waved a flippant hand. 'Yes, I'm very mean. Hurry up, Claire.'

Claire knelt beside the bed and brushed a gentle kiss across my mouth. Even with the painkillers – and the actual pain – my cock stirred against the bed at the soft touch, wanting more. 'He's still allowed the screen, right?' she said over her shoulder.

'I'm afraid not,' Willow said gently.

She looked taken aback then, like she'd just realised this was serious. 'We'll work something out,' she whispered to me, pressing her forehead to mine. 'We'll come back and see you, Kyin.'

'I know you will, little one.'

'*Claire.*'

'Fuck, Maeve, *okay*,' Claire said crossly. 'I'm coming.' She squeezed my fingers one last time, then stood. 'Just ... *Please* let him have a book or something. He'll go insane if he doesn't have something to do.'

Willow's reply was lost as Gydion crouched down beside me, stroking my hair back from my face. 'Ky.'

I searched his expression. 'I'm scared, Gyd.'

'I know.' He kissed my forehead, my eyes, my nose. 'We won't let this happen.'

'It's already happening, *core*.'

He looked frustrated; this wasn't something he could fight with his spear and claws. 'I'll talk to Ashton. I'll get as much information as I can. Try to figure out our options.'

I closed my eyes. 'Just ... Look after Claire and Lanir, Gyd.'

'Kyin.' He took my chin; I let myself get lost for a moment in the lovely green of his eyes. 'We'll get through this. The Goddess wouldn't have given you back just to snatch you away again.'

Wouldn't she? I thought.

Ashton helped Lanir from his bed; he swayed when he stood. I hated seeing him like that, especially when I couldn't do a thing about it. Every instinct in me screamed to get up, to help, to nurse him back to health, but instead I was stuck in a stupid position in a stupid sickbed, and even when I could walk again, I'd still be imprisoned.

Lanir reached down and touched my face, running his fingers along my jaw. 'Have faith, my love,' he murmured.

'You and Gyd will have to forgive me, but I find my faith rather thin at the moment,' I said tersely.

Lanir gave me a serene smile. 'Not faith in the gods, Kyin.' He bent and pressed a kiss to my cheek, swaying again when he straightened. 'See you soon.'

A moment later, the room was empty, and the door gave a reproving beep as Willow gave me an apologetic look and locked it behind him.

'Fucking fantastic,' I said glumly.

# CLAIRE

'MAEVE. *MAEVE*,' I SAID, hurrying after her. I took a deep breath. 'Maeve, I don't understand. You said you *liked* Kyin. I'm really … That really upset me. *You* really upset me. I don't know when I'll be able to see him again, and I didn't get to say a proper goodbye.'

'I know,' Maeve said, striding down a corridor I hadn't seen before. 'I'm sorry I upset you, Claire. And I *do* like Kyin. He's fun.' She turned a corner. 'But the faster we get this done, the better for everyone.'

'The faster we get *what* done?' I said angrily. 'I don't think you're listening to what I –'

Maeve stopped before a door and banged loudly with her fist, despite there being a communication screen on the wall. 'Anna! Open up!'

'Anna?' I repeated, confused. 'Maeve, what –'

The door opened a moment later, showing a sitting room the size of my entire apartment. The walls were covered with blossoming vines, and fairy lights hung from the ceiling, making it look like a faerie's grotto. Anna and Alcide were sitting at a table; Anna was looking towards us with a curious smile, while Alcide continued flicking through something on a screen he held before them both. A mouth-watering scent filled the air, coming from another room; I assumed Anna was responsible, if only because she got territorial about her kitchens. Vesper and Callan were sitting cross-legged on the floor, playing ...

Chess?

'The pawns don't move like that, Vesper,' Callan was saying, exasperated.

'Why not?'

'Because of the *rules*.'

'But I *want* that one to move like that,' Vesper said, unrepentant.

Callan's nostrils flared.

Alcide looked up from his screen. 'Hullo, Maeve,' he said levelly. 'From past experience, I'd say you have approximately seven minutes before that game turns into an all-out brawl or an all-in fuck, and either way, Vesper won't care whether you're watching. What can we do for you?'

'Kyin Crace,' Maeve said without preamble. 'The Council have taken him into custody. Make it stop.'

I gaped at her.

'Make it stop?' Alcide frowned. 'How, exactly?'

Maeve waved a hand. 'I don't know. In a *kingly* way.'

'I'm not sure it works like that, Maeve.'

'My Captain said she vouched for him. Do the same. Tell the Council he's of good character and sound mind or whatever, and that you don't think he's guilty of his father's crimes.'

'The Council is annoyed with me,' Alcide said carefully. 'I've already asked them for rather a lot. I'm not sure that –'

'Kyin fixed the comm systems so that *your* troops would know your orders,' Callan interjected.

'Claire spotted the stolen burrower well before the radar picked it up,' Vesper pointed out. 'And we *know* Kyin's big blue mate saved your ass on the field.' The starling jumped one of his knights to the opposite side of the board to flick Callan's king over. 'You weren't winning before he did that, husband.'

'Thanks, Vesper,' Alcide muttered.

'I didn't say you weren't doing *well*. Nor that it wasn't an ass worth saving. That outfit really is – '

Callan cleared his throat. 'Perhaps you could petition the Council. Let them know what Kyin did.'

Alcide's frown grew deeper. 'I don't think –'

Anna stood, and the three males fell abruptly silent, turning their faces towards her. '*I* think,' she said softly, 'that Claire and her mates helped give you victory, Alcide. And now one of them needs *your* help. *I* think,' she went on, 'that you can petition the Council *and* ask Morgan's mother to do the same. Kyin and Lanir helped save Natare's crown prince, after all. She owes them, too.' Her eyes flickered to me. '*And* Claire helped deliver her granddaughter. The least the Queen can do is add her signature to your petition.'

Maeve grinned. I stared at Anna, trying to keep my jaw off the floor.

Anna flicked her hair over her shoulder. 'I'm going for a walk with Maeve and Claire,' she announced. 'I imagine I'll be gone long enough for you to write the petition and contact Morgan's mother. Don't distract him,' she said to Callan and Vesper.

Vesper grinned. 'Yes, lodestar.'

Alcide caught her hand and pressed a kiss to her knuckles, his black eyes flaring. He didn't say anything, but Anna flushed, letting him brush another kiss over her palm before she pulled away.

'Anna, I'm sorry,' I said anxiously, once the door had slid closed behind us. 'I didn't know ... I didn't mean to cause an argument.'

She flicked me a surprised glance. 'Oh, Claire, no. That wasn't an argument. Alcide is so focused on fixing Scytha that he's not thinking properly about anything else. Sometimes he just needs a reminder that other things are important, too.' She smiled. 'And it means he'll take the night off to apologise for neglecting his wife and husbands, which means he might actually sleep tonight. That was a win for everyone.'

'I *definitely* meant to cause an argument,' Maeve said, still grinning. 'Also, Tessa is pissed off that you haven't come to see her yet, Anna.'

Anna blinked. 'I thought she might want space.'

'I think she needs *interruptions*. Morgan is being ... well, *Morgan*, and there's only so much of it any being could take. He tried to *feed* her the other day, for fuck's sake. Tessa almost stabbed him with her fork.' Maeve turned a corner. 'His wound didn't help. She was almost as overbearing with *him* as he is with her.' She stopped outside Tessa's room and knocked. The door slid open, but Maeve didn't go inside. 'El?' she said instead, surprised. 'What are you doing, beautiful?'

Elswyth was standing at one of the room's huge windows, Tessa's daughter in her arms. '*Karia*. Do you want to hold her?'

'Um,' Maeve answered blankly. 'Not just now.'

Anna coughed, stifling a laugh. 'Where is Tessa?'

Elswyth inclined her silver head towards the bathroom. 'Having a shower. The males are giving her a break.'

'Sensible,' Maeve muttered. A crease appeared between her brows. 'I thought you were on the peacekeeping ship, El.'

'I was,' Elswyth said, smiling at the bundle in her arms. 'But she's so sweet, Maeve.'

'Fucking hell,' Maeve said under her breath.

'It's just a *baby*, Maeve,' Anna said archly, dragging us both into the room. 'Anyone would think you're *scared*.'

Maeve shot her a glare and waved the door closed behind her.

'Oh, thank God.' Tessa's voice came from the doorway; she was wrapped in a robe and raking product through her wet curls. 'I thought you were Morgan.'

'How are you feeling, Tessa?' Anna said.

Tessa considered it. 'Okay, I think. I'm still very weepy and occasionally a bit sad. And even though Cy and Willow healed me after, I still feel like I've run a fucking marathon. And then there's the whole business of my organs returning where they belong, which is fucking *weird*.' She winced, then smiled at Elswyth. 'The lack of sleep probably doesn't help, but having three partners and an extra auntie certainly does.'

Elswyth beamed, light shimmering from her hair.

There was a sunken lounge in one corner of the room; Anna led us there, smiling as Elswyth passed the baby to her. 'Goodness. She is the sweetest thing,' she said softly, touching the baby's fine blonde hair. 'Does she – ah – is she –'

'Does she have tentacles?' Tessa offered, smiling, wiping her hands before joining us on the lounge. 'She hasn't shifted yet. Apparently, it's fairly normal for cephalopod babies to stay in one form for months before they begin to shift between them and try to swim.' She exhaled. 'That will be a *time*. Morgan and Aster can deal with that part.'

'Claire?'

Anna offered me the baby and I took her, cradling her in the crook of my arm. She really was beautiful, with her tiny nose, her dusting of blonde hair, and her lips pursing as she slept. 'She's lovely,' I said softly. 'Have you thought of a name?'

Tessa hesitated. 'I thought maybe Naida,' she said shyly. 'It means *water nymph*, from the ancient Greek naiads.'

'Naida,' Elswyth echoed. She smiled. 'Perfect. Absolutely perfect.'

We stayed with Tessa and Naida for half an hour or so, until Morgan burst into the room as if he'd been gone for months, Aster and Cy following more sedately behind him. Morgan took Naida carefully from Elswyth, rocking his daughter until his limbs changed from scarlet back to their usual sea-green. Cy crossed the room, giving Tessa the searching look that I knew to be him using his scanners to check for harm; Aster's expression remained anxious until Cy checked Naida, too, and gave the starling a tiny, relieved nod. For all she'd complained about needing a break, Tessa welcomed them back with enthusiasm, letting herself be wrapped in a nest of Morgan's limbs while Cy and Aster had a turn cuddling Naida.

'Well, I'm out,' Maeve said, standing. 'This is nauseatingly domestic, Tessa.'

Elswyth raised a silver brow. 'You say that as if you didn't spend last night letting Willow and Ashton feed you star berries and rub your back until you fell asleep.'

Maeve narrowed her eyes. 'Traitor.'

Elswyth kissed her cheek. 'I need to visit my heartree. I'll bring more berries when I come back.' She disappeared in a swirl of white light.

Tessa, Anna, and I looked at Maeve.

'Oh, fuck off, the lot of you,' she said. She sobered, glancing at me. 'Claire, can we do anything for you?'

I shook my head; I hardly knew what to do myself. Lanir would need to stay in the infirmary until Willow let him out, and Kyin wasn't going anywhere. I'd find Gydion and we'd sit with Lanir, but other than that, my mind was blank. 'Not unless you know where I can find some paint, or a tablet and stylus,' I said wistfully.

Anna studied me, looking thoughtful. 'I'll find you something. That's perfect, actually.'

'Perfect?'

She nodded, though she didn't elaborate. 'Come on,' she said, holding a hand out to me. 'We'll go and visit your Illisae, and if Alcide hasn't petitioned the Council by tomorrow, I'll take matters into my own hands.'

Tessa extracted herself from Morgan's limbs long enough to give me a hug. 'I never thanked you,' she said softly. 'For being there while Naida was born. It meant the world.'

'You did all the hard work.'

She shook her head. 'Just knowing you were close by ... It helped a lot. Made me calmer. Let me focus. Thank you, Claire.' She glanced at Morgan, who raised a questioning brow. 'He'll call his mother later. About Kyin.'

'I'll do it now,' Morgan said quietly.

I bit my lip to keep from crying. 'Thank you. All of you.'

Maeve walked Anna and me to the infirmary, leaving us outside so she could train with Ashton. Lanir had been moved to one of the main wards; Gydion perched on a chair next to his bed. While the ward wasn't crowded, there were a handful of wounded Roth who called out to Anna.

Gydion pulled me onto his lap and I watched her speak to them. She wasn't trying to be regal; she simply *was*, speaking to the injured Roth with gentleness and grace. It had always been there, I realised, but her life on Earth hadn't let her shine in the way she did here. It was plain to see that the Roth admired their *Little Queen*, as they called her; for a species I'd heard so many bad things about, they treated her with reverence and respect, each of them basking in her attention when it came to be their time.

'She's perfect at this,' I murmured.

'She's found her place,' Lanir agreed.

I looked down to see him watching *me*, not Anna, his violet eyes thoughtful. He blinked and the expression fled, but not fast enough for me to wonder what he was pondering. I took his hand. 'How are you feeling?'

'Like I want to be in our bed,' he said, bringing my knuckles to his lips. 'I'm on the cusp of becoming as annoying as Kyin.'

Gydion snorted. 'That's simply not possible.'

My fingertips traced Lanir's bottom lip. 'Anna is going to try to help. She convinced Alcide to petition the Council, and Morgan is going to speak to his mother, too.'

'That's ... That's excellent news,' Gydion said slowly. 'The Council might listen to the Nataran Queen.'

Willow appeared on the other side of the bed. 'I know he doesn't think he needs it,' he said apologetically, 'but Lanir really should rest. Perhaps you could come back tomorrow, and we could assess whether he needs to stay longer?'

'That's the politest way I've ever been kicked out of anywhere, Willow,' I said, smiling. I leant down and kissed Lanir, shivering when he cupped my face and let his tongue trace my lip. 'We'll come back tomorrow.'

Gydion gave him a less restrained kiss, his hands bunching in Lanir's silver hair until Willow cleared his throat and ushered us rather more pointedly from the room. I waved to Anna, leaving her smiling at a Roth who'd lost an eye, then yelped as Gydion picked me up, cradling me close to his chest.

'Sorry,' he muttered, nuzzling my neck as he walked. 'I need … I just *need*.'

'It's fine,' I whispered, because it *was*, and I felt the same. I hooked my arms around his neck and let him carry me back to our room.

He settled me on the bed, then took my chin in his hand. 'You are not second choice,' he said quietly. 'I don't need you because I don't have Lanir or Kyin. I need you because I need *you*. Do you understand?'

I nodded, my eyes prickling.

'Words, little one.'

'I understand.'

'Then tell me what you want right now.'

'I want a shower, and then I want you in bed with me,' I said. 'I want you to finish what you started the other day. I want to feel you inside me. I want to feel –' my breath caught '– I want to feel safe. And you make me feel that way.'

He swallowed, his eyes flaring. 'I'll make you feel that way forever, if you'll let me.'

He stripped my jumpsuit off slowly, kissing me with excruciating gentleness, like butterfly wings on my lips, his tongue sending tingles through my body. When I was bare before him, he ran his hands over me, tracing the shape of my shoulders, my breasts, my waist, my thighs, his chest resonating with a deep purr. Without warning, he picked me up again and carried me to the bathroom, waving the shower on before stripping off and stepping in beside me.

We didn't speak; I didn't feel that I needed to. Gydion watched my every reaction so closely that words weren't necessary, not this time, when his attention was solely on me. It was the best kind of overwhelming, like his world had narrowed and I was his entire universe. When I tipped my chin up, his lips found mine. When I trembled, his hands found my ass and lifted me from the ground. When I bit back a moan, the head of his cock found my entrance and he pushed slowly inside.

I'd had sex before, some of it good, some of it bad, but I'd never made love. Not until I'd been accidentally abducted and known Kyin's playfulness, Lanir's gentle touch. Not until Gydion's cock was buried to the hilt inside me and he was leaning with his back against the shower wall, his arms holding me up, holding me close, giving me something to work against as I moved my hips in a slow roll, my body stretching slowly around his width.

It wasn't just *making* love, I realised. The ache in my heart simply *was* love. I loved Gydion, loved Lanir, loved Kyin. I'd seen them at their worst, broken and desperate, and I wasn't afraid.

I'd meant every word I'd said to Gydion when we arrived at the Spire. When it came to them, I wanted *more*.

I suspected I always would.

'Claire,' he groaned. 'My tie –'

I kissed him quiet. I knew what would happen; he'd explained it before. 'I know.'

'It might hurt.'

'I know.'

He rested his forehead against mine. 'I'll come inside you.'

'I know.'

He groaned again, this time wordlessly. 'I'll want it again. And again. I'll fill you up and keep you full.'

I kissed his cheekbones. 'I know.'

His eyes fluttered open; when he spoke again, his voice rasped. 'You're sure?'

'I'm going to talk to Willow tomorrow about contraceptives, but yes. I'm sure.'

His eyes flared. 'Other than our mates, don't say another being's name while I'm inside you,' he growled, nipping my neck playfully. 'The only words I want to hear are *Lanir, Kyin*, and *yes, Gydion, just like that.*'

I rolled my hips. 'Better make me say them, then.'

He spun us so that my back was against the shower wall. I watched him through half-closed eyes, delighting in the contrast between the coolness at my back and the heat of him before me. He held my gaze, then moved one hand up to cup my cheek; a moment later, he began to move.

His tie swelled as he did, stretching me slowly, rubbing up against some sweet spot inside me with every roll of his hips. He wasn't thrusting – he couldn't, not once his tie was starting to swell inside me – but his hips moved slowly, smoothly, his cock lodged so deep I could barely breathe, the pleasure-pain of the stretch flaring with every movement. I'd talked a good game, but deep down, I hadn't been sure that I *could* take his tie, but it expanded so slowly that my body adjusted as Gydion moved, my internal muscles clenching and softening as they ceded to his sweet intrusion. He was so deliberate, so controlled, as if he knew exactly how every shift of his body was lighting up my nerves, as if we'd done this a thousand times before.

'God, Gydion, *yes*, like that,' I moaned.

He chuckled. 'The next time you say those words,' he purred, 'I want you coming on my cock.'

The words sent a fresh stab of lust through my body; he changed his angle slightly, pressing against my clit with every roll. His free hand slid down over my breast, gently pinching a nipple between his thumb and fingers until every tug demanded an answering throb deep inside me.

'Goddess, I can *feel* that,' he grated out as my core clenched. 'Don't stop, little one. Let go, love.'

I whimpered as he tugged harder, rubbed against me faster, rolled deeper, and a handful of moments later, my body tensed and my core tightened and I broke apart in a crashing climax that left me boneless. Gydion held me still, rocking against me, driving me further and further, higher and higher, until I came again, the waves of the first climax barely breaking before he pushed me into the second, pleasure flooding all the way to my toes and fingertips, making me lightheaded.

When I came back to myself, I realised he'd carried me to the bed. He was still lodged inside me, stroking my back as I sprawled on his chest. 'Perfect,' he whispered. 'So perfect, little one. So beautiful, so lovely, so strong, so smart. So perfect, love.'

'Gydion,' I whispered.

I pushed myself upright, biting my lip as the position shifted his cock deeper. I couldn't move up and down, so I rocked back and forth instead, watching his pupils dilate, the diamond shape darkening the green iris. His hands went to my hips as I rode him, his eyes on my face, his lips parted as his breath came faster. His tie swelled further, stretching me to the point of pain, but I rocked until my body surrendered and the pressure broke into pleasure once more. Gydion gritted his teeth, his claws pricking my skin and his hips pushing up as his cock pulsed and warmth painted my inner walls. I studied the beautiful arch of his bared throat as he hissed my name, rocking gently until he caught his breath.

When he stopped shuddering, he touched my face. 'What do you need?'

'That again,' I breathed. 'You. *Please*, Gydion. Please.'

'Thank the Goddess,' he said hoarsely. 'Because I don't think I could stop, love. I don't think I can *ever* stop.'

'Then don't,' I said.

It wasn't until hours later that his tie calmed and he could slip his cock from inside me. He'd carried me back to the shower by then, which turned out to be practical; I was an utter mess and when he pulled out, my thighs were worse.

'Kjidja males are all over the breeding thing, hey,' I said, realising I'd probably be messy for some time. I ached all over, and my internal muscles were throbbing. I didn't think I'd be fucking *anyone* for a couple of days; at least, not until my core forgave me for asking it to do things it wasn't strictly designed to do.

Gydion slid soapy hands over my stomach. 'It's not usually so ... intense.'

'I like it.' I turned in his arms. 'But I *am* asking Willow for a contraceptive.'

'Ask Cy instead.'

'Cy?'

Gydion nodded, flushing slightly. 'Aster had a ... *chat* ... with us when he realised we had a human mate. Cy worked out a way to prevent pregnancy in humans, but it didn't work with Tessa because of Aster. He said it should work for you and Maeve, though.'

'Is it permanent?' I'd never really wanted kids, but I also wasn't keen on the idea of irrevocably changing my body.

'No. It doesn't have to be.'

'I'll talk to Cy.'

He buried his face in my neck. 'Out of all the humans we could have picked up, how were we so lucky?'

I couldn't answer that.

We tried to sleep, but after some time tossing and turning, Gydion wrapped me in a blanket and carried me back down to the infirmary. Despite my still-shaky legs, I didn't *need* to be carried, but I didn't exactly hate it, either, taking the opportunity to bury my face in Gydion's neck.

Lanir was awake, staring at the roof while the Roth around him slept. The moment he felt us, he rolled on his side, a smile flashing through the dark.

'That felt like a fun evening,' he whispered. Gydion settled me on the bed; Lanir wrapped his arms around me.

'You'll be there next time,' Gydion said quietly.

'I'm not jealous, Gyd,' Lanir said, as Gydion settled against his back. He pulled Gydion's arm around his waist. 'We've always needed time alone, as well as time with each other. That's the way we work.' He pulled Gydion's arm tighter. 'But I want your tie next time.'

I let out a surprised, breathy moan; the Roth across from us stirred.

Lanir chuckled under his breath. 'Needy little human,' he murmured into my neck, his voice full of affection. 'Lucky Gydion's not the only one of us with a breeding kink. If you let Kyin know that you're open to it, you won't be walking straight for weeks. I know from experience.'

I shifted restlessly, pressing myself against him, worming my way further into his arms.

He sent a wave of affection, calm and heady, then pressed a kiss to my skin. 'Sleep, Claire.'

And even though three of us were sharing a bed barely big enough for one, I felt as if I'd never been so comfortable.

KYIN

The Council waited until I could sit upright before calling their trial, which was nice of them.

Willow refused to clear me for an in-person sitting, and surprisingly, they listened to him, *but* it meant that I was questioned from the same room I'd been in for a week, when I would have agreed to go almost anywhere in the universe just for a change of scenery.

I'd never been before the Council, nor had anything to do with them directly, but they were imposing, even from behind a screen. Made up of the heads of state from across nine different Sectors, the Council was supposed to uphold the Intergalactic Pact, which immediately put me at a disadvantage, having recently abducted a being from a Category-3 planet, one of the things the Council strongly discouraged.

I didn't think they'd care it had been accidental.

'Kyin Crace,' the Council head intoned; I stared at them, fascinated. Lanir was the only Illisae I'd seen before, and this Mage was different to Lan in almost every way: small where Lanir was tall, slender where he was broad, their features rough where Lan's were sculpted. They were a rippling grey, with the white light of *elya* shining in the veins beneath their skin. 'You are charged with assisting your father, Xanthin Crace, with various criminal activities, on eleven separate occasions. We will go through each charge one-by-one, and –'

'We don't need to do that,' I interrupted. 'My claim for each is the same. I did not know what my father was doing. I do not dispute his involvement in illegal activities; in fact, I alerted Captain Peony of the Tirian fleet to his actions when I realised. But whatever *I* did, I did it unknowingly, believing that my father had the requisite approvals from official bodies. I had no reason to question his actions, or his motives, as no one else had done so, including, I might add, this Council, who benefited multiple times from his work. Each time, he presented me with the relevant approvals and dispensations, so you can add forgery to his list of charges, if you haven't already.'

The Illisae blinked. 'We'll cut to the heart of the stone, then. Crace, we know you alerted Captain Peony, but it seems highly unlikely that you were unaware of your father's actions on *eleven* different occasions.'

'With all due respect,' I said, as levelly as I could manage, 'I know that my father is smart, ruthless, and uncaring. What I *didn't* know was that he was acting illegally. As I said, he gave me what I thought were all relevant permissions. I thought I was acting within the bounds of the Council's laws and the Universal Pact. While I'm not denying I did those things, I was deceived into thinking they were legal. I can't give you my ship, and therefore the actual evidence, but I believe my mates have already provided testimonials swearing that they sighted the permissions. Please feel free to add the theft of my ship to my father's list of crimes, too – I paid for that Sidereal with my mother's money, so it certainly doesn't belong to *him*. I'm not sure what else I can give you, or what else I can say.'

'And the human?'

The question came from a Luncest male, his four eyes blinking as one; his iridescent scales glittered under the lights in the Council room as his antennae swivelled slowly.

'Do you mean my mate?' I said pointedly.

'The *mate* you took from a Category-3 planet,' the Illisae answered.

'Yes. I took her. She belongs with us.'

'We'll be asking her that,' the Luncest muttered.

I didn't answer.

'Three are willing to speak in your defence, including one of the Council,' the Illisae went on. 'We have signed declarations from Captain Peony of the Tirian ship *Forest Souls*; from the new Roth King, Alcide Severson; and from Her Majesty Orla Eventide, Queen of Natare. All speak of your good character and the assistance you gave willingly to the Roth King, assistance which ultimately helped support his victory. But we are not so convinced, Kyin Crace.'

Fuck.

I lifted my chin, inhaling, waiting.

'We have reviewed the evidence – such as it is – and as we cannot prove either way what your intentions were, and what you knew, the Council is pressed to act on the side of caution. Therefore, we sentence you to incarceration on the planet Everrule for six Darnagh years, with a review and the possibility of early release for good behaviour after four and a half Darnagh years.'

The words hit me like a blow. Everrule was a low-security prison planet where the inhabitants lived fairly normal – if closely supervised – lives, but *six years*. Six years without my mates?

I could barely last six *minutes*.

My tail thrashed behind me as I tried to gather my scattered wits. 'Councillor –'

'If I may.'

The interruption came from Alcide via a livestream; his stern face popped up on screen. I hadn't even known he was watching.

'The Council has recently granted me several favours and concessions, and I am grateful for each and every one. I come here today to ask for one more.'

The starling Council member let out a very organic-sounding sigh. They were in their trueform but had grouped their darkness together in a vaguely humanoid way, their eyes glowing golden. 'You are testing our goodwill, Alcide King.'

Alcide bowed his head. 'I am aware, Council member Astra. I would not risk testing it if I did not believe that Kyin Crace is innocent of these charges. I would, therefore, humbly propose that instead of incarceration on Everrule, Kyin Crace is instead restricted to Scytha, and spends his six-year sentence helping to rebuild the planet which his father most recently caused harm.'

I froze. If I had to be restricted, then Scytha – with Alcide in charge – wouldn't be the worst place in the universe. Maybe – *maybe* – I could still see my mates.

'I will, of course, be personally accountable for him at all times. He will be housed in the Spire, and his daily activities will be prescribed and monitored. During the six-year period, I will arrange for him to be presented to the Council without delay, whenever they should wish it.'

The Neph Council member's wings twitched behind them, their large eyes darting sideways to Astra – Vesper and Aster's parent. 'Is Scytha to become a refuge for criminals?'

'Only two of them, at my count,' Alcide answered calmly. 'And you are welcome to try to capture my husband again if you wish, though your latest attempts have not gone smoothly, and I can assure you from personal experience that he makes an exceedingly poor prisoner. In the last few weeks, he has returned everything you have asked for, along with quite a few things you did not. As his past … associates … seem unwilling to give evidence against him, your files on Vesper are now fewer than your files on Kyin Crace. I would also note the *lack* of criminal activity my husband has undertaken since his attachment to myself and my claimed. If the point of this Council is to maintain a peaceful universe, then you must admit, Councillor, that our marriage has done more to support that aim than the many years of law enforcement before it.'

I bit down hard on my lip so I wouldn't grin.

'If the Council would like to add other stipulations as part of Kyin Crace's restriction to Scytha, I am happy to consider them. However, this course of action would save the Council money, as *I* would be responsible for Crace's upkeep; it would recognise the tenuousness of the charges against him; *and* it would offer an appropriate reward for Crace's role in maintaining peace within this Sector. I should not have to remind you what would have continued, had the outcome of this war been different.'

The Luncest looked thoughtful; the Neph, nervous. Astra's golden eyes dimmed and brightened slowly as the starling blinked.

'We would be happy with this outcome,' the head of the Tirian Grove said, sitting back in their chair, their knuckles lined with thorns. They were white-haired with age, rather than with *elya*, and their skin had begun to mottle like bark.

'As would I,' the Nataran Queen announced, flicking her hair over one shoulder with a light-green limb. Morgan's mother was just as beautiful as her son, just as blonde, and looked just as likely to punch anyone she didn't like squarely in the face. I'd heard she ate her lovers – afterwards, one would assume – and that as a Princess, she'd lived for four years straight in the Pleasure Houses of Kirkoss, for which she certainly had my everlasting admiration. Most beings barely lasted a night.

'We will vote, then.' The Illisae gestured to his screen. 'You all know the rules; *yes* or *no*, with no abstentions.'

I held my breath. There was no way for me to know who else might agree, and who wouldn't. The Luncest didn't seem to like me much, the Neph clearly had some concerns, and the representative from Darnagh would no doubt have strong opinions about my father. I looked up, meeting Willow's calm gaze. He gave me a smile, but I noticed his fingers were curled into loose fists.

'The vote stands at ten *yes* and eight *no*,' the Illisae Mage said, seemingly a lifetime later. 'Kyin Crace, the Council has voted that you be placed into the care of Alcide Severson, Roth King, and are restricted to the planet Scytha for a period of six Darnagh years. The Council will send your official sentence – along with its stipulations – to you and to King Alcide within one

Scythan week. Until this has been finalised, you are to remain under constant watch and in isolation. Do you understand?'

I dipped my head, trying to look contrite. 'Yes, Council member.'

'Hmm,' the Illisae said, and cut off the comm without warning.

I stared at my reflection on the black screen, hardly able to believe my luck.

'Well,' said Willow, 'I'd start thinking of a *thank you* gift for Maeve, if I were you. No doubt she'll suggest some options, if you ask her.'

I got up and pulled a startled Willow into a bone-crushing hug. 'I'm officially a criminal and borrowing all of my credits from Lanir, but I'll buy Maeve whatever she fucking wants.'

# CLAIRE

'*What?*'

'The Council sentenced him to six years restricted on Scytha,' Maeve repeated, her voice gentle. 'They were going to send him to a prison planet, but Alcide intervened and offered to keep him here, instead.'

I was sitting down already, but my head still swam. 'So ... it's good,' I said blankly.

'It's better than it might have been, yes,' Maeve said.

I stared at my hands. It was still odd to see them clean of ink or paint, as they had been for some weeks now, but even without that, they were the same hands I'd always had – long, thin fingers, with callouses and slightly swollen knuckles.

'They were going to take me back to Earth,' I whispered. 'As soon as they could.'

Anna touched my shoulder. 'Someone will take you back, Claire. If that's what you want.'

I chewed on my bottom lip.

'I could ask the Captain,' Maeve offered. 'We were supposed to be heading to Tir, but I'm sure there's another Tirian ship that could take you. You'd be safe, and I could ask to escort you.'

'Or Morgan's mother could send someone,' Tessa chimed in. 'I don't think Aster could jump another being that far, but I'm sure that Orla could send a ship.'

Anna took a deep breath. I looked up to see her studying me, her hands clasped together. 'Or,' she said slowly, 'you could stay.'

I stared at Anna. 'Stay?'

I'd been assuming I'd go back to Earth, go back to my own life.

Go back to bookkeeping, and to my small bedroom in my shared apartment, and making art that I rarely shared. Go back to lonely nights and being frozen out by my family.

Go back without my friends, and without my males.

'On Scytha.' Anna lifted her chin. 'I've been thinking, and I talked to Alcide, and to Vesper and Callan, and we have some suggestions.'

'Some suggestions?' I repeated, before I could stop myself.

You're not a fucking parrot, Claire.

I inhaled slowly, catching the negative thought. *You're surprised. You're allowed to verbalise that. Extend yourself kindness.*

'Yes,' Anna confirmed. 'Some suggestions.' She paused. 'Kyin, obviously, will be staying here for four years, until the Council reviews his behaviour and decides whether the extra two years of his sentence are necessary. They have requested that he remain in Scytha City, and he reports to them every week for the first year, and fortnightly after that.' Her eyes were on my face, her expression very serious. 'Alcide thinks there's enough work Kyin could do for twice that time, so he won't be bored. But he wanted to offer something else, too.'

I waited, holding my breath.

'He knows Gydion trained as a Divine Guard, and Lanir completed his time within the Illisae diplomatic corps, too. Alcide wants them to help train his own personal guard. And to offer them positions within it, if they choose.'

I exhaled.

'And for you ...' Anna trailed off, smiling. 'This offer is from me, though Alcide very much hopes you will accept. The frescoes in the Spire. We want you to restore them, and use any blank walls you choose to paint more.'

A mixture of hope and excitement flared in my chest as I considered it. Those frescoes were beautiful, and if I could have my own wall space, too ...

I could paint scenes of the battle, I realised. I'd watched the entire thing unfold, and I could watch the footage again. I could paint Alcide facing Fiach Redhands, Callan and Vesper standing behind him. I could paint Maeve and Ashton, fighting back-to-back. And I could paint my own males, Lanir towering above a flattened field of warriors –

But people will see my work. What if I fuck them up? What if everyone hates them?

My heart started to pound and a flush of heat made me sweat. I inhaled slowly.

Acknowledge five things around you.

Tessa, sitting on the sunken couch opposite, her ash-brown curls flowing over her shoulders. Naida, nestled in her arm and propped up with a pillow, feeding quietly, her fuzz of blonde hair covered with a tiny yellow beanie. Maeve, perched on the edge of a couch cushion, her hair pulled back, her blue-green eyes intent. Anna, sitting next to me, light glinting off the circlet in her hair, a tentative smile curving her lips.

I looked down.

My hands, still free from paint or ink, poised, as if waiting.

What if I succeed?

'I don't know how to restore frescoes,' I blurted.

'Um,' said Maeve, wearing a strange expression, 'this is going to sound wild, but my mum took me to Italy when I was younger, and that's what we did. For six weeks straight. There are a few different processes depending on the level of damage, and I don't claim to be *good* at it, but I've done it before. I'm pretty sure I remember the steps.'

'And I know how to mix lime plaster,' Tessa chimed in. 'And what programs they use to create a digital image of how it should look, and how to colour-match the paint.' She shifted Naida from one side of her body to the other. 'I can ask Cy to create something similar.' She smiled at me. 'We can all do it together. You're such a fabulous artist, Claire. I know you'll create something amazing. You're the perfect person for this.'

Anna looked at me, expectant. 'What do you think, Claire? Will you ask your males?'

I hadn't been able to cry, not the entire time I'd been away from Earth. I'd been abducted, been dropped in the middle of a war, fallen in *love*, and I hadn't cried.

I burst into tears.

I cried until I was a shaking, sobbing mess, my nose running and my neck wet with tears. I cried until I was hiccupping, my throat was sore, and my eyes were swollen and stinging. I cried until I was wrapped in a nest of arms, and Tessa had tucked Naida into mine. Knowing my friends were there, supporting me, meant absolutely everything.

I didn't have to go back to Earth; everything I needed would be close by.

After a while, I heard Maeve's voice. 'Anna offered her a job, and she broke. She needs a bath and a backrub and to drink about two litres of water. You're good?'

'We've got her,' Lanir murmured, and then it was *his* arms around me, his lips on my forehead, and his chest I was nestled against. 'We've got her.'

'I know you do,' said Maeve.

I barely noticed the journey back to our room; I was too busy sniffing and rubbing my cheeks and generally trying to appear like someone who was holding it together.

'Claire,' Lanir whispered, as the door slid open. 'We have you. We're here. You don't have to hide from us.'

I looked up at him, swallowing.

'Plus,' he murmured. 'You *can't* hide from me, my love. Not even if you wanted to.'

'I don't want to,' I croaked.

He brushed a kiss over my forehead. 'I know.'

'Claire.'

The whisper echoed through the empty corridor. I turned, searching.

Nothing.

I frowned. I'd spent the day practising making plaster before studying one of the smaller frescoes, taking pictures of it and planning to recreate it in our bedroom before I moved on to restoring one of the real things. I'd been in the corridor for hours; my body was chilled, I hadn't eaten since breakfast, and it was possible I was hearing things.

'This is your warning, Claire.'

Not hearing things, then. 'Gyd?' I turned again. 'What –'

A low chuckle thrilled through me. I turned once more, but he was nowhere to be seen. 'We've waited long enough, Claire.'

Warmth flooded my body. I licked my lips, unsure. 'Gyd?'

'There's no one around, *cora*.' My toes curled at Kyin's low rumble. 'You're ours.'

'Kyin –'

'No one to save you, little one,' Gydion purred.

I spun, but the corridor remained empty. My heart fluttered like a bird; my breath stuttered. I pressed a button to close my tablet, then shoved it and the stylus into my bag. 'Where are you?'

'It doesn't matter where we are,' Kyin whispered. 'All you need to do is *run*.'

In a swirl of lust and nerves, I finally caught on. 'Kyin –'

'We're going to count down, Claire,' Kyin crooned. 'Five. Four. Three. Two –'

'*Run*,' Gydion growled.

I turned and fled.

A laugh echoed after me, low and filthy; a rush of footsteps followed. I sprinted towards our room, through the unusually quiet corridors, my uneven breath rasping in my throat even as my body flooded with adrenaline.

'You'll need to be faster than that, *cora*,' Kyin crooned; a hand glanced off my hip.

I didn't look behind me, just increased my speed as much as I could.

'I like you running, love,' Gydion agreed, his fingers brushing mine. They weren't even out of breath, the assholes; as I turned a corner, I wondered how much longer I could sprint for – or if I even wanted to.

Something – Kyin's tail, I suspected – flicked my ankle, and I stumbled. Gydion's hands found my hips and steadied me; he swiped his tongue up my neck then let me go. 'Run, Claire, or I'll devour you *right here.*'

I gave a breathy pant – it wasn't that much of a threat – then pelted around another corner, just outside our room – until I ran straight into a pair of huge blue arms, arms that caught me and swung me up. 'You'll need to be faster than that next time,' Lanir murmured. He adjusted me until I was hanging over his shoulder.

'Next time?' I said breathlessly.

'Gydion will want this often, little one. And Kyin just enjoys chaos, generally.'

'And chaos involving Claire, particularly.' Kyin ran a hand up my back. 'You look lovely like this. Our beautiful prize, just waiting to be played with.'

I shivered, though I was anything but cold now.

'She's trembling,' Gydion said. 'Inside, Lan.'

His voice was laced with command, and Lanir didn't hesitate. I wonder if it affected him the same way it did me, with the sudden and complete desire to do everything – *anything* – that Gydion asked, to give into his every whim.

Lanir shuddered beneath me, and I suspected that answered my question.

I thought I'd be thrown straight on the bed, but Lanir carried me into the bathroom and turned on the shower. I *was* trembling, so I supposed it was fair enough, but when Lanir proceeded to strip me naked while taking the opportunity to touch and kiss every part of my bare skin, I realised the shower wasn't *just* to get me warm.

'I caught you, so you're mine,' he murmured, as if he'd heard my thought. He bent to take a nipple between his teeth, biting gently before he straightened, his eyes on my lips. 'For a few moments, at least.'

I reached to pull him down for a kiss. 'You cheated.'

'Absolutely,' he agreed, his lips curving against mine. 'And I'm sure there'll be consequences. I can't say that I'm sad about it. Tip your head back, little one. There's plaster in your hair.'

I let my head fall back, standing still as Lanir gently rinsed my hair. I'd dyed the ends again, but chosen different colours this time – blue and violet and green and golden blonde to match my males' eyes and Lanir's blue skin.

'Mmm,' he murmured, his fingers twining through my hair, keeping my back supported with his free hand as my body curved like an offering. 'That's a very beautiful sight, Claire.' He bent to trail his tongue up my neck as his fingers left my hair, travelling down. 'Open for me.'

I spread my legs, giving him access; he wasted no time in pushing a long, thick finger inside me. I shuddered, trying to keep my breathing steady, but it was almost impossible when he touched me like that, so possessively.

'I'm taking you here tonight,' he said softly. 'Will you like that?'

I moaned.

His thumb found my clit and pressed down. 'You're not quite wet enough yet, Claire. You're going to come, just you and me, and then I'm taking you out for Gydion and Kyin to play with.' Inside me, his finger curled slightly, brushing over my g-spot. 'I don't think the game will last long tonight. They've been waiting for Kyin to be cleared for … physical activity.'

'Please tell me he didn't ask Willow to be cleared for sex,' I gasped.

'It's Kyin. Of course he did.' His thumb started moving in small circles, just where I wanted pressure; my hands came up to hold him, my fingers digging into his biceps as he played my body like an instrument he'd practised for a decade. 'More than once. He told Willow exactly what he wanted to do, in excruciating detail, until Willow discharged him from his care completely. I've never seen a being turn that shade of green.'

'Fucking Kyin.'

'That was rather the point, yes.' Lanir grinned, his pupils dilated and his skin glowing softly as he watched me writhe under his hands. 'Let go, little one.'

I moaned in answer, closing my eyes. A wave of lust and love – Lanir's – swept through me, and the fire of his arousal pushed me over the edge. My body clenched around his finger as I whimpered and he groaned, teasing shudders from my body with his thumb until I was clinging to him so my knees wouldn't buckle. He made a wordless satisfied sound, so pleased with himself that I bit my lip to hold back a smile.

'I can feel that,' he reminded me, pressing down again in a sweet act of revenge. I shuddered as an echo of pleasure shivered through me. He moved his finger, a caress followed by a gentle withdraw. He licked it clean; arousal surged through me at the sight. 'I think you're wet enough now.'

I let my hands wander over his shoulders, tracing the planes of muscle. 'Let the fucking commence, then.'

He laughed softly, then picked me up and carried me – dripping wet in every way possible – to the bed. Kyin and Gydion were already on it, kissing in their usual clashing way amidst the chaos of pillows and coverlets. Kyin seemed to think that humans required cushions for comfort, so he'd taken to stealing them from elsewhere – with Vesper as his accomplice – and leaving them on the bed for me. I'd return them to their rightful home the next day, but he wasn't inclined to kick the habit; he seemed to enjoy the challenge.

Lanir lay me down gently, claiming my mouth in a caressing kiss that left me just as breathless as his fingers had. It was always that way with them – their gentleness left me just as desperate as their hunger.

'What a lovely prize you claimed, Lan,' Kyin drawled, running his hand down my side, tracing the dip of my waist.

'Perfect,' Gydion agreed, his eyes flaring. 'Are you sharing?'

'Naturally,' Lanir said, nipping at my ear. 'She's made for sharing.' He gently pushed my knees apart and sank his fingers inside me; I flushed as three pairs of eyes narrowed on where his fingers disappeared.

Kyin traced my blush. 'I see you've staked your claim,' he said to Lanir. 'Do we get to choose ours?'

'Gydion's been inside her before,' Lanir answered, pumping his fingers as I gasped. 'It's our turn.'

Kyin's tail thrashed. 'Together?'

'Always,' Lanir said, and leaned across me to kiss him.

I panted as they kissed above me, so passionately my toes curled as Lanir's fingers continued to move. 'I, um, haven't done that before,' I managed.

'We'll be gentle,' Gydion promised, bending to trail his tongue up my calf before moving higher. 'If you want.'

'You're always gentle.' I closed my eyes as he kissed a line up my inner thigh.

His tongue licked around Lanir's fingers. 'Then lie on your side, Claire.'

The command was back in his voice, so I did as he said, Lanir pulling his fingers free and settling in front of me. I reached to unbraid his hair, kissing him deeply as the silver strands slipped through my fingers like silk. Kyin had thankfully divested Lanir of any remaining clothing, and Gydion reached between us to palm his cock, wrapping his fingers around Lanir's thickness. His size made me slightly nervous, but my body was aching for him, ready and willing, and I was almost dizzy with the need to have him – have *them* – inside me.

Gydion guided my knee up with his free hand, shooting me a rare smile as he did. 'I can't help myself,' he said, as if I minded – as if I wasn't silently begging for him to take charge of me, of *us*, to direct our pleasure and take his own. Because when it came to me and Gydion, that was the dynamic: Gydion said *jump*, I asked how high, and he made me scream with pleasure all the way down. I suspected that Lanir felt something similar, though Gydion pushed him harder, further, touched him more freely, more roughly. Kyin played on Gydion's side when it suited him, and against him just for fun, injecting his own brand of delicious chaos into every interaction.

I couldn't imagine how it could ever be less than perfect.

Lanir bent to seize my mouth as Gydion positioned his cock outside my entrance. 'Claire?' Lanir murmured against my lips. 'Yes or no?'

I shifted my hips so that Lanir's swollen head nudged inside me, Gydion keeping it in place. 'Yes, Lan. Please.'

His breath stuttered as he pushed forward. I gasped as he worked his way into my body; I wasn't the only one, Gydion giving a wordless hiss as he watched.

'Oh, Goddess,' he grated out. 'That's ...' He closed his eyes. 'I'm going to need a moment.'

'You don't have one,' Kyin said practically. He pressed a line of kisses down my spine, his hand caressing the small of my back before moving down. His fingers were already slippery with some kind of oil and when he circled me, I pushed back, a small sound of pleasure escaping my throat as Lanir rolled his hips at the same time, thrusting further inside.

'Slowly, Ky,' Gydion cautioned.

'Do you want *slow*, Claire?' Kyin enquired politely, as if he wasn't already on the way to pressing a thick finger inside me. 'Or do you want Lan and I to fuck you until you can't think straight?'

Lanir's hand went to my hip, holding me still as he thrust up. I shrieked as he bottomed out, throwing my head back and arching my body as it stretched to accommodate him, then Kyin pushed his fingers further inside me. Gydion's hand slipped between us and found my clit, pressing and pinching until I wasn't thinking about how big Lanir was, or how Kyin was stretching me, just whether Gydion would keep doing *that* until I came.

Lanir groaned. 'Gyd, you're severely overestimating my resilience right now.' He pressed his forehead to mine. 'You feel divine, little one. You *are* divine. But if you keep clenching around my cock like that, this is going to be over in less than a minute.'

'You didn't answer, Claire.' Kyin withdrew, then bit my neck gently as something that was decidedly *not* a finger pushed against my back entrance. 'Slow, or ...?'

I hooked my leg around Lanir's hip, then pushed until he lay on his back and I was spread on top of him, moaning as he shifted inside me. My body protested at the new depth with a sweet ache; I rocked back and forth until I adjusted, leaning on Lanir's broad chest. 'Not slow,' I begged. 'Kyin, not slow.'

I *felt* him grin as he positioned himself behind me. 'My perfect *cora*,' he whispered, and pressed inside my body.

Despite what he'd said – and what I'd begged – he took his time, pushing in inch by inch, giving a dark laugh every time I cried out or Lanir groaned. Lanir stayed still as Kyin worked his way in, murmuring a mess of endearments and expletives as my internal muscles clenched and Kyin nudged against him. When Kyin was fully seated inside me, Lanir pulled me down gently for a kiss; the tip of Kyin's tail stroked my thigh, then found my clit.

'Perfect,' Gydion crooned. He stroked Lanir's hair back from his face. 'So perfect. All of you.'

'What's it to be, Gyd?' Kyin said, rather breathlessly, moving slowly as Lanir rolled his hips and I panted. I was so full I felt pinned in place; I raked in air as if I were sprinting down the corridors again. Sensation sparked through me as Lanir made a strangled sound when Kyin rubbed against him, my males separated by a thin wall of muscle. 'You've got choices, *core*.'

'Such delicious choices,' Gydion crooned. 'So delicious, in fact, that I'm not going to choose at all.' I looked over my shoulder as he kissed Kyin, nipping at his bottom lip. 'You're simply going to suck me first.'

I whimpered, closing my eyes as Gydion positioned himself and pushed between Kyin's lips. Kyin groaned around his cock; his tail faltered for a moment, then resumed its teasing presses between my legs. A wave of pleasure rolled through me, my core clenching around Lanir and Kyin, the feeling spreading from somewhere deep and secret as they filled my body so completely I couldn't move, couldn't *think*.

A moment later, pleasure that wasn't mine shuddered over my skin.

I opened my eyes to find Lanir's gaze on my face. 'What –'

I broke off with a shriek as my body answered his wave of pleasure with another of its own. Before it had finished, Lanir was pushing another wave, and my body responded to *that*, until I was clawing at his chest and tears were streaming down my face. My body was at breaking point, pleasure building in endless coiling spirals inside me, every muscle tense against the continuous swell as Lanir pushed me higher and higher with shallow, rocking motions of his hips and waves of his own sensation.

Very carefully, Kyin's tail pressed down.

I screamed as I came, the feeling almost painful as the waves broke and I fell apart with them. Lanir gave a rough groan, grinding as he pushed the feeling of his own climax over me, pumping me full of his release. Kyin gave two hard thrusts before he did the same, his shout muffled around Gydion's cock. There was so much pleasure I was almost high on it, my body shaking and shuddering at its strength. Lanir was merciless, pushing the echoes of Kyin's climax until I was begging again and Gydion roared as he came, Kyin's tail working my clit until I followed him again.

When I came back to myself, the sun had set outside our open window. My body felt tense and loose all at once, empty and sprawled out with my cheek pressed against Lanir's chest, listening to the thunder of his double heartbeat. There were hands on my back, stroking and kneading, and another in my hair, teasing out strands and sending shivers down my spine.

'I didn't know you could do that,' I croaked.

'I was waiting for the right time to show you,' Lanir said, kissing the tip of my nose. 'It felt like now.'

'You've ruined me. You realise I won't settle for normal orgasms now. I'll never be able to fuck anybody else, because it couldn't ever compare to *that*.'

'Claire, *cora*,' Kyin said with uncharacteristic gentleness as he gathered me up and walked towards the bath, 'that is entirely the point.'

CLAIRE

I STEPPED BACK FROM the wall and studied my work, taking in the new colours with a critical eye.

It was good.

Better than I'd thought it could ever be.

It had taken time, but I'd finally reached a place where I was happy with my work. With Cy's image generation program, Tessa's advice on plaster mixing and colour matching, Maeve's guidance on the restoration process, a whole lot of research, and trial and error in my own technique, I was getting *good*.

The fresco was an important one, showing the Roth Sun King triumphant over a fallen battlefield. It was in one of the Spire's cavernous entrance halls, so it was important to me that it was restored well. And if I'd made the Sun King look a little like Alcide, and the Sun Queen look a little like Anna ... Well, no one would blame me, and the Roth King and Queen certainly wouldn't complain.

'Fuck.'

I turned, smiling as I wiped my brush on a cloth. 'Hey. I didn't think I'd see you again before you left.'

Maeve was looking over the fresco, her now-green eyes wide. Her hair was pulled back, showing the thorns along the pointed shells of her ears. They looked all kinds of badass, but she'd complained that she'd had to remove some of her piercings to accommodate the change in the cartilage beneath it. She'd have to start wearing her hair down once they got to Earth, I realised, and I knew that Cy had already made some contacts in her old eye colour.

'It's fucking amazing, Claire,' she said abruptly. 'You've kept what was there, but somehow made it yours all at once.' Her eyes followed the border of flowers I'd added around the outside – Nataran sea lilies, Tirian arcadias, Roth desert flowers, and Kjid ivy blossoms. 'Anna's going to lose her shit.'

'She already is.' Tessa appeared behind Maeve, shifting Naida on her hip. 'God, Claire. This is incredible.'

Anna stood to the side, her eyes bright with tears. 'Alcide is going to be so happy,' she breathed. She shot me a watery smile. 'I *knew* you were the right one to do this.'

I cleared my throat, flushing. 'One down, four hundred to go,' I said jokingly. 'Good thing I practised in our bedroom first.'

I'd painted and stripped our walls so many times that I was surprised they were still standing; Kyin swore he'd be coughing up plaster dust for the rest of his life.

I wasn't too worried; I'd made Willow check him the last time they'd visited, and Willow had informed me that everyone in the universe could perish and Kyin would still be standing, searching for someone else to irritate.

It was extraordinarily funny to watch Kyin poke and prod until the measured and diplomatic Willow snapped back. You wouldn't know it to watch them, but they were the best of friends; Kyin always moped for a week after the Tirians left.

Maeve shook herself. 'I could stare at this for hours,' she muttered. Naida held out her arms, and Maeve took her wordlessly from Tessa, settling the toddler on her own slender hip. 'I came to check that you're *sure* you don't want to come with us.' She glanced between me and Anna. 'Either of you.'

Anna shook her head, smiling. 'Not this time. I have too much to do. Thank you, though.'

I swiped the back of my hand across my forehead. 'Not this time,' I echoed. 'Probably not until we can take Kyin. He wants to go to Melbourne. He's developed an obsession with trams.'

'God, don't let him talk to Aster,' Tessa said. 'I've already had to convince him that we can't *just get on* the Gahn.'

'He and Elswyth are going to be trouble.' Maeve pressed a fingertip to Naida's nose; Naida giggled and stuffed her fingers in her mouth, chewing. 'As if it's not going to be hard enough convincing your daddy not to shift and frighten all the humans with his tentacles, we're going to have to manage those two and their habit of just fucking off whenever the fancy takes them, no matter where they happen to be.' She switched Naida to the other hip. 'You're much better behaved.'

Tessa flicked me a glance, her lips curled up at the corners, as we all pretended not to stare at Maeve. 'Another two years isn't too long to wait.'

I smiled back. 'No. Not long at all. Give your mum a hug for me, Maeve.'

She nodded. 'I will, seeing that I'm fairly sure Tessa's cousin will have *words* when he sees me. I'm going to need all the hugs I can get.'

'Rian will be perfectly polite,' Tessa said mildly. 'He's a gentleman. And luckily, Naida loves hugs.'

Naida solemnly smeared her saliva-covered fingers down Maeve's cheek.

'Okay, that's me out,' Maeve said, and gave her back to Tessa. 'Let's go, before Morgan gets his tentacles in a twist.'

Tessa gave me a one-armed hug. 'This really is beyond words, Claire. See you in a few months.'

'What she said.' Maeve pulled me into a tight embrace. 'Send us a cast if there's anything you want us to bring back.'

'A sackful of chocolate,' Anna reminded them. 'The generators just don't do it right.'

A thought struck me. 'Will you visit Advena?'

Tessa and Maeve exchanged a glance. 'We thought we'd leave that until we were all there. We thought ... We thought we'd wait to do it. Together. Whether the club is still there or not, it's still the place that everything started.'

I nodded. Even though we hadn't left Advena as a group, it *felt* as though we had. With Tessa and Maeve spending six months of each year on Scytha with Anna and me, we were closer than we had been on Earth, bound not just by work friendships, but by experience and adventure and love.

It was nice. It was *more*, somehow, than it ever could have been back home. We were part of each other's lives, part of each other's *families*. I surreptitiously eyed Anna, whose face had rounded slightly in the last month, and who seemed to be favouring looser clothes than she normally did. Soon, it wouldn't just be *us* who would rely on that; it would be the next generation, too.

Maeve and Tessa gave us one last hug – I let Naida pull on my rainbow hair for good luck – then they left the hall for their first Council-sanctioned visit to Earth.

'Next time,' Anna said.

'Do you miss it?'

She smiled at me. 'No. I think ... Even though we didn't choose to leave like Tessa and Maeve did, I can't help but feel it was still the right thing. I've made a difference here, and I don't think I ever would have had the courage or the opportunity to do that on Earth. And you, Claire ...' She trailed off. 'You were always brilliant, but here, you give yourself permission to live up to your potential in a way you didn't at home.'

'I couldn't,' I said softly. 'Give myself permission, I mean. Everything felt heavy there, like I was dragging weights around with every step. Here ... Here, I'm free.'

Anna took my hand and squeezed it. 'That's how I feel, too.'

We stood there for a moment, looking up at the ancient Roth King and Queen.

It wasn't just the place that had made me free, I knew. It was the journey here, too, and the things I'd experienced, and what I'd learned. It had allowed my strength to shine, given me space to prove to myself that I could do more than just cope with life; I could *live* it. I could take opportunities and make something of them, make something new, make something *beautiful*, and I could show that beauty to the world. I might still be anxious, but I could often acknowledge that feeling and move past it; I didn't have to feel it drag me down.

I still had bad days – weeks, sometimes. I always would. But I was better able to deal with them now, especially when I was surrounded by so much joy.

I glanced at Anna. 'So, when will you tell them?'

Anna flushed. 'How long have you known?'

I shrugged. 'A month or so. You're glowing.'

She gave a rueful smile. 'Vesper knows. And in exchange for keeping his mouth shut, he made me see Cy and Willow to check that everything was okay.' She squeezed my hand again. 'I suppose I should tell Alcide and Callan before Cy breaks down and we get a cranky cast from Tessa and Maeve.'

'Good plan.'

'You know Alcide will want another portrait, right?'

I grinned. 'I'll keep a booking open.'

I washed my brushes when she left. There were still a few details I wanted to add, but seeing the fresco all but finished gave me a sense of peace. I'd spend the next few days perfecting it, and then I'd move onto the next one.

'Fuck, *cora*.'

I turned to see Kyin walk into the hall, hand-in-hand with Lanir, Gydion following.

'By the Goddess, Claire,' Lanir said, studying my work.

Gydion slipped to my side and wrapped an arm around my waist. 'This is incredible,' he murmured.

I flushed. Even after two years, their praise made me hot in all the right places. 'Do you like it?'

'It's fucking amazing,' Kyin said, snapping an image with his wrist screen. Though he was technically serving his sentence, the Council had gotten more lenient with his access to tech after his father had been captured and sent to one of the prison planets. Kyin was allowed to contact his mother, and he loved showing us off, sending her casts of Gydion and Lanir training, whatever I happened to be working on, and just ... pictures. All the time. Of us doing completely boring, everyday things, like walking down corridors, eating, reading, lounging around.

He said those were his favourite.

I relaxed back into Gydion's arms. 'Which one should I do next?'

He nuzzled at my hair. 'I think the next one should be new. One of Alcide's battle against Fiach Redhands, maybe. So that anyone who visits will know what happened, and those who fought can see themselves remembered. And,' he continued, 'so you can create something that's all your own.'

I turned, linking my arms around his neck. 'That makes me nervous. Creating something from nothing. It's a big responsibility.'

He kissed my forehead. 'It makes you nervous, but not afraid.'

He was right. I wasn't afraid.

And I was already sketching the scene in my head. 'Lan, can you –'

He handed me my tablet and stylus before I'd even finished the sentence.

I slid down onto the floor, flicking open a new page to draw on. I outlined it swiftly, changing the composition a couple of times until I was happy, placing Alcide and Fiach Redhands in the centre, their swords clashing.

And to one side I sketched Lanir, waiting, glowing bright with *elya*. Gydion and Kyin were by his side, with Ashton and Maeve before them, their staffs held ready.

I didn't realise how long I'd been sketching until Kyin prodded me with his tail. 'It's getting cold, *cora*.'

They'd all settled on the floor with me; Lanir had stretched out, his head in Gydion's lap, his eyes closed as Gydion ran clawed fingers through his hair. Kyin's tablet showed he'd been working on improvements to the climate systems again, but had evidently gotten bored.

'I'll make you *limere* if you take a break, Claire,' he coaxed.

'You mean we'll get to the kitchen and you'll ask me to make coffee,' I said, fighting back a smile.

He waved a hand. 'Either way, we both win.' Without warning, he scooped me into his arms, making sure my sketch was saved before he plucked the tablet from my hands.

I mock-frowned. 'You're incorrigible, Kyin.'

He grinned at me. 'I believe that has been said before.' He turned, making for the kitchens.

'My brushes,' I protested.

'All cleaned,' Gydion said calmly.

'The paints –'

'All covered and put away.' Lanir grinned at me. 'It's almost like we know what to do, Claire.'

They *did* know; they'd done this before, too many times to count. So many times that they knew the way I liked to stow my brushes, that they knew exactly how long the paint could be left out before it dried, that they knew how to store the plaster I used.

'You're the best,' I said, resting my head on Kyin's shoulder. 'All of you.'

'That has *also* been said before. Usually you're naked, though.' His tail stroked my cheek. 'I told you we'd give you one hell of an accidental abduction.'

Extended Epilogue - Ten Years Later

A WARM HAND SLID over my hip.

I stirred, my eyes fluttering against the artificial dawn. 'It's not morning,' I croaked. 'I only just went to sleep.'

'Then it's still nighttime,' a voice murmured, breath tickling my ear. 'Everything is dark and quiet, and you're still tucked up in bed, warm and comfortable.'

The hand slid over my soft belly to settle between my legs, its fingers hot. Arousal spread through my body, sweet as mulled wine. My hips pushed up, seeking more. 'Aster,' I whispered.

'Shh,' he hushed, brushing kisses over my cheek and lips. 'I know you're tired, starlight. Let me make you feel good.'

I sighed, spreading my knees for him. 'Okay.'

His fingers danced lightly over my clit before moving down. They withdrew, and I heard a soft click before they returned, slippery with lube. Aster worked it over me, his breath coming quicker as his fingertip slipped inside. 'Stars, I've missed this,' he murmured. 'You're the heavens themselves, Tessa.'

I gave a strangled moan in answer as his fingers moved back to my clit and began to work. 'Oh, god.'

Morgan shifted beside me. 'You promised you'd wait,' he slurred grumpily.

'My cock is nowhere near her,' Aster said, moving down the bed to lavish kisses on my neck as his fingers kept working.

'It was implied that *everything* counted, Aster, not just cocks,' Cy said, a hint of reprimand in his voice. 'We wanted to do it together.'

'We're together now.'

'Were you three planning this behind my back?' I gasped. 'Because if you were –'

'There was no plan, *elyn*,' Cy said, placating. 'We just wanted to make you feel good *together*, that's all.'

I made a humming sound, pleasure sparking through my core from where Aster was touching me. A limb curled around my knee, holding me open. I heard Cy move on the bed, coming to sit near Aster, then bending to press a line of kisses up my calf.

I sighed again, melting beneath the combined weight of my male's attention. My body had been ready for this for a while now, but my mind hadn't; giving birth to twins would do that for you. Even though Cy and Willow had healed me afterwards, my body had changed, and was still changing. It had taken a while for me to get used to the new heaviness of my breasts, the increased softness of my stomach, my thicker waist and wider hips. And while I'd been learning my body's new parameters, I hadn't really felt like being touched, not when I was reticent to touch myself.

A hand brushed my cheek – Morgan's. 'I swear that every time I see you, you get more beautiful, starfish,' he rumbled. 'I don't know how it's possible, but it's true. Every morning, you're more divine.'

'Morgan,' I whispered, then cried out as Aster slipped a finger inside me, the heel of his hand pressing down where I needed it.

I was wet now, not just with lube. Aster sat back to watch my face, his unruly black curls falling into his glowing eyes. I pulled him back down for a kiss as Cy's lips caressed my knee, and then my thigh. Morgan dipped to trail his mouth over my belly, his limb snaking up to caress where Aster's finger was buried inside me.

'Fuck,' I said breathlessly, as my core tightened. 'Aster –'

'We've got you, starlight,' he said softly. 'All of us.'

I came with a moan, my body clenching on his finger. Morgan gave an approving rumble as the tip of his limb traced over my wetness; he leaned across me to give Cy a swabbing kiss. I watched them through heavy-lidded eyes, pleasure tingling through my limbs.

'Mmm,' Aster purred. 'This is my favourite way to start the morning.' He gently withdrew, then sucked his finger straight into his mouth, closing his eyes as he licked my moisture from his skin. 'And the most delicious breakfast.'

'Please tell me you'll eat something else,' I said drowsily. 'We have a big day ahead of us.'

There was a bang at the door. '*Mu-um!*' Naida shouted from the hallway. 'Aunt Claire said I had to ask you if I wanted another bowl of cereal.'

I tugged up the blanket to cover my body; Cy rolled off the bed reluctantly. 'How many bowls have you already had?'

'And of which cereal?' Cy added, pulling on a pair of jeans.

There was a pause. 'Two,' Naida said, disgruntled. 'Of the chocolate one.'

I bit back a laugh. 'Then no more, love. You can have fruit or toast instead.'

'Or I'll come and make you eggs,' Morgan added.

'Eggs, please, papa!' she sang, as I'd known she would. 'And mama – the twins are awake. They're with Aunt Maeve, but they're making hungry cries.'

'I'll get them,' Morgan said, pressing a kiss to my forehead. 'You three stay here.'

I grabbed him and dragged him down for a proper kiss. 'Tonight –' I started.

'Yes,' he growled, two of his limbs tracing my shape through the blanket as his eyes devoured me hungrily. 'Tonight.'

He pulled away and dressed quickly, then went to find the twins. They slept in the room adjoining ours, but Maeve had taken one look at the shadows under our eyes and offered to help as much as she could, which usually meant carrying them around the halls of the ship with Ashton when they woke up.

'I'll get you some breakfast,' Aster said, disappearing in a surge of darklight to reappear a moment later fully dressed. 'Toast? Or eggs? Or both?'

'Both,' I decided. I didn't usually eat a lot at breakfast, but breastfeeding made me fucking *hungry*.

He gave me a gentle kiss. 'I think Gydion made more of that juice you like,' he said, and disappeared again.

I sighed happily, then snuggled into Cy when he sat back on the bed. 'You were up for most of last night.'

He wrapped an arm around me. 'Just thinking about something,' he said vaguely. 'I'm sorry if I kept you up.'

I shook my head, breathing in the clean, fresh scent of him. 'You didn't. The twins did, and then I couldn't sleep.'

'Were you thinking about today?'

I nodded.

'How do you feel about it?'

'I'm not sure,' I said. 'I'm feeling a lot of things, all at once.'

Cy hugged me tighter. 'That sounds like a pretty human thing to me.'

A pair of matching wails came from outside the room. I caught Ashton's deep voice as he tried to soothe the twins.

I smiled. 'This is chaos, isn't it?'

Cy smiled back, his grey eyes bright with happiness. 'I didn't think I'd like chaos,' he said. 'But with you ... With you, it's perfect.'

'No fucking way.'

I bit my lip, staring.

'This has to be a joke.' Maeve stepped forward, shading her eyes so she could stare through the window. 'How –'

'They couldn't possibly know,' Anna interrupted. She frowned through the glass. 'Could they?'

'There's no way,' Claire pointed out. 'Like, *no way*. This is just a coincidence.'

'This is the *mother* of all coincidences,' Maeve muttered.

I started to laugh.

I couldn't help it. Advena was long gone, but in its place was another bar – and this one was *alien themed*.

The interior had been transformed into an otherworldly landscape, with tiny lights shaped like stars hanging from the ceiling; sparkling and smoking cocktails advertised at the bar; glowing lights around small, circular daises on the black dance floor; and ivy backlit by green light covering the walls. The booths each had their own colour theme, with their own flickering UFO-shaped lights casting gentle coloured flashes on the patrons below.

It was completely cringeworthy and somehow *wonderful* at the same time.

'What the fuck is that?'

I turned to see Morgan frowning into the bar. 'It's a bar, babe.'

He rolled his eyes at me. 'I know what a bar is, starfish. *That.*' He pointed.

I squinted at something hanging from the ceiling.

Cy cocked his head, studying it. 'It looks like a healing wand.'

I spun to face Aster, whose face was already split into a grin. 'It's a *probe*,' he said, delighted.

I laughed again; I couldn't help it. In the carrier, Stella stirred against me, her skin giving off a faint golden glow; I kissed her tiny dark head until she settled. Morgan had her twin, Sirius, cradled in one arm; Sirius hated both the carrier and the pram, but was perfectly happy to be carried about by one of his fathers, who were all equally happy to oblige.

'Do we ... *go in*?' Anna said hesitantly.

We all stood in silence for a moment.

'It's weird,' Maeve said, 'but I think I'd prefer to remember Advena how it was.' She squeezed Elswyth's hand. 'Good things happened there, after all.'

'I want to see the garbage bin Callan kidnapped you from,' Vesper said to Anna.

'For the last time, Vesper, I wasn't in a bin.'

'That's not what I heard.'

Anna made an exasperated noise, though her lips twitched up. '*Fine.*' She dragged him down the street and presented him with a nondescript corner, bin-free.

'Why did we bring him, again?' Aster muttered.

'Because he's your twin and you love him,' Cy said. 'Also, no one could work out how to leave him behind.'

Morgan snorted. 'Look,' he said to Sirius, who was completely and entirely asleep. 'This is where your daddy first saw your mama and convinced her to have sex with him.'

'Morgan,' I hissed, trying not to laugh again as a human walked by, eyeing him.

'What?' Morgan said, unrepentant. 'They should put up a plaque.'

'*The first Advena Abduction, Tessa Wilding, who is completely fine and living a very happy life several Sectors away, decided to have sex with an alien here,*' Maeve said, grinning. 'Really flows off the tongue.'

'Don't you *dare*,' I muttered to Aster, whose face had taken on a familiar *this-is-happening* look.

He grinned and kissed my forehead. 'I promise nothing, starlight,' he murmured.

I stared at the door, no longer cherry-red, the white neon sign above it simply reading *Open*. 'I've always wondered if there was something special about it,' I mused. 'Advena, I mean. Whether there was something magic that brought us all here, so you could find us.'

Cy kissed the top of my head. 'You brought us here, *elyn*. You're the something magic.'

'If we're not going in, can we go somewhere else?' Kyin pulled Claire into his arms. 'We're not supposed to call attention to ourselves, and I, for one, don't want to be put under surveillance for another six years. The cameras in the bedroom really dampened my imagination.'

Several people were staring through the glass at us, wondering why we were ogling them while they tried to drink their post-lunch cocktails in peace.

'Train,' Aster said immediately. 'Let's go on a train.'

'Aster, oh my god,' I said. 'You went on a train yesterday.'

'A *different* train.'

'Fine,' I sighed. 'Let's go on a *different* train.'

An hour later, we'd split into groups, agreeing to meet back at a restaurant at the city centre for dinner. Maeve and Elswyth had caught a ride share to the arboretum, Anna had convinced Vesper to see a film, and Claire and Kyin were heading for the state art gallery. The rest of the males were still on the Tirian ship in orbit; Gydion was sending me five-minute updates on what Naida was doing, which seemed to involve getting covered head-to-toe in paint as she used her sucker-lined limbs to make a mural – her hands were paint-free – but she was smiling in every cast.

Willow sent me a message assuring me he'd deal with the paint before dinner time, then added an image of Lanir, whose face Naida had also painted.

I sent that one to Claire.

Ashton was in the background of the pictures of Naida, protectively cradling Anna's year-old daughter and Princess Royal of Scytha, Elyna. At three-to-one, my children made up the bulk of the next generation of Australian intergalactic ex-pats so far, though I supposed their citizenship might be a little muddy, given their planets of birth.

The last ten years hadn't always been roses. Anna had gone through two miscarriages before Elyna; the Tirian Grove had taken exception to some of Willow's research and tried to remove him from his post; the government on Machina had finally traced Cy and demanded he returned to be permanently shut down; and there'd been a small intergalactic incident when one of Vesper's criminal friends resurfaced with a rather large bone to pick with the starling ex-con, but, on the whole, we abducted humans were happy.

Often deliriously so.

We let Aster pick the train, which he did seemingly at random. I didn't suppose it would matter; we'd ride it to then end and then turn around and go back the way we'd come; the direction was largely irrelevant. More important was the cluster of seats that Morgan managed to coerce from a random man, shamelessly gesturing to me holding Stella in the carrier until the man got up and found somewhere else to sit – probably as far as he could manage from my cephalopod.

I settled in. Aster grinned out the window as Morgan and Cy had a soft conversation, punctuated by equally gentle kisses over the top of Sirius' sleeping head.

Even after ten years, my heart still melted when they did that.

'How's the research going, starlight?'

I snuggled into Aster's shoulder, breathing in his familiar scent as I adjusted Stella carefully. 'It's okay. They still won't let me into the Council records, though.'

'Because they're hiding something,' Morgan said, his foot pressing gently against mine.

'Very probably. We have enough evidence from elsewhere to make a fairly strong case, but it would be nice to have official confirmation.'

Willow had sparked the idea. We'd been talking one day, and he mentioned he was spending his time researching similarities between Tir tree species and those on Earth, trying to prove that there was enough cross-over to support his theory of prior contact. I'd thought about it for a while, and decided to look into Tirian art history to see whether I could find anything to back up Willow's research.

I found it. And not just in Tirian art history; it was the same across several species.

When I'd spoken to Anna about it, she suggested looking into literary history, too, and I'd found even more. I'd been in the process of collating everything when I'd fallen pregnant with the twins, but I'd picked the project up again a few weeks ago.

I wasn't really trying to prove anything, not in any formal way. I just thought it was interesting.

'Has Willow mentioned any of his other research?' Aster said casually.

I frowned. 'No?'

He started glowing slightly, then realised and cleared his throat, clearly forcing his excitement down. 'Cy?'

Cy's brow furrowed. 'It's too soon,' he said softly.

'I agree,' Morgan rumbled.

My frown deepened. 'Too soon for what?'

None of them answered.

I raised an eyebrow and waited.

Morgan broke first, because he always did. 'Obviously there's no expectation, starfish,' he began, 'but –'

'Willow's been working with Cy,' Aster interjected, 'and –'

'He thinks he's done it,' Cy finished, his grey eyes steady on mine.

Something unfurled in my stomach: *hope*. I'd always rolled my eyes when Aster talked about each of them having a *turn* at a baby; it had been to cover the sadness that Cy wouldn't get one. But –

Aster nodded. 'He thinks he's worked out a way,' he said happily.

'Something about Cy's genetic sequence bonded to a type of protein,' Morgan added. 'No interventions required.'

'And it would be a normal pregnancy,' Cy said in a rush. 'Nine human months. And our baby at the end.'

'And you want that?' I said softly, studying him.

He swallowed. 'More than almost anything, *elyn*.'

My heart swelled with love; I sat back. 'Not this year.'

Cy shook his head. 'Of course not.'

'And probably not next year, either.'

Morgan shifted Sirius as he stirred. 'Not until these ones can be handed to Uncle Vesper to look after.'

'That isn't happening until they're forty-five,' I said. 'Just so we're clear.'

Aster took my hand and kissed my knuckles. 'It doesn't matter when,' he murmured. 'We have forever, starlight.'

THE END.

Notes on the Text & Acknowledgements

If you're reading this, thank you. This is my first completed series, and it's incredible to me that you've journeyed the whole way through. So thank you, thank you, thank you. While I won't say this is the *end* end – I have a few ideas waiting in the wings – the main series will stop here.

(For now, at least. I'm not good with absolutes.)

I'm one of three siblings, and we all have anxiety. It manifests in all of us slightly differently, but has, at various times, made our lives quite complicated. I was hesitant to write a heroine with anxiety, as I know my experience is not that of everyone else, but it felt right for Claire. Anxiety isn't something you just *get over*; for many people, it's a lifelong relationship, with its own highs and lows. I've tried to represent this in Claire as authentically as I can, though I recognise and understand that the experience may look different for some of my readers. For anyone struggling, I see you, and you have my love.

My husband is an artist, and so it feels natural to me to include artists (or art historians, like Tessa) in my work. Any errors regarding art practice (and fresco restoration) are entirely mine.

Claire's *Pinup* series – along with her imagined portraits of her males – take inspiration from artists Jana Brike, Lisa

Lach-Nielsen, Caitlin Hackett, Lauren Marx, Maria Dimova, and Aykut Aydogdo (I strongly recommend checking out any and all of the artists listed, especially if you'd like to know what Claire's art might look like), with a dash of my own love of pinup aesthetics. Lanir is inspired by the empaths in Isobelle Carmody's *Obernewtyn Chronicles*, which was my favourite fantasy series growing up, and her empath misfits' powers have always stuck with me. The priestess/Divine Guard relationships on Kjid have their roots in Arthurian legend and notions of courtly love; Kyin was inspired by the first alien romance I read including tails: Chloe Parker's *Alien Rogue*.

As always, a massive thank you to my wonderful alpha reader, Kelly, without whom I could not function. An identically-sized thanks goes to my beta readers, Hannah, John, Erika, Claire, and Charlie; as always, you are amazing and I am so grateful for your considered feedback. A shout out, too, to Erika, Amy, Anne, Kacey, Wini, and Marian, whose kindness and consideration for my awkward AF self makes bookstagram feel more like a place I'd like to be.

And again, to you: thank you, thank you, *thank you*. If all goes well, I'll see you again soon.